Isle of Kapre

A Novel

By Kevin E Lake

Edited by Wallace Dunn

For Dearly and Daniel.

For saving my life.

Every day.

1

Twenty eight.

Twenty nine.

Thirty.

No wait. That wasn't blue. It was like, aqua.

Twenty nine.

What am I doin'? I'm counting slippers. Blue ones. What do you think I'm doin'?

No. It just *looks* like I'm sittin' in my yard in my boxers with a pair of gardening shears in one hand and a broken screwdriver in the other.

Why?

It keeps me from thinkin'. Thoughts can be dangerous, ya know. Especially when your mind has been wired and programmed and brainwashed since birth.

Like mine.

I'm workin' on that though.

Yours is like that too. You probably just don't wanna admit it. Or don't wanna face unpleasant facts.

No offense.

And plus, I still have some *anger issues* as they've been called. I don't know why. Hell, I graduated from three different anger management classes that the almighty U.S. Government forced me to take.

But having to go to them just pissed me off more.

And I'd rather count slippers, or smiles, or green shirts than take all those damn meds they used to have me on. Man. That was no way to live. I was in the Army, see, and… well… I'll get into all that a little later.

I'll get into a *lot* a little bit later.

You wanna go for a walk? We can stop and get a drink or three somewhere. It's almost noon now, and it's always noon somewhere, right?

We can stop by and see if the princess is home, and I can help her count rocks. That'll calm me down a bit. Then we'll go on for that drink.

Or three.

But I gotta count somethin' or I'm liable to go punch that… that man next door in the face!

Who's the princess?

No. Not my wife, who isn't really my wife, even though she's pregnant and we've been livin' together for a couple years. I'll explain that all later, too. Part of the culture here in the Philippines.

Well, yeah, the livin' together without being married, but that's everywhere any more, right? It's the title part. Wife. Whether it's legal or not. That's part of the culture here.

Lots of 'splainin' to do.

What's that? You wanna know why I count things first?

Fair enough.

I guess you could say it keeps me from thinkin' too much. I have a tendency to think the way others want me to. We all do. And I just don't wanna think like that anymore. Especially after some of the things I've seen. Because if I listen to the powers that be, and the so-called *reason* they beat into my brains for almost forty years, then I'd convince myself that the things I've seen I haven't seen. And then I'd start believing everything they wanted me to again.

And that's where the princess comes in. I'll get to her later. Just wait. I don't wanna get too far ahead of myself. It makes my mind race and I go right back to where I was before with my stinkin' thinkin'.

Have you ever thought about how hard it is for an individual- and I mean anybody- to think the way they want to think in the world we live in today? Think about that! Man, the bravery it takes! 'Cause for sure, everyone'll think you're crazy.

Anyway. Back to the slippers.

I'm countin' individual slippers, not pairs, because people here in the Philippines, once you get outta the cities anyway, rarely wear matching slippers. That's a luxury most of 'em can't afford. Hell, most of 'em find their slippers washed up on the beaches or along the road from where they fell off'a someone else's foot while they were ridin' a tricycle.

No, not that kind. The kind that's like a sidecar hooked to a motorcycle. It's one of the main forms of public transportation here. That and jeepneys.

Anyway, I'm countin' slippers because I'm pissed off, because I've gotta replant my damn vines. At least on one side of my yard. And I'd planned on readin' all afternoon, 'cause I'm almost done with this book, and it's got a hell of an ending.

I read a hell of a lot.

See? Here, under my chair. Workin' on this one, and I'm almost to the end. "Sphere" by Michael Crichton. It's one of his earlier works. Man was a genius. Medical degree from Harvard. He liked to write though, so he never practiced medicine. He followed his passion.

Now *there* was a man who could think for himself and didn't give two flyin' turds about what others thought of it.

How much do I read? Oh, about ten books a month.

Why?

I just like to read, but also, few people here speak English. So it's kinda how I get my English fix. There've been times when I've had to stop and think a minute to recall simple words in English, because I rarely speak it much these days.

That's why I'm so happy you're here!

No, not Tagalog. I mean, I know a little of that, and it's the national language, but down here in the Southern Philippines the language is Visayan. Some of the words cross translate though. There are actually more than one hundred languages in the country.

Kinda like the California public schools system.

Anyway, back to why I'm countin' slippers. It calms me down. I'll defuse in about twenty minutes or so.

It used to take longer.

And at least now I'm *able* to defuse. Once upon a time, I was always pissed off.

Always!

And it was killing me.

But I liked it.

I wouldn't've admitted it, but if I hadn't liked it, I wouldn't have lived that way for so long. If people are truly unhappy they make changes. If they just bitch and moan, but don't make changes, well, then I guess they just haven't had enough yet. That's one of the lessons I've learned here in the Philippines, and I was that way for a while myself.

And the drugs I mentioned earlier didn't help. When I took those I was just pissed off and high and then the next day I was pissed off and hung over. But I got most of 'em at those stupid anger management classes, and when I was still on the U.S. Government's dime- that means still in the Army- I *had* to take 'em. Direct orders.

And if I hadn't taken 'em?

Loss of rank and pay, and possibly jail time.

Hell, they'd threatened to charge me with treason for disobeying a direct order during a time of war once while I was in Iraq for trying to refuse a vaccine shot. No kiddin'!

The shot they'd given me before that one had made me sick as hell. Broke me out in smallpox. It was *supposed* to be the dead cowpox strain, but I was so fit and healthy that I got to be the one out of every ten thousand soldiers- U.S. Government property, ya see- to get the *real* smallpox, so that the government could see how far the strain had mutated since it's 'eradication' in 1979.

Eradication my ass.

Weaponized, more like it.

Anyway, don't get me off on that yet, or I'll never explain about the vines.

Happy thoughts. Happy thoughts.

What a nice view of the tree line I have here, huh? Look over there. I like how you can actually see it all the way to the beach. Then it just drops off. This is a pretty big island, but we're close to the coast here. On a clear day I can actually see some of the islands all the way over in Indonesia. That's how far south we are.

Well, let me reword that. On a clear day that is also clear on the island *in between* the island I live on and the islands across the way that are part of Indonesia, I can see into Indonesia. And the days in which there are no storm clouds brewing on the back of *that* island blocking the view are few and far between.

See? If you tippy toe, you can see some faint lightning strikes in the distance. Look there where the clouds are blackest.

Ah, now you see 'em.

Oh, I can tell you all about that island, and I will. It's the biggest part of my story.

But first, I have to explain about the vines. And why I'm countin' slippers. And I have to tell ya all kinds of other stuff too, so you'll understand what life is like here, in case you decide to stay awhile. And I have to tell ya about the things that happened on that Island. Isle of Kapre it's called.

What's a kapre?

You know about Bigfoot, right? Well, Kapre is the Philippine version of Bigfoot. Every major culture around the world has a Sasquatch type creature in their folklore.

Did you know that?

Probably not, because I didn't either until I researched it after I spent some time on that island over there.

You know what's really neat about what I found in my research? All of these different cultures- all on different continents- have had these folklores and legends in their history going way back to before world travel was known to be possible. If you ask me, this is proof enough in itself that the story wasn't spread from culture to culture, but rather, there was actually truth to the creation of the legends. As in, the creatures exist!

But I don't need convincin'. I know. And after I share this story with you, you'll know too.

Okay, first off. Before I explain about the vines, I need to point out that there are some major cultural differences between Americans and Filipinos. And just so you'll know through this story what I'm referring to, I'll point out now that there are a few different forms of that word- Filipino.

A "Filipino" is someone from the Philippines. However, "Filipino," when referring to one person as opposed to a group of people, means male, and "Filipina" means female.

Now, part of rewiring my brain and my thought processes, and being able to live here peacefully with the locals and with myself, is understanding so many of these cultural differences and not making more out of 'em than they really are. You gotta learn not to take things so personally, or it'll turn your heart to stone, and you'll begin to hate. And that's ugly.

I was gettin' dangerously close to bein' one hateful sumbitch once upon a time and the little trip I took to the island I'm gonna tell ya about later made me realize that. I changed my ways after that, and I gotta make sure to keep those ways in check.

You've got to understand the great paradox of the Filipino people. They are, without a doubt, the friendliest people on earth. I've been to many, many countries, and rarely have I run into people who are as friendly as Filipinos as a whole. The closest I've come, really, are folks back in the southern part of the U.S.

However, at the same time, Filipinos are very unaccepting, and they can come across as very rude. But you've got to understand that this is nothing personal. It's cultural. And it's taken me years to really grasp this, and now that I understand it more, I try not to let it piss me off when it happens.

But it's hard.

You don't follow me?

Okay. It's like this. They are tolerant, say, of white foreigners. But by God, you'd better believe that you can't walk down the street without being reminded by complete strangers, dozens of 'em a day, that you are not a Filipino. That you are different. As if perhaps you've forgotten.

But if you follow the old axiom of seeking first to understand, rather than to be understood, you'll see yourself that it has nothing to do with you, or the fact that you're a foreigner. It's just because you're different. Listen, they do it to people within their own race who are different.

How do they do it?

Oh, you'll see when we go for our walk. They'll point out to us that we're different, and we'll probably get an example or two of them pointing out to someone within their own race that they are different too. I hope not, 'cause it can break your heart.

Okay, I'll give you an example now then.

Down 's syndrome.

I'd just gotten here, and I was walking down the sidewalk with my girlfriend. This was several years back.

What?

No. Not my wife, that's not my wife. There've been several. And I'll get to all that.

But anyway, I'm walking down the sidewalk with *my girlfriend at the time*. How's that? Better? And here comes the most beautiful little girl you'd ever seen. She was maybe ten or so. And she had Down's Syndrome.

Well, just as we get to her, I see her big, beautiful smile, and I smile right back at her, and her smile gets even bigger, and then my girlfriend at the time points at her and says, very loudly, "Look, Pete! She is abnormal!"

And the smiles disappeared from both of our faces.

Yes! I am dead serious!

I stopped and looked back to make sure that the little girl wasn't crying. She'd put her head down, I mean, you could tell she'd been hurt, but she wasn't crying. And then I saw one of the most disgusting displays of human behavior I'd ever seen.

Every other person was pointing at this beautiful little girl and saying something as they passed her. Every other person!

So that's what I mean by they are not accepting. It's anything that is different. Not just white people. It isn't personal.

But boy, when it happens, over and over, day after day, it sure does start to feel personal.

And it's not limited to the Philippines. It's common throughout Asia. I researched that too. Google it yourself.

Studies have found that certain psychological disorders that are not accompanied with physical pain in the West *are* accompanied with physical pain throughout the East. Why? It's because of the social stigma placed on the one who suffers the psychological disorder by their peers.

In the West, we would *never* point out a person with disabilities, or differences they had no choice in such as Down's Syndrome. Never! And if it *did* happen, the person who did it would have everyone else in close vicinity on top of 'em, beatin' holy hell out of 'em before they could take two more steps!

Not here.

I know of a lot of white foreigners who've developed agoraphobia from living here. You know. Fear to leave your house? I have to watch that one myself. I mean, when you need a loaf of bread and a dozen eggs, it ain't about just walkin' down to the store and pickin' 'em up and comin' home. It's about walkin' to the store and back and having a dozen or more people remind you that you are different.

Okay, I'm kinda veerin' off in the wrong direction again. They'd given me meds for that while I was a Government mule, but I don't remember it being this bad before I was on 'em. I honestly think that all that crap made me worse, even after I came off of it. And that *may* have been part of the plan. I've not ruled that out.

For the most part, life is very good here. Tropical weather. It's summer every day of the year. Low cost of living. One dollar's worth forty two of their pesos. And the overwhelming majority of the people are wonderful. They really are.

And the women? Oh, they are beautiful and sexy and if you're a white man, no matter how old, bald or ugly, they'll chase you down the street! Sometimes it pays to be different in that sense, I guess.

But you've got to be *very* careful with that. Don't worry. I'll get to that too. Lost my ass and all my shirts a couple times in that area.

Okay, so understanding the cultural difference is a start. Great! But *dealing* with the cultural differences? That isn't so great. Sometimes certain things just get old.

Okay, one of the things that get old is bein' stared at as if you were a freak in a carnival exhibit.

At first, it's flattering, because when you ask why people are staring, they will tell you it's because you are so guapo. That word means handsome. And at first, before you really learn about the place and the people, you're dumb enough to believe that you *are* handsome, and that that is why they are staring at you.

But after a while, once you get burned a few times because of your naivety and white guilt, and you see them staring at the eighty year old, four hundred pound white foreigners as well, you start to understand that, no, they aren't staring at you because you're the hottest thing since Brad Pitt. They're staring at you because you're different, and they don't give two rat shits if they're offending you or not. It's how it is here.

Okay, so. Back to the vines.

My wife and I moved into this house a year ago. Now remember, she's not really my wife, but it's disrespectful in this culture to call a woman with whom you live and share a child with anything other than 'wife,' and since we're expecting, well, I'm just gettin' used to calling her my wife. And I was callin' her that before she was pregnant anyway. The culture thing.

Every time I move into a new place I go through the same crap I've gone through everywhere that I've lived before on these islands. And I've been here for about five years now.

When a white man- I'd say person, but you'll find few white women here. Hell, they're rarer than Sasquatch. So when a white man moves into the neighborhood, or barangay (pronounced burr-un-guy) as they call it, everyone in the neighborhood comes out and goes to the fence and gawks. They'll even bring chairs and sit there for hours if you're out in the yard. If there's shade. But trust me, if there's no shade or cloud cover, you ain't gonna be out long yourself.

You can ask 'em if they have a problem, or if there is something you can help 'em with, and they'll just shake their heads and say, "No, Joe. No problem," and then just keep starin'.

See, if you're white, they call you Joe. It stems from WWII, when the U.S. Army was here in full force routing the Japanese from these islands. It's the second time in the past, oh, just over one hundred years or so that we've given them their freedom. The first time it was to end Spain's 433 year rule during the Spanish American War.

Joe is the nickname of the lower enlisted guys in the military. It's all part of taking away your personal identity. Make you all the same. Stockholm syndrome. It's part of the mind control in the Army. Trust me, I know about it, all too well. And it sucks. And it's why I can get so pissed off at times when they say, "Hey, Joe!" here.

So anyway, I learned early, you can be offended, you can get pissed off, but you ain't gonna change it. You have to accept it and move on.

However, it *is* frustrating, and I'll dare say, nearly impossible to accept being stared at as if you have a third eye all the time. It actually makes you go a little crazy. Or in my case, craz*ier*.

I know of other foreigners here who've not left their houses in a year because they've gotten a full blown case of agoraphobia, and it's because of the stares and the heckling.

So, here goes. There's a beautiful vine that grows here, and it grows quickly. It has these little white flowers on it that look like morning glories. It grows almost everywhere, and it grows fast. I mean it'll bury a flower garden or take over a whole yard in two weeks if you don't keep it cut back.

Well, about six months ago, after I'd ignored bein' the central theme of entertainment for my neighbors for as long as I could, I went into the jungle and pulled a dozen or so of these vines up by the roots and brought 'em into my yard and planted 'em around the inside of my fence.

See, everyone has fences here, and you'd better keep 'em locked if you wanna keep what's inside the fence. If you take anything outside of the fence, you'd better keep your eye on it or it'll be gone.

It's odd. People here aren't afraid of their neighbors being violent or being sexual predators that are going to rape them and their children like everyone is back in The States. It's just that your neighbor will rob you blind the minute they think they can and not get caught, and everybody knows it, so they keep their yards locked up.

So, while I'm planting these roots, all the natives are staring at me even more intensely. They go back to their houses and pull all their family members out and have 'em come watch the foreigner.

That's our other name here; foreigner. We have three really; Joe, foreigner, and Americano. And even if you're from Europe or Australia, you're an Americano to the natives. Only two countries exist to them; The Philippines and Foreign Land. And Foreign Land is also known as America, or the U.S. I'll get into that more, later.

So, it was quite the stir when the foreigner was out in his yard, in all his white skinned glory, planting vine roots. But six weeks later?

A-lah!

That's what they say when they're shocked, or surprised, "a-lah!" But not like the Muslim God. That's like, awe- law. This is quicker and snappier, like a-lah! And you go up in pitch on the second syllable, whereas when pronouncing the name of the Muslim God you go down in pitch on the second syllable.

But anyway, six weeks later they're all like, "A-lah! The foreigner has disappeared!"

Well, I didn't go anywhere. But the vines grew and they covered my fence and they gave me privacy. I've since been able to get out in my own yard, and I've planted a beautiful garden with eggplant and squash and string beans. I have papaya trees, banana trees, and mango trees. This is important to me, because I want to grow most of the food that I eat. The world governments are poisoning the food supply, and if I grow my own fruits and vegetables I know I'm safe. Nothing I eat these days, as far as I know, has been genetically or synthetically altered with any of that Monsanto bullshit.

And I have grass! So when it rains my yard doesn't flood. The locals pull their grass up by the roots so they never have to cut it. So when there's been no rain, their yards are like asphalt. But when it rains, their yards flood and turn to goo for a week, because there's no root system to absorb the water.

They understand this. It's not an issue of ignorance. They are very intelligent people. I mean, people the world over have the same brain. As far as I'm concerned, there's only one race.

The human race.

Anyway, the whole pullin' their grass up by the roots in spite of the repercussions of it? Throwin' their garbage everywhere and making one of God's most beautifully created spots on earth look like one big landfill? All of these things?

Apathy!

They just don't care!

Now, that apathy is good when it comes to not sweatin' the small stuff. They've got us on that one. I mean, we spend our lives tryin' not to sweat the small stuff, right.

There's something about me though. I don't know what it is.

One of the aspects of the culture that I love the most here, that I wish I could adopt, is how they just don't sweat the small stuff. And to them, it's all small stuff. As long as they have their rice and a roof over their heads, they're content. I wish I could be more like that. And I've tried to be.

I don't know if it's because I'm an American, or if it's simply because it's who I am, but I cannot settle for mediocrity. I've never accepted being second best if I had any say in it.

And don't we always have a say?

All I know is that I feel like our time here is limited and I cannot be content with the bare necessities. I want to leave my mark in the annals of time, and I want that mark to read, "I was here! And while I was, by God, I gave it every fuckin' thing I had!

Now, if only I could figure out how to leave that mark.

The problem here is, they view it *all* as small stuff, and they don't sweat anything. They have to know that it's not right to throw their trash on the ground. There has to be some part of their being that knows it's not okay to point at a ten year old little girl with Down 's syndrome and say, "Look! She is abnormal!" The fact is they just don't care!

Have you ever read Ayn Rand? Man, she can go on and on. Like I am now. But she said something once that sums it all up. She said, "You can choose to ignore reality, but you cannot ignore the consequences of ignoring reality." Now, she was talking about communism and socialism, but you could say the same thing about the mindset of apathy. Just not caring. Not caring will catch up to you.

But, anyway. Back to my vines.

Someone reached through the fence and cut the main stems of my vines a couple days ago so I no longer have privacy, and I'm sitting here right now with this broken screwdriver, because I use it to poke planting holes for seeds, and I've been planting some string beans while I've been cuttin' the grass. That explains the sheers. I can't remember the last time I saw a gas powered lawn mower and I wouldn't even know where to buy one.

And I'm bein' stared at by no less than fifteen natives.

They're making fun of my nose. It isn't big by Western standards, but this ain't the West. Filipinos have these flat little pug noses. They don't like 'em, but frankly, I think they're cute. Especially on the pretty girls.

They're making fun of my hairy arms, which aren't overly hairy by Western standards, but through tens of thousands of years of adaptation, these people have lost all body hair, or simply never developed it, because of the lack of a need for it due to the incessant tropical heat.

I've lost the battle, but I've not lost the game, so to say, because I'll plant more vines, but I've certainly seemed to have lost this round.

But damn, I keep losing a hell of a lot of rounds.

Who cut the vines?

Oh. well, what happened was, the man next door didn't like havin' to pick up a leaf or three a day that dropped to the ground on his side of the fence. It took him all of, oh, one minute each day to do it. But that was one minute he could've had his tuba glass in his hand.

Tuba- that's this really cheap, rotgut wine the locals live on. It's made from fermented coconut tree juice. And notice what I said. Not coconut juice, but juice from the tree itself. It's gross and it'll kill you by age fifty. Its American counterpart can be found in prisons and is called squeeze.

Now, the old me- the stinkin' thinkin' me- would have walked over and punched him in the face. Or wanted to at least.

No.

Would have.

Okay, but that's because I would have viewed his actions as an insult, or a slight. But remember. Apathy.

The man didn't take the *time* to think that he may have been pissing off his neighbor by cutting the vines. He simply saw it as, well, if I cut these vines, eventually I won't have to pick up leaves.

Seriously.

That's the truth of it. It's *that* simple. To think for a moment that he thought any further ahead than simply killing the vines to keep from having to pick up the leaves would be to give him way more credit than he deserves. He *did not* think that far ahead.

This is not an insult to the man's thinking capabilities, either. Intellectually, he's as smart, if not smarter, than me. He just thinks differently than me, and it's because he's from a different culture than me. And the way a people think is just as cultural and society driven as the way they dress, act, dance, eat, etc.

One of the smartest people I've ever met in my life was a Filipina named Rose. And I'm gonna be tellin' you all about her. But she couldn't think past the confines of her culture, and she ended up doing something that greatly and negatively affected her entire future because of it. At least as far as you and I would think.

Oh, you'll see for yourself when I tell ya about it. I'll do so over that drink or three.

So, anyway. If I were to go over there and punch my neighbor in his little pug nose, he would have no idea why I did it.

And I'd end up in jail.

Again.

And that's always fun. Basically, anyone here can have you thrown in jail if you harm them or their property in any way and then they name the price you pay to get out. You kill their rooster because it won't shut the hell up? They have you arrested, and all of a sudden a two hundred pesos filthy bird becomes worth twenty thousand pesos.

They calculate how many chicks it would've produced for however many generations they want, and the jailers, who'd not allow it if they tried it with another Filipino, laugh and tell you not to worry about it, because you are so rich anyway, and to just pay or you stay in jail.

And jail here sucks. It's a twelve by twelve room with twenty other guys who are all so high on shaboo- that's like cheap meth (I know, meth's already cheap, so think about *that*)- and they stink because they haven't bathed during their week long binder, and so you pay just to get outta there. It's like five hundred dollars.

One hell of an expensive chicken, huh?

But I've created a game to take care of the roosters that keeps me out of jail.

What's the game?

It's called "Ferals versus Feathers."

I've taken in some of the feral cats that run the place like rats do sewers, and I've trained 'em to go into the neighbor's yards and kill the roosters. At least I've tried. Some of the cats have been befriending some of the chickens, and on more than one occasion I've found chickens roosting in my garage at night.

Cock fighting's the national sport here, so there's a hell of a lot of roosters, and good luck sleepin' through the night.

So, anyway. Back to my vines.

Now my task is to figure out how to win the next round of "Are you smarter than a third world peasant?" and do so before all the staring drives me crazy again.

Well, craz*ier*.

Anyway, I'll figure it out. I always do. And I've accepted the fact that I can never really permanently win the game, but rather, simply stay ahead for a while.

But that's how life works, right? No one ever really wins, because to do so you'd have to make it out alive.

And no one's getting' outta here alive.

But I'll figure it out. And while I'm working on it, I'm gonna tell ya my story. Or stor*ies* rather. As I've already alluded to during this ramble, there're several stories.

I'll start with who I am, and why I'm here.

My name is Pete Richards. I'm forty years old. I spent most of my time in The States as a public high school teacher. I taught U.S. History. And I was a soldier in the Virginia Army National Guard. An airborne infantryman.

Oh? You recognized the southern accent? Yeah, I guess I've not dropped it.

Anyway, I deployed to Iraq where I learned that everything I ever thought of as truth, and what I'd been passing on as truth to so many young minds in America for ten years or so as a history teacher, wasn't quite so.

And don't read into that as if I'm a commie! Furthest thing from the truth! I'm a patriot! A Mark Twain kinda patriot!

What's that?

Oh, you know. What he said about patriotism. He said, "Patriotism is supporting your country all the time, and your government when it deserves it."

Anyway, I went home from Iraq confused and injured and in pain and half crazy- well, maybe all the way crazy- and was treated like a lunatic, a threat, and later would be demonized and criminalized, and I finally said the hell with it all, and I came here.

And now I'm on a mission. That mission, like I've already told you, is to see the world around me as it really is, not how someone or some*thing* like a lifetime course in soviet history wants me to see it.

And that island over there that I told you about? The one with all the lightning and thunder?

Man! The things I saw there. You talk about gettin' thrown for another loop. Just when I thought I was startin' to get things figured out! What's real and what isn't. Fact versus fiction. That kinda thing, ya know. I end up over there on that island with Rose, and…

Yes. The girl I'd mentioned earlier.

I get over there with Rose, and I start seein' things I'da never believed I'd seen if I hadn't seen 'em with my own eyes.

Oh, look at me. Gettin' ahead of myself again. Don't worry. I'm gonna tell you all about it. Over that drink or three.

You can choose to believe it or not when I do. And if you don't, that's okay.

But I believe it. Because I was there, and I saw it all.

2

Okay, next thing...

Oh, wait. That's my asawa coming out now. That means wife. Ain't she a beaut!

I know. Back home she'd be a pinup model. But here, and I say this with respect, girls that beautiful are a dime a dozen.

While they're young.

The rough lifestyle here ages 'em. Too many kids, too much time doin' laundry by hand in the sun. Too much stress, worryin' about where the next meal for those kids will come from. Poverty will kick your ass and age you fast!

But if you can get one while she's young, like mine. That's the key. And don't have all those damn kids.

What's that?

Oh, she's twenty five now. She was twenty two when we got together. She's the best damn woman I could ever hope to have on this continent or any other, I'll tell ya that! And she...

Hold on a minute and let me see what she wants. She's 'high blood,' as they call it here. That translates in American English to 'pissed off.'

Unsa! (What?)

Unsa mun, ditto! (What are you doing there?)

Pagbibilang ng sapatos! (Counting slippers!)

Bakit? (Why?)

High blood ko! (I'm pissed off!)

Bakit? (Why?)

Sa utin ditto cut ako vines! (That dick over there cut my vines!)

Go count rocks!

She's not there!

How do you know?

She's out collecting rocks before it gets hot.

Lakow ka. (Go for a walk.)

Sigey, sigey. (Okay. Okay.)

Okay, come on. We're gonna take that walk.

There's really not much else to do here. I have a mountain bike, and I ride that a lot, but I don't have one for you, and I can tell you all these stories while we're walkin'.

Don't worry. We'll take lots of breaks. Ya have to, because of the heat. Or the humidity rather. As we used to say back in Virginia, 'it ain't the heat, it's the humidity!' And man, is it humid here! Seems like one hundred percent every damn day.

Except for the rainy season. That's June and July. It rains every day for two months straight. You're happy for it for the first couple of weeks, because the clouds block the sun and the heat lets up. But after a couple weeks you start to get down as the serotonin levels in your brain drop.

Oh, I have pills for that, too. Serotonin. Well. I used to. They were part of the nearly one dozen different types of pills our Uncle Sam had me on after the war. But I reckon the combination of all of 'em were driving me crazy, so I flushed 'em all one day.

Oh, and that's figurative speech by the way. Flushed 'em. Because other than the few times the asawa and I've stayed in a hotel somewhere, I can't remember the last time I had a toilet that flushed. And I can't remember the last time I was able to use figurative speech with someone who understood it was figurative. Guess that's why I pointed that out. They're taught English literally here, and they take it literally, so you really have to be careful what you say. You might say, "I'm gonna kill you," to someone, just joking, and they'll run the hell away from you and avoid you forever more. Hell, they might even go to the cops.

Here, now. Don't let the gate hit you as I shut it. An open gate invites thieves, remember, so I have to shut it and lock it. I used to say that the Filipino people were all thieves, but again, that brought some negative energy with it, so I've changed the way I address that issue. What I say now is, 'there's only one thief in the Philippines, but the bastard seems to follow me around.'

And I keep the gate closed and locked at all times, 'cause I know he's around here somewhere.

Okay. We'll head this way. It goes to the park. You'll like the park. You can get your feet massaged there. Costs about a buck U.S., and they spend half an hour on each foot. Hurts like hell at first, especially if you've never gotten it before. It's called 'reflexology.'

What's that? Never heard of it?

Listen, I'll be pointing out some of the pitfalls you have to watch out for, livin' here as a white foreigner, but understand, life can be marvelous here as well, as long as you know how to live it. And goin' to the park a couple times a week for some reflexology therapy is part of that.

Known also as "zone therapy" it's a type of massage where pressure's applied to certain points of your feet, hands and ears, and these points are each associated with different parts of the body. For instance, the arch of the foot is linked to the lower back and sciatic nerve. The tips of the toes are linked to the frontal sinus region. And the bottom center of the foot, just behind the toes, is linked to the lungs.

Oh yeah, I got it all memorized. I used to only go for a drink to calm my nerves, but after my time spent on that island I'm gonna tell ya about, I learned to go other routes. Healthier routes. And I was goin' three days a week for almost a year for reflexology. Don't have to no more.

Why not?

Oh. That's where I met my asawa. She was my reflexologist. That's where we got to know each other. Still took me six months of askin' 'er out to get a date though.

Why?

She said I talked too much and couldn't stay on topic. Drove 'er nuts. Still does.

But I'm workin' on that.

The concept behind reflexology is that your life's energy flow, or Qi, can be unblocked by asserting pressure on the various points of the feet, hands and ears, thereby expediting the healing process of illness and injury by allowing your Qi to flow throughout your body more smoothly.

Like most forms of alternative medicine, the great minds of the West have tried for years to discredit reflexology, claiming there's no actual medical or scientific value to it. Perhaps it interferes with the overmedication of Western populations, which garners Pharmaceutical companies hundreds of billions of dollars per year? That's my guess. But it's done me more good than all those pills I used to be on ever did.

I've found that for me, reflexology does work. The severe lower back pain I suffered from chronically inflamed lower disks, incurred due to the massive body armor that I wore for a year while in Iraq- pain that I used to take several different medications for back in The States- has ceased to exist. I know that the subtropical climate of the Philippine Islands has helped with this as well.

I used to practice my Visayan with the reflexologists that speak good English, and they likewise practice their English with me back when I went there all the time. I actually learned most of the Visayan I know sittin' over there getting' my feet massaged.

But ya know what? It was the therapists who didn't speak a word of English who were perhaps the most helpful to me during my times of frustration in which I felt I simply needed to vent.

Why?

Because I could bare my soul and share anything and everything with 'em, and I knew I had their complete confidentiality, because they didn't understand a word I was sayin', and that always ended up leadin' to a free session of "laughter therapy." And ya know what they say. Laughter's the best medicine.

Often, as I'd rant and rave about whatever problem I thought I had, the reflexologist would say, "Walla ko kasabote! Walla ko kasabote!" (which means, "I don't understand!"), over and over, and laugh, and like a sneeze, laughter's contagious, ya know. I'd catch their laughter and then I'm laughin', and I'd no longer remember why I was frustrated. Then I'm sittin' there, havin' my life's energy unblocked by the reflexology treatment, enjoyin' laughter therapy, and havin' just shared my concerns with someone who I know will never breach my confidentiality about a problem I no longer remember havin' anyway, my day would be better and life would be good.

It's always pleasant speakin' with friendly locals during reflexology treatments. And there're so many of 'em here. Remember, these are the friendliest people on earth. I can learn more about the local culture, geography of the region, or history of the country, and when I'm lucky enough to speak with an elder, I often learn more about life.

One time during a reflexology session, I was sittin' beside an old Filipina lady who appeared to be in her early seventies. We were lookin' across the way at some young people, early twenties perhaps, who were dancin' in the park. Oh, how the Philippine people love to dance. I said to the old woman beside me, "You know, if your people danced less and worked more, they would have more money." She sat silently for a moment and then said, "You are right. And if your people worked less and danced more, they would have more happiness."

I certainly got my dollar's worth of therapy that day, and afterward, I danced the whole way home. No kiddin'.

Before we pass the park, we'll stop off along the way and have a drink. We'll save reflexology for another day, 'cause I got some stories to tell ya over that beer or three.

I don't drink much these days. I'll actually go for six or eight months without a drink- once I made it a year- and then I'll decide to have a refreshment or two. Then one or two becomes three or four, which becomes eight or ten, which then becomes I don't know how many, because I black out and wake up in the park the next day, and so I stop again.

For six or eight months.

But one time I made it a year.

But today's a special occasion. I have someone to talk to in English. Do you know how rare that is?

Sure, there are other foreigners here who speak English, but to be honest with you? I avoid most of them like the plague.

Why?

Two reasons.

Numero uno. Most of them are here to drink themselves to death, or fuck themselves to death, or both. That sounds like a harsh assessment, but it's true for about ninety percent of 'em.

Letter B. Everytime foreigners get together, it's just a matter of time before the conversation turns to Filipino bashing. And that ain't good. If you want to have any chance of living here without losing what little bit of your mind you have left when you come here, you have to accept that things are the way they are and that you can't change 'em.

Listen, do I like the fact that the price on everything goes up for me because of the color of my skin in eight out of the ten places I shop? Hell no! And we call that the 'skin tax' by the way. But I have to accept it.

And all those foreigners? Man. They were so great in their own countries. Rich. Popular. You name it.

I call bullshit!

If things were so great for 'em there, they'd still be there. Hey, I was a nobody at home, and I'm a nobody here. The difference? I'm honest about it.

And I'm honest about all the times I've been taken advantage of by the locals here too. Most foreigners'll pump you for your stories so they know what to watch out for and then laugh at you and call you an idiot and claim nothing like that's ever happened to them.

Bullshit again!

They just don't admit it, 'cause they don't wanna look like fools!

Look, most of us came here for a girl. I didn't per say- I came here for other reasons, and I've already covered 'em- but sure, I made sure to have one waitin' on me when I got here. Found a beautiful young thing on one of those chat sights.

And man, was she ever waitin' on me! And her family, and her neighbors! That small village took me for nearly five grand American money in a month!

How? Oh, they had me haulin' 'em around everywhere and doin' all these touristy things. That was on the island of Bohol. Most beautiful place I've seen here. The girl would ask if I'd take her and her family to see the Chocolate Hills. They're these really amazing landforms. Mountains that look just like chocolate gumdrops. That's where the name comes from.

So anyway, I'd say, "Sure, I'll take you and your family to see the Chocolate Hills." And I'm thinking she means her and her parents. A few siblings. Next day, four jeepnies and fifty people show up to go to the chocolate hills! Seriously! They'd clear out the whole barungay! And while we were out? We'd eat at the nicest places. Everyone would buy souvenirs. And I got the tab for all of it!

And they nickel and dimed me to death. We'd go by to see an aunt or uncle, and they'd ask if I'd like some coke and donuts while we were there. I'd say "sure" to be polite. Then, when we were leavin', they'd tell me to give 'em money for the coke and donuts.

They took me to the cock fights once. I had a blast. Me and these ten guys were in a van. I was the only one without a cock. Well, you know what I mean. But then at the end of the day, they charged me a thousand pesos for the van fee. And one of the guys had won ten thousand pesos that day at the cock fights!

I refused to pay it. And the driver was one of the uncles of that girl, and every day for the rest of the time I was with her, he'd call her and harass her to get a thousand pesos outta me. I never paid it.

Could you imagine? We're back home, and someone visits us from another country, and we ask 'em to join us at a baseball game? Then after the game, we charge 'em for takin' 'em?

They'll tell you it justified because they are so poor and we are so rich, but you can never justify takin' advantage of someone. If they were gonna charge for donuts and coke and van fees, they needed to point that out upfront. Give me the option of either sayin' yes or no. It's not justifiable.

And remember. They're not all like that. That's what ya gotta learn. You just gotta watch yourself.

Never hook up with a girl you meet on chat! They're scammers! I've since met girls here who've told me all about it, even though I'd already found out from experience.

I know one woman that has four husbands. One in the Philippines, two in The States, and one in Germany. She makes more than twenty grand U.S. a month scammin' lonely western men online outta their savings. Flashes her perky little boobs on the webcam, tells 'em how much she'll take care of 'em in their old age if they take care of her while she's young.

Look here. We're passin' an internet café now. Just come over here and peek in the window.

See there? Look. Terminal eight. You can see her screen. See how she has six different tabs open? See the different men on each tab through the webcam?

Look at her fingers. Watch how fast she's able to go back and forth between 'em.

Let me tell ya. Any guy in America or anywhere else who's chattin' with some young beautiful Filipina over here and thinks he's the only one she's talkin' to is a fool! But look. You can see it there for yourself. It's a business. Some girls freelance- the smart ones do- but mostly there are men in charge. They recruit half a dozen different girls to scam and then he gives 'em a commission. Half of the intake usually.

Why do they work for him instead of themselves?

Listen, if someone Western Unions money, you have to have a valid i.d. to pick it up, right? You'd be amazed at the number of people over here, who on paper, do not exist.

Birth certificate? Driver's license? Really?

Most of 'em have no i.d. You get a guy with a driver's license, and most of those are fake, and he can run quite a profitable little venture.

Come on. Let's go.

What's that? They're getting what they deserve?

Ha! Well look across the street there, and tell me if all those good hearted Christians back home are getting what *they* deserve?

Of course it's just a street shop sellin' clothes. But let me tell ya about the clothes and where they came from and where they're *supposed* to go.

The shop is called a ukay ukay. Or black market.

You know all those clothes and shoes and coats that well intentioned folks back home donate to their churches and the Salvation Army? So it'll go to the needy for free? Well, you're lookin' at its final destination.

The stuff gets shipped here through the Red Cross, or the Salvation Army, or churches back home will raise funds to ship it over, then as soon as it gets here, the people workin' on this side of the transaction make a killin'! They don't go around and give it out to the needy as they're supposed to. Oh hell no! They sell it for about two hundred and fifty dollars U.S. per pallet to street vendors who then turn around and mark it up and sell at a price so high the needy could never afford it.

What?

Oh, I know it's all used and half worn out. But it'll last longer than that made in China bullshit you can buy new around here. See, you guys bitch back in America and England and everywhere else in the West that everything's comin' from China and it ain't no good. Boy, if you only knew the other half of the story.

See, you guys get Class A Chinese imports, because of the strict importing laws in the West. And if you think that shit's defective, try class C. All that class C crap, which is *most* of it, gets distributed to the third world, like here in the Philippines, and down in Indonesia, and up in Cambodia and Vietnam.

How bad is it?

You can buy a set of brand new class C batteries for your camera and they're dead after five pictures. No kiddin'.

So, anyway, the people here'll pay a mint for a pair of authentic Levi jeans from America, even if the knees are worn, 'cause they know they'll last another ten years. You buy a pair of brand new Chinese class C jeans down at the mall, and they'll last through about two washes and then fall apart.

So, there's big money here in ukay ukay.

But don't blame their Salvation Army or their Red Cross. It's a mindset that's infiltrated the culture. That girl I told you about in Bohol? You know where her mom works? A couple weeks out of the year at least?

She's a cook at an orphanage run by her church. The orphanage was set up by some good Baptist missionaries who'd come here from my native state of Virginia. They saw the poverty, all the poor kids, and they found a local Baptist church and told 'em they wanted to help.

Well, the local Baptist church told 'em to open an orphanage. They said that if they'd sponsor 'em from America, their congregation would gather the orphans and run the orphanage here in the Philippines.

The Baptists from Virginia went back to their church, got approval, and started sending a shit ton of money back to the Philippines. The people in the church take pictures of *their* kids eating rice and chicken and drinking milk in the church hall, and reading brand new books and learning how to use computers. The whole nine yards. And they send these pictures back to the Baptists in Virginia. Hell, they have a Facebook page now. And the only time the kids are really there, other than when they want to take some pictures to update their Facebook page, is twice a year when the missionaries come over for two weeks each time.

None of the damn kids speak English. The girl told me that their parents just tell 'em they're havin' a sleep in at the church for a couple weeks when this happens and spending time with their sponsors from America. So none of the kids would even be able to tell the good Baptists that they're bein' scammed if they wanted to. They don't know what's goin' on anyway, and this is where they learn this shit. There's the next generation's training for ya.

Now, I ask you again. All those well intentioned people back home goin' to bed all warm and fuzzy at night after donating some jeans and tee-shirts and a couple pair of shoes for the needy? Not knowin' that it's all gonna come here and be black marketed by some opportunists while the needy sleep on the sidewalk at night by the shop sellin' what was meant for them at prices they'll never be able to afford? Do you think they got what they deserved?

Okay, the creepy old divorced guys who can't get laid back home who chat online. Maybe. But the people givin' their shit to the Salvation Army and the congregations raising money to help the needy? I don't think they do, but that's just me.

Makes ya feel a little different about foreign aid, huh?

Anyway, that girl and her friends and family who were waitin' on
me gave me one hell of a 'hit the ground runnin' learning experience
that's no doubt saved me a ton more money than I'd lost since. Oh,
I've been taken a time or two since then, and the biggest time way
after I should've known better. And it all has to do with that Island I
pointed out back there from my yard. And Rose.

No, it's not that *Rose* took me as much as it was her family. And the
fact that it's her culture to allow it, and she never stepped in to stop
it.

But I'll get to that.

That reminds me. Back to my story.

Do you believe in Bigfoot?

Well, I ask because it's kinda relevant to the story I'm gonna tell ya
about that island.

No, I won't laugh at you.

You think there's a possibility?

Well. You're certainly more open minded than I thought you'd be.
There may be hope for you to make it here yet, should you decide to
stay.

Oh look. Here we are already. Let's stop in here and get a cold one.

What's that?

Still not noon yet?

I beg to differ. We're exactly twelve hours ahead of U.S. east coast
time, so actually, my biological clock is telling me it's past prime
time hours and I'm late in wettin' my whistle. And you are too, so
have a seat.

Oh, don't pay any attention to those girls behind the counter pointing and laughing at us, and ducking down behind the bar. Yeah, I saw your eyebrow wrinkle. Of course they know we're here. That's why they're laughin'. Don't take it personal at least. Remember I was tellin' ya back in the yard about how every time you leave the house you have to be reminded that you're different? As if you'd forgotten?

Voila! Here it is!

It's just something you have to get used to. They'll laugh and point at us and fight over who has to wait on us, and then someone'll come over.

See, that's something that used to drive me bat shit crazy my first couple of years here. Bat shit craz*ier*. How they'd always laugh at the sight of me. At first I thought it was me personally, but I came to understand quickly that, again, it was the tone of my skin, and then, just because it's different. It's that whole lack of acceptance thing that is deeply embedded in Asian culture, not just Filipino culture.

I used to view it as blatant racism, and I used to wonder what it was about white skin that made them laugh so much. But again, that fueled my anger, and that was leading nowhere good fast. And I was still on all those pills back then, and I was drinking heavily all the time, not these little bi-annual binges I go on these days. And I'd like to eliminate those too, by the way, at some point. So when I got off the pills and *tried* to get off the booze, and went on this soul searching mission to reprogram my mind- for the sake of my own survival really- I had to change my way of thinking about that too. The laughter and the pointing.

So here it is. This is what I tell myself when it happens.

'White people make brown people happy.'

Yup. That's it. It really is that simple, and I'm sure politically uncorrect back home. But that's another thing about this place. All of Asia again. Political correctness does not exist here, and the people view it as the weakness that it is. They are actually taught in their business courses how to manipulate it- that and white guilt- to their advantage. And they're good at it. Hell, Japan almost took over all of America in the 1990's doing it. Manipulating P.C. and white guilt. Michael Crichton wrote a novel about that. It's called "Rising Sun." I read it a couple months ago. You should read that one.

Here in the Philippines, I've seen people with second grade educations- third world second grade educations mind you- take every damn thing from college educated, professional westerners. Hell, I fall into that category. And I'll tell you all about it. Promise. That's part of the story, I just gotta tell it all in order.

Anyway. The girls are shy, too. That's the thing. They make fun of you, and view you as less than human- you're more in line with an ATM machine than a human being if you haven't figured that out- but they are shy as hell to talk to you, almost as if you have celebrity status.

A lot of it stems from the fact that they think their English isn't very good, but most of 'em speak very good English. And I always blow their minds by speaking to 'em in Visayan. There are a lot of people down here that speak Visayan and English, but not Tagalog, even though it's their national language. And I'm talking about Filipino people.

Sometimes I go overboard with the whole language thing and tell 'em I'm German, and that I don't speak English. Just to get 'em to have an entire conversation with me in Visayan. It's a great way- the best way actually- to learn.

And that's real world learnin' friend. None of that classroom bullshit that comes with a piece of paper afterward that says you're qualified to do something that you've never really done before. God, to think that I used to take part in such a system of incompetence and artificial proclamation of qualification.

And sometimes I'll speak only English and give no sign that I know any Visayan if I want to know what they're sayin' about me. Because you'll never really know if you don't understand their language. They'll tell you that you're so guapo, which means handsome remember, and then turn around and say to each other in Visayan that you're 'pangit,' which means ugly.

But remember. They're not all like that.

Anyway, I digress.

And get used to it, because I do it a lot. I've already told ya that, and you've already seen it. That's why my asawa wouldn't agree to go out with me for six months at first. I already told you that too, though, didn't I?

Oh look. The really cute one finally got the nerve.

Ma-ayune Buntag! (Good morning)

You speak Visayan?

Deli. Deli. Walla kasabote Visayan ko (No. No. I do not understand Visayan).

….silence…

Char lang! (Joke only!)

See what I mean? I just tell her that I don't understand her language, *in* her language, and she has no clue what I'm talking about. So I tell her I'm joking, and she just stares at me. It's that damn figurative speech thing. Give me a sec…

Palit Ko dako Pilsen. (I buy big beer.)

Isa lang? (One only?)

O O. (Yes.)

Baso? (Glass?)

Deli. Deli. Enum ko echuck akow kamote (No. No. I'm going to drink from my hands.)

…silence…

Char lang! (Joke only!) Doha baso. (Two glasses.)

See. I just miss being able to joke around a bit with a pretty young waitress. I mean, these girls are pretty, sure. But it's that whole literal minded thing.

Anyway, I ordered us a liter of San Miguel Pilsen. You've got three main choices of beer here. That, or San Miguel light, or Red Horse. And they're all brewed by San Miguel.

The Pilsen tastes like Coors. The San Miguel Light tastes like Coors light, and the Red Horse? Well, that tastes like horse piss. And it actually has a little horse piss in it. It's what the Filipinos like to drink when they can afford something more than Tuba, which only costs seventy five cents a gallon by the way.

Why Red Horse?

Because it's strong as hell! Seven and a half percent alcohol per volume. Like malt liquor. And when they drink, they don't drink like we do. To relax. They drink to get drunk.

Spoken like a true alcoholic huh?

All right. So, back to Bigfoot. Or rather, the fact that you are at least willing to believe in the possibility of Bigfoot.

That's good.

Now, before we get there, Let me ask you a couple other questions. And it will all add up by the end of these stories. Hell, which may take to the end of the day. But that's okay. Because you'll find that here on the islands, all you have is time.

Sounds nice, don't it?

In time it'll drive you crazy.

Or craz*ier*.

Okay, next question. If I were to have asked you, on September 12, 2001, who was responsible for knockin' down the world trade towers the day before, what would you have told me?

Exactly! Me too!

No one knew.

Yet.

But if I would have asked you the same question two weeks later, what would you have told me?

Exactly! Al Qaeda!

And why?

Of course. Because that's what we were told.

And we'd been trained by then, hadn't we?

No, I'm not talking about the two weeks where we didn't know. I'm talking about our entire lives before that.

Conditioning! That's what I'm talking about. All those years in school, where we were taught to respect and listen to authority, but by God, don't ever question it!

And the majority? Oh, now the majority is always right. Right?

So you and I and the rest of the American people are thinking Al Qaeda, right? Two weeks after the attacks.

What about now?

I mean, what about now? Who do you think was behind the attacks of nine eleven now?

Ah- you're hesitating. Your mind is working.

Why? Why aren't you so sure?

Well, I commend you. You may not have thought for yourself too much early on, but you've learned over the past decade or so to do so.

Okay, let me tell you about nine eleven.

No. I don't have any crazy conspiracy theory, though most of the ones I've read about make more sense than what a lot of the government has said.

Anyway, no, I don't have any more proof about nine eleven than you do that points to it being someone other than Al Qaeda. But I want to tell you about an experience I had in the month leading up to those attacks. An experience with a very beautiful and mysterious woman. An older woman.

And I swear on my life, this is true.

Oh, look. Our beer's here. Just in time.

Put ice in it. I know, we don't do that back home. But if you don't, that beer'll be warm as piss in about ninety seconds. And you remember I said it tastes like Coors? You let it get warm and it tastes like Schlitz.

There ya go. Take a sip.

Not bad, huh?

After a few it gets better 'cause you can't really taste it as much.

Okay, here goes with the story.

And of all the things you're gonna hear from me today, or ever, this is the scariest story I will ever tell!

3

It was the summer of 2001, of course, and it was hot as hell! Not like here, but hot.

I was in my late-twenties that year, though if it weren't for my business suit, cheap as it was- I mean, I'd bought it on a teacher's salary- I'd have passed for nineteen. I've always looked younger than I am.

Well, until after the war. Or some point during the war really. Dealin' with that asshole Lieutenant we had as a platoon leader in Iraq. There's another story to add to the list of stories for ya. Stress'll really age ya, and man, was that little prick stressful! Lieutenant Bee, his name was. I'll tell ya all about him later.

See? I told you ya. Ya need ice in that beer. Yours has already melted.

Here. Have more.

So, anyway. I was seriously considering gettin' out of teachin'. Had been. Too many people makin' the rules who'd never taught. They were legislators really, not educators, and they were comin' up with some pretty dumb ideas. Had been all through the nineties really, but the stupidness was reaching epic levels.

Plus, my wife. Yeah, I'm happily divorced, and the whole experience the first time around's probably why I've not made things legal eagle here with the 'ol asawa, who's not really my asawa, but hey. Anyway, my wife wanted me to get out of teaching and do something a little more upscale, as she called it.

So I'd taken a year off. No biggie. Just wanted to try something different and get my wife off my back for a while. And hell, everyone was makin' money on Wall Street back in those days, so I thought I'd try it. I had a couple buddies who were brokers for a regional firm and I got one of 'em to let me apprentice for him.

My first thought was, 'man, look at me moving up in the world. Goin' from teachin' history in a little country high school in backwoods Virginia, to working on Wall Street!' Well, I soon found out that I was nothing more than a salesman.

A door to door salesman, at that.

Knock, knock. Who's there? Yes ma'am, yes sir, my name's Pete Richards, and I offer a fine line of stocks, bonds and mutual funds, and bank issued CD's. But you'd be better off buyin' some municipal bonds over those, because the rates are the same, but the interest is tax free. And you're not really lockin' your money up for thirty years. You can redeem 'em any time!

There're a lotta retirees out there holdin' on to some 6% tax free bonds right now that're thankful that I came by peddlin' a dozen years ago, I'll betchya! If their bonds haven't been called, they're still earnin' six percent tax free. Hell, the best ya can get these days is less than half that.

Anyway, I remember one particularly hot day from that summer as if it were yesterday. It would have a major impact on my way of thinkin', and how I would forevermore view what is real and what isn't for the rest of my life. It would at least lay the foundation. I'd build on that foundation later in Iraq. And I think I've reached the steeple in my time over here.

At least I'd thought.

That island over there? Boy, just when I thought I had things figured out, that island let me know I still don't know shit.

But we'll get to that.

So I'd been calling on small business owners that day. Mostly because it involved sittin' for long spells in air conditioned offices trying to get past the gatekeepers. Most people would know them as secretaries. The amount of contacts I could make during an hour dropped when I went this route- it was my goal to make twenty five contacts a day- versus makin' house calls in residential neighborhoods, but did I mention the air conditioning?

Anyway, I'm sittin' in this used car lot showroom when I look out on the lot and I see what had to be the most beautiful woman over the age of fifty that I'd ever seen in my life.

Remember! At the time I was nearly half that age, so fifty was old. But still, my heart skipped a beat when I saw this beautiful, olive skinned woman, with nearly waist long silver hair, and the most beautiful, big brown eyes I'd ever seen.

Well. Until I came here. Have you looked at some of the big brown eyes some of these girls have? Look at the girl that brought our beer. Over there laughing at us with her friends.

What's that?

No. It never gets old to 'em. They'd laugh at us until closin' time if we stayed here. But we're not going to. I never stay in the same place too long. They get comfortable with you, and you do with them, then the next thing you know you start feeling like you actually have a real friend, and then BAM! They hit you up for money.

It's always posed as a loan, but they have no intentions of payin' it back. And if you give it to 'em, they never will. If you press 'em on it, they'll actually quit workin' here and work somewhere else, just so they won't have to put up with you pesterin' 'em about the loan. Seriously. I've had *friends* here who've thrown away a year's worth of friendship for a thousand pesos. That's about twenty two dollars.

But the truth is- they were never really my friend. They were just friendly to me, and the minute they saw that I was softened up enough, they pounced. Remember, I'm less than human. I'm more closely related to an ATM machine than a homo sapien.

But remember. They're not all like that.

I told you I digress a lot, didn't I?

So anyway, this beautiful woman out on the car lot caught me lookin'.

What'd she do?

She smiled. She liked it. You could tell.

I went out on the lot and I gave her a card and told her I was an investment counselor, and that I'd love the opportunity to earn her business. And I just kept gogglin' over her.

She took my card and smiled and then asked me how old I was. I told her twenty eight, and she laughed and said that was nice and perhaps she'd be in touch. The owner of the lot came out to greet her, too. She pointed at the car she'd been lookin' at and said, "I'll take this one," and then they went into his office. They came out about ten minutes later, and she drove away in the like-new mini-van.

I asked the owner who she was, and he told me he wasn't really sure. And that she came by every summer and bought a like-new car, with cash, and put more miles on it in a year than anyone else he knew. But she always paid cash, and cash is king, so he never asked too many questions.

"Is it just me, or is she like, the most beautiful older woman you've ever seen?" I asked him.

"She sure is one pretty young lady," he said. I turned to look at him and realized he was pushing seventy. I mean, she had me *that* hypnotized. Then he asked me what in hell I wanted.

I told him I was just passin' by.

A couple weeks went by, and I kept thinkin' about her. And just as I started to forget about her, she called. Isn't that the way it always is?

Hey now!

You'd better slow down on the brewski there. It's not Red Horse, but it's stronger than that domestic stuff back home. And we've got a long day ahead of us, and I've got several stories I wanna tell ya.

Especially about that island over there.

Damn, you're fast. Here, let me order us another beer.

Guapa! (Beautiful!)

Unsa? (What?)

Palit ko e-sapa. (I buy another.)

Okay. It'll only take her five minutes to stop laughin' at us and bring it over, but it'll be here by the time you drain your glass. I'll finish this little story- I swear to God, this is the scariest story I'll ever tell- and then we'll keep walkin'.

Oh, don't worry. We'll get another drink up the road. I wanna take you to one of my old stompin' grounds to tell you about that island. It's okay to go in there now. Jo Jo's gone.

Who's that?

No, not another foreigner. That's good though. Shows you're payin' attention.

He used to manage the place. Total maggot. Stole from everybody, especially me. Guess the owner caught 'im stealing from her a couple years ago and fired his ass. That's when I started going back. But again, not often. Just when I go out on my bi-annual binges. They'll be happy to see me.

See? Here's our beer now.

Salamat. (Thank you.)

Walaysa-payan. (You're welcome.)

So anyway, the woman from the car lot calls, and she says, "You might remember meeting me at a used car lot a couple of weeks ago."

"Oh yes," I said. "How could I forget?"

She giggled. Girlishly. You could tell she liked that.

"I wanted to ask you what kind of money you're used to investing?" she asked.

"Any amount," I said, hoping I sounded convincing. "I'll work with young people who are committed to as little as $25 a month into a mutual fund, but I work with some old people who have a million dollars!"

I wasn't lying. I had a *ton* of young couples investing $25 a month, and two old people that had a million dollars they kept in a money market at my office with strict rules for me to never call them and harass them about investing the money or they would move it elsewhere.

They never heard from me.

"Hm," she said. And she sounded disappointed.

"How much do you have to invest?" I asked.

"Thirty million dollars," she said.

Yeah! I nearly choked on my coffee like you just did your beer.

I mean, that would've given me sixty thousand dollars in gross commissions! My take home, even after taxes would have been more than thirty thousand dollars! That was more than half a year's pay at the time for a teacher, and I stood to make that with an afternoon's worth of work.

I asked her when she could come in and talk and she made an appointment for the next day. Man, I'll tell ya. I didn't get a wink'a sleep that night. The wife and I stayed up counting all the ways we were gonna spend the money. And she seemed so proud of me. It was the only time in our marriage that she seemed proud of me. And it had to do with money. As much as it felt good for her to be proud of me, the reason she was proud of me made me feel kinda sick.

So anyway, this woman. I'll call her Darlene. That's really close to her real name, but I'm changing it a little bit, because this story, more than any other I'll ever tell, can get me killed, and quickly. Anyway, Darlene comes in the next morning.

And this is where it gets really weird.

"This money cannot go into the stock market, because it is going to crash in a month, and I do not want to pay any taxes on the income it generates, because I am not paying for the goddamn war!" That's the first thing she says.

Mind you, the tech bubble had just burst a couple years before this, but the markets had been recovering and were marching on to new highs. Hell, war? We were havin' our longest period of peace in post WWII history! The good times were here again, Jack!

I asked her, in a nice, professional way, just what in the fuck she was talking about. And of course I didn't use the "F" word, but if she hadn't been a lady, I woulda.

"There is going to be a major terrorist attack next month," she says. Mind you, this was August. August of 2001.

"It will be an attack like the American people could never imagine," she continued. "After the attack, we are going to be plunged into the longest, most costly way in history. And I don't want my money in the markets when they crash after the attack, and I don't want to pay taxes to fund the war. That's what I mean."

"Okay," I tell her. Real slow. Like, "Oooooooo-kaaaaaaaaay." You know, like she was crazy? And I tell her about tax free municipal bonds. They're insured, free of taxes, and with the rates where they were at the time, she would be looking at roughly $1.8 million a year in tax free interest.

"Great!" she said. "I'll take it!"

"It'll take me a few days to work up a portfolio," I told her. "I'll need to call our bond desk and work with them directly on this, because it's such a big amount."

"That's no problem," she said. "I don't have the money just yet anyway. But I'll have it soon."

"So where are you getting this money?" I asked her.

Now, by this point I thought she was half crazy, so I was a little scared of what she might say. But what she said wasn't what I expected, and it kind of scared me more because of that.

"It's my money," she said.

"I know, but where is it coming from?"

"You don't need to know that," she said.

I told her that I know my home office would ask, and that I was kinda curious, and then she says, "You know why I'm dealing with you? Instead of some big wig down at Merrill Lynch?"

I told her no, and she said, "I'll tell you why. Because you're young, and I can tell you're hungry. You don't ask me any stupid questions, and I won't tell you any stupid lies."

"Sounds good to me," I said. And I told her how much I stood to make in commissions, and that the missus and I already had it spent in our heads. She just laughed and relaxed and started opening up.

She told me that her job was to go around to all these different prisons and put on classes for men who were serving life terms and couldn't read or write. She said her efforts were funded by certain interests that were not *part* of the government, but that were certainly *associated* with the government.

I didn't really understand most of it. What I gathered was that she was spending a lot of time in prisons, talking to a lot of potentially bad people- I mean, you don't get life for grand theft auto, and that's bad enough- but I could understand where all those miles on her car were coming from.

"So who funds you?" I asked her. "And what's the purpose? What does society stand to gain by having a literate lifers populace?"

She leaned back and asked me if I'd ever heard of...

Oh, look at that. Out in the street.

Yeah- the guy walking down the street jerkin' off.

Bet you never seen that back in The States, huh?

Now watch everyone around him. They get out of his way- I mean hell, wouldn't you?- and then they point and laugh, and heckle and ridicule.

My friend, you are seeing third world mental healthcare in action. Remember what I was sayin' back in my yard about different? Well, that's pretty different wouldn't ya say? And you see how he's bein' treated.

Oh sure, I've seen that before. I've seen *him* do it before. That's why I'm not shocked.

It was the first time. I seen him comin' up to me with his hand out, beggin' for money. But what I didn't see at first was that his other hand was wrapped firmly around his prick, going up and down as he was coming at me.

Man, I jumped back and told him to get the hell away from me before I broke a bottle over his head. He just kept on goin'. Went up a couple shops, laid down in the parking lot and finished his business. Hell, everyone gathered around, laughin' and pointin', and takin' pictures with their cell phones. Even the guards.

Yeah, you noticed that did you? Armed guards at every business. Don't let the guns intimidate ya. Number one, most of the guards- most as in all of them- have never fired their weapons. They're more decorative than anything. And letter B, most of the guns are so old and rusty they'd be as inaccurate as a pre-civil war musket anyway.

So even the guards were recording this poor bastard bustin' a nut right there in the parking lot.

Oh, I've seen others drop their pants and take a shit on the sidewalk. I've seen couples- homeless, mentally ill couples that is- having sex in the park. The locals act the same way as you just saw 'em act with jerkoff man. They point and laugh and take pictures. No one tries to get these people any help. They provide too much entertainment.

Yeah. I know. It's sad as hell.

But you aint gonna change it!

And remember. No matter how much ya see, you gotta keep tellin' yourself. They're not all like that.

So anyway. Where was I?

Oh yea, she asked me if I knew this guy. Now I am definitely not gonna say *his* name.

Why?

'Cause no way in *hell* would I live for forty eight hours afterward if I said this guy's name. That's if it got out to the wrong people.

Look, I'll tell ya this much. The guy she was asking about, she was asking about because it was her uncle. Well, I'd never heard of him at the time, and I told her that, and she threw her head back and laughed and told me I *was* young and then just started going on and on about how her uncle and his friends had the whole world played, and that he was really a prick, but he paid her well to be a message runner, etc. etc.

So, at this point, I'm convinced the bitch is completely insane. I mean, terrorist attacks? Wars? Going into prisons under the guise of teaching prisoners while the whole time allegedly being some sort of message carrier for some sort of secret society?

Nuts, right?

But I couldn't afford to write her off as such, or treat her as such, because my wife and I had already fantasized about the new car, and the new big screen television, and paying off the credit card debt. You know, all that. I was a middle class schmuck back in those days, and those things were all important to me.

So anyway, she leaves, and I call my bond desk and tell 'em all about it. They ask me where this woman's gettin' the money, and I told 'em she had a rich uncle. Which really was the truth. I just left out the part of how her rich uncle was Lex Luther.

A few weeks go by. I'm still countin' the money in my head, my commission that is, but she's not called or stopped back by. So, on September, 10'th- and I shit you not- on September 10'th, 2001, I call her. I told her some lame shit about how I wanted to make sure we got her all the bonds we'd planned on buyin' in her account, but I was afraid that they were gonna sell out of inventory, and I asked her if she'd gotten the thirty million dollars yet.

"Not yet!" she said. She almost screamed it. But she wasn't mad.

She was frantic!

"Not yet! But I'll have it soon! Really soon! Something is going to happen soon, and I'll get paid. I have to go!"

And then she hung up. Just like that. And I wrote her off as crazy.

And then the next day, my world, your world, everyone's world changed instantly when those planes flew through those buildings.

Man, I'll always remember that day. Just like you. I was on the phone talkin' to a mutual fund wholesaler out of Newport News, Virginia. My buddy Craig with the American Funds Group. He's readin' me somethin' off the net about a plane flyin' through one of the world trade towers and then we start comparing hangovers, and laughing, and wasting away precious selling time like we did on way too many mornings. I mean, we assumed it was some drunk bastard in a Cessna.

All of a sudden, Craig says, "Uh-oh." I'm like, "what's up?" and he says he's just read that another plane hit the other tower, and that he had to go.

I got off the phone and turned on the television in my office. Stan, that's the guy I was apprenticing for, and who, by the way, is a teacher himself now back in Virginia- at least last I knew. He'd actually spent some time as a preacher before that. Stan comes back, and we stand there and watch on the news the destruction of that day.

I remember that we stayed glued to the tube that whole week. The markets were closed you'll remember, so it's not like there was any work to do. So we watched the television, smoked cigarettes- and I wasn't even a smoker- and drank beer. Yep. We drank beer, right there in our place of business, and I don't think anyone would'a said a thing about it that week. Matter-a- fact, there was a Baptist church right beside our office, and the preacher'd been comin' over to watch the news, and *he* drank a few beers with us that week, though I told him I'd never say a word.

Oops.

So toward the end of that week, Stan looks at me, and he says, one word.

"Darlene!"

I didn't have to tell him about all the crazy shit she'd been talkin' about the terrorist attacks and the war. He used to hang out on the other side of the door of my office- I'd never shut it- and listen to my appointments so that he could critique me on 'em afterward.

So I race to the phone, pick it up and dial, and I get a disconnection sound. Her line was dead.

Considering everything that'd happened that week, I decided to call our field compliance office. They dealt with legality and stuff like that. So I call 'em, I tell 'em the story, and they tell me not to go anywhere, because they were gonna call me right back after talking to one of the firm's managing partners.

So five minutes later, dude calls back and tells me to call the F.B.I. I felt my blood go cold, but I knew he was right, so I did.

In less than an hour, I had two F.B.I. field agents in my office. And you wanna know the weird thing? You remember the old X Files show? Well, these agents could've passed as doppelgangers for Mulder and Scully. Seriously! They were both in their mid-thirties and had those boy next door/girl next door good looks. She was a redhead, and he seemed to wear one of those, "I know something you don't" smirks on his face, just like Mulder.

So I tell 'em the story. And the whole time I'm talkin' they're both takin' notes, and they have a recorder goin'.

So when I finish the story, I ask 'em if I'm crazy.

"Oh no!" Doppelganger Scully says. "This is the exact dollar amount…"

And then Doppelganger Mulder elbows 'er, and she catches 'erself and shuts up.

"We can't really say," Doppelganger Mulder says.

"Can you give me some follow up when you find out what's up?" I asked 'em. I mean, I was really curious. And since I'd already lost my thirty thousand in commissions I'd never gotten, I was kinda hopin' they'd be sending little miss beautiful older woman Darlene into one of those prisons she was so fond of visiting. But not to teach classes.

"We can't do that," Doppelganger Mulder says. "Thank you for your time."

And then they got up and left.

#

Guapa! (Beautiful!)

Ulit ko bali. (I go home.)

They'll have the check here in a couple minutes. Go piss and I'll pay and then piss myself, and we'll head on up the street.

As long as jerkoff man's moved on.

4

No, I never found out anything else about Darlene.

Who was her uncle?

Watch out for that hole there. That's the thing about the sidewalks here. They'd be better off without 'em. They're all so uneven. Hell, I've done some pretty dangerous odd jobs here before, and I've never gotten hurt doing 'em, but I've sprained my ankles more than once just from walkin' down the street. Sober.

What kind of odd jobs?

Oh, I'll get to that. That's part of the main story. About the island. It's how I got there. Doin' a job.

Oh, the uncle?

Okay. I said I wouldn't say his name. But have you ever heard of the Trilateral Commission?

Of course you have. I knew you were mindful of things when you said you believed in the *possibility* of Bigfoot.

Well, Darlene's uncle was one of the co-founders of the Trilateral Commission. Now you know why I've changed her name and won't even mention his.

And now you see why I say that that day changed the way I viewed things. A combination of that day and what happened later on September 11, and seeing that that woman actually *wasn't* crazy, but informed, and may have even played a part. And why is it that our government agencies had no problem shouting, "Bin Laden! Bin Laden!" at the top of their lungs, but they'd not tell me peep about Darlene?

But look at how conditioned I was to never question the possibility of all the things she told me about in her forewarning. Like a sheep bein' led off to the slaughter.

Hey, just to appease my asawa, let's go see if the princess is home before we swing by the Green Room. She's probably not, but at least I'll be able to say I went there

Yeah, the Green Room. That's where the story about the island starts, because that's where it started. We call it the Green Room because all the walls are painted green.

But let's go see if the princess's home first, so when my asawa asks I can tell her I did.

Who's the princess? Oh, she's probably the closest thing to a friend among the natives that I have. She's one of a kind. Never asked me for a single peso!

Actually, I think she's a piece of stardust trapped in a human shell. No, really. I know that sounds nuts. But I believe it.

No! I'm not on any drugs. I flushed 'em, remember? Well, threw 'em in the jungle. That whole flushing toilet thing, remember?

Oh, it's not far. Just up this alley actually. She lives under a tarp up here at the end beside this banana field.

Okay, I'll tell you about the princess, and more of why I'm here. She's played a big part in my recovery slash reprogramming my mind, so to say.

I'm crazy.

I'm completely insane.

But I've already told you that, and you've probably figured it out on your own.

At least that's what certain U.S. Government agencies have told me. That I'm crazy. They've even given me as many as a dozen medications at a time for my 'isms, the use of which always led to other substances. But I already told you about that, too.

More than once they've kept me for study. In-patient *they* call it. Incarceration *I* say. All to determine just which label to pin on me, in the hope, of course, of coupling the right medication to said label. It's all about the drugs anymore. Let's put a band aid on somethin' that needs stitches, then sit back and watch as they fuck their lives up even more after gettin' addicted to the band aid.

I've managed to escape what Ken Kesey referred to as 'the combine' in his 1962 novel, "One Flew Over the Cuckoo's Nest." Now *that's* a great book! Go read it if you haven't. And no, the movie's no substitute! Though I do love 'ol Jack!

I've not changed here, because wherever I go, there I am, but I've shed the labels simply because I'm no longer around those who would want to label me. For the purposes of profit at least.

Living here in the Philippines I've taken on a whole new slew of labels. I've told you about these already, and you've noticed it yourself while we've been walkin' down the street. They include; foreigner, Joe, rich, Americano, and yeah, sometimes, crazy American, but they don't lock me up and shove pills down my throat here when they call me these things. They simply stare, and laugh, and then go on with their lives, allowing me to go on with mine, and that's okay. I'm gettin' more and more used to it the longer I'm here, though there are days I won't leave the house 'cause I just don't want to deal with it. And that's not okay. I worry about that sometimes, actually.

However, it wouldn't be a bad idea, I don't think, if they could lock up jerkoff man and a few others for a while. I guess some people *do* need some inpatient incarceration.

Living here in my self-imposed exile I've discovered my own form of therapy. It doesn't involve any mind altering medications that make me gain weight, or lose weight, or want to sleep all day, or stay up all night, Like Huey Lewis sang about. Or worse! Make me wanna kill myself or others, like some of the medications I was on in the U.S. did- all in 'their' attempt to make me 'normal,' whatever the hell *that* is.

My therapy?

It's simple. Reprogramming my mind, like I've told you already.

What does this involve? Reprogramming my mind?

You mean specifically?

It simply involves a strong desire and an open willingness to see the world around me as it truly exists; not how corporations, political parties, religious institutions, the byproducts of my upbringing, or my own warped way of thinkin' wants me to see it.

A keyword to keep in mind during this form of therapy is "perspective."

You see, in life, there really is very little good, and there is very little bad. There is, however, lots of perspective. And perspective, if it's inaccurate, can be very damaging and misleading. It can make things that are not true appear to be facts.

Now, let's talk about my 'crazy.'

My kind of crazy, I was told, stems from having so many 'problems.' Not enough fill in the blank. And you can fill that blank in with anything; money, food, healthy relationships, material objects.

Okay. Now according to whom?

Those telling me these things were missing, that's who.

As a middle aged American, who'd spent almost all forty of those years placed in the box of the American middle class, I became convinced, as convinced as I am that gravity exists, that I needed the two cars, a house of a certain size, certain appliances in that house, etc. to be whole. Why, this message was sent to me from the television, the radio, the internet. It came from my neighbors across the street, from my neighbors to my left and right, from my family members. It came from my colleagues, my peers, my superiors, and my subordinates.

DO this, HAVE that, and you will BE all that you can BE.

No one would have ever guessed that this formula was completely backward, and that it should read thus: BE who you are, DO what your heart leads you to do, and you will HAVE a life of contentment and you'll know no want.

So who taught me this? Well, it's come from my therapy- rewiring my brain- gettin' away from the onslaught of corporate advertising and political horse rubbish most Westerners are subjected to. And you'll do well to kill your television to accomplish this. But I'll admit, I've had some help.

I'll get to Rose. The girl on the island. She was a big help, even though things ended up the way they did. But one of the biggest helpers I've had with this new concept of living without labels and boxes and medications and constant want and awareness of problems is a woman I've spent time with- quite a bit of time in the last year or so- yet with whom I've never had a single conversation.

To my knowledge, she can't even speak.

I call her the Perspective Princess of the Philippine Islands, and that's who we're on our way to see.

A year ago I would've referred to her as a homeless beggar, but that's only because I'd not come as far as I have today in reprogramming my mind. A lot of it's that I'd started judging the people of the Philippines the same way they judge me. And that's not good. That's one of the biggest dangers of constantly being treated the way you are here as a white foreigner. You start to reciprocate. And I'm keepin' my eye on that as closely as I am the whole agoraphobia thing.

Anyway, the princess isn't homeless. She has a home, albeit one she's constructed herself of plastic bags and tarps she's found here and there. It's just right up here a little further. See the tops of the banana trees on the horizon? Just there.

And a beggar? Perhaps. But she's never asked me for anything.

I first noticed her one afternoon, about a year ago, when I was walking into a local store to buy something- I can't remember what- but I do remember I was frustrated, worrying about some problem or another I was convinced that I had. Being harassed the whole way to the store for forgettin' to put my brown on that day hadn't helped.

"Oh no," I remember thinking as I prepared to walk by her. "Just don't make eye contact. Just don't make eye contact."

I passed her, and her hand did not come out. I glanced down at her, sitting in the small amount of shade provided by the building, and she was looking up at me, smiling, but not begging. And man, what a smile! Her face was scarred, she had burn marks or birth defects of some sort all over her skin, and she was as grubby as an old doll that'd been left out in the weather on the playground for a few months, but what a smile!

I wrote her off as mentally insane, like so many others have me. She had to be crazy, right? How could someone with so little be smiling so big? She was so dirty and scarred; I wouldn't even begin to be able to make an accurate estimate of her age.

"She'll get me on the way out," I mumbled to myself. But when I came out, she was gone.

I'd see her again, off and on, while I was out and about, and ironically, it was usually during times when I was worrying about some problem or another that I thought I had.

Once I saw her in front of a JolliBee restaurant. That's kind of like the McDonalds of the Philippines. They sell fried chicken and cheap rice like everyone else, and the burgers suck. Don't waste your money on the burgers.

She was chewing on a chicken leg while I was on my way in. I looked down at her, sitting there eating on the curb, expecting her hand to come out, and it never did.

But she gave me that smile again.

I asked her if she wanted some food. She looked at me like *I* was the one who was mentally insane and held her drumstick up for me to see, as if I hadn't seen it, and shook her head no.

"Weird," I thought. "She'll get me on the way out." But when I came out she was gone.

I was starting to think that perhaps my Perspective Princess of the Philippine Islands was merely a figment of my imagination. I told you at the beginning of this rambling that I'm crazy. I'm absolutely insane. And I know you've figured it out for yourself.

Then, one day, while out for a walk, thinking about how much I missed hot showers, real pizza, and those flushing toilets we've talked about, I found where she lived. There, under a tarp tied down to a wall and gate of what appeared to be an abandoned property, sat my Perspective Princess of the Philippine Islands. I watched as she did what appeared to be her daily chore. She was taking small stones, pebbles really, from one shoe box, one at a time, and then placing them into another shoe box. Every time she did this, she'd make a tally mark with a pencil in a notebook she kept.

She noticed me staring after a few minutes, and she offered me the same smile she'd always given me when I'd seen her before. She waved me over and motioned for me to sit with her in the shade.

"Asa emu bali?" I asked her. "Where is your house?"

She motioned around her with her hands, never speaking, letting me know that this *was* her house.

"Asa tuloog ka?" I asked. "Where do you sleep?" She pointed to the ditch in front of her bench. It was lined with palm leaves, and there was a tarp on top of the leaves. I could tell that the makeshift bed was actually slept in regularly due its indention into the ground, proof of regularly bearing weight, though I doubt that weight was more than seventy five pounds.

She smiled again, and then continued counting her pebbles. She was keeping the tally marks in traditional sets of five; four lines, side by side, and then the fifth crossing through the four, from top left, to lower right. I watched for a few minutes, and I felt a feeling of peace wash over me. One I'd rarely felt and one I'd never experienced from any of the mind altering medications I'd been given in The States. I offered to take the note book and keep the tally as she moved the stones from one box to the other. She gave me that smile again, showing how happy she was that I was willing to help.

I've never intentionally gone looking for my perspective princess of the Philippine Islands at times when I've been flustered and needed my perspective reset, but she's always seemed to appear, like magic, at times when I've needed it the most. I don't think that intentionally going out to compare myself with someone less fortunate would work, because frankly, I think that is disgusting and the act of doing so would have negative energy attached to it. I do think, however, that the great consciousness of the Universe puts us in the places we need to be, and in contact with the people we need to be in contact with, when we are supposed to be there and when we are supposed to be with them.

When the student is ready, the teacher will appear.

I've come a long way in reprogramming my mind, and it's led to a more peaceful life. I still have a long way to go. Nearly forty years of programming cannot be undone in the five years that I've been here. And I have to watch it with the locals. If I go out, and I'm not in just the right mood to be able to ignore 'em, a little heckling from a few of 'em can set me off. But I've come a long way, even with that.

I'm more comfortable in my own skin than I've been in many years, perhaps ever, and it's taken no pills, no therapy, other than my own which I've been describing, and I've not been locked up in any antiseptic smelling wards or clinics. I've been walkin' around, enjoying the fresh, sea breezes of this beautiful archipelago in the south Pacific, a free man, with no addictions, minus that bi-annual binge I've mention, with a simple understanding that in life, things happen. We can label them as good, or we can label them as bad, or we can simply accept them, and not label them at all.

Because remember, it isn't about good or bad. It's about perspective. And at times, when I lose sight of proper perspective, I have a friend that I can visit to regain it. We can sit, count rocks, and enjoy the shade. Doing so always seems to put everything into the proper perspective.

Now you understand that whole slipper countin' thing I had goin' on back in the yard. Replacement therapy.

Well, here we are. There's her tarp, and it looks like she's not here.

Yes, she really does sleep down there in that ditch. And I don't know how, but I guarantee you she sleeps better at night than you and I do.

She's got somethin' you can't pick up at any clinic or in any church. I don't know what it is, but I want it.

Let's go to the Green Room.

5

Okay, now the Green Room is one of the places where I only speak English.

Why?

Well, remember I told you that I stopped going for a long time, because of Jo Jo? The old manager? How he was always cheatin' me outta money? Well, pretty much everyone else in the place is like that too. It's safer to let 'em think I don't understand Visayan so when they start schemin' I can catch it before anything happens. If they know I speak Visayan they'll switch over to Tagalog and I won't know what's comin'.

Oh, they'll never hurt you physically. I swear to God, in spite of all the bullshit State Department warnings about comin' to the Philippines, you and I are safer here than we are on the streets of our own country. We can walk down this same street we're walking down now, at… look there, it's mid-afternoon already, so you won't have to feel guilty about havin' the next drink. But we can walk down this street at 2 a.m. and no one'll touch us. The Filipino people are a very non-violent people.

If you're a foreigner, and you get physically attacked in the Philippines, it's probably because you're an asshole and deserved to have your ass kicked anyway. I know of only one foreigner who's ever gotten in a fight here. He got the shit kicked out of him and it was his own fault.

What happened?

Oh, he's one of the typical foreigners I told you about earlier, that makes me avoid most foreigners. Here to drink himself and screw 'imself to death.

One day, he's drinkin' with some young guys, early twenties maybe- he's in his mid-fifties- and they run outta booze. So he gives 'em a thousand pesos to go buy some more alcohol.

Well, they come back two hours later with fresh haircuts, a new tee-shirt each, but nothing to drink. He gets all pissed off and starts pushin' 'em around, so they beat the shit out of 'im.

I know, right? I mean, it was twenty two bucks. Chalk it up as a cheap way to know you can't trust those guys and they're not really your friends, and have nothin' to do with 'em in the future. I mean, that's what I'd do. Trust me. I've had lots of cheap lessons on friendship here. And the lessons finally took.

But not this guy. He gets his ass kicked, then on the way home he stops and asks these three other guys if they know the guys that just beat 'im up. Well sure they do. They're all cousins.

See, that's another thing too. Families here are huge. These people will *not* use birth control. And that whole Catholic Church still havin' a choke hold on the country thing's part of it, but not all of it. Gives a lot of 'em an excuse to be irresponsible. Next time a man with ten kids tells you that crap about birth control bein' against his religion, ask 'im when the last time he went to mass was. He'll laugh and give you a high five, which means, "You caught me."

My wife who's not really my wife has six brothers and sisters. No kiddin'.

So anyway, these three guys knew the other three guys because they were cousins. Dude offers 'em all a thousand pesos each to go down there and beat their asses, as long as they put 'em in the hospital.

What do you think happened? That's a lot'a damn money to a Filipino. They go down there and beat their asses and put 'em in the hospital.

So it looks like the foreigner's gotten his revenge, right? Like he came out on top, right?

Wrong.

That will never happen here. Get that in your head right now. If you are a foreigner in the Philippines, you are not allowed to win, be it in a successful business, or a conflict or disagreement, or even a damn game of pickup basketball.

What's that?

Well, I'll tell you what happened. The cousins in the hospital told the cousins who put 'em there, that if they didn't pay 'em two thousand pesos each, they were gonna file a complaint with the police. See, that's another major difference in our countries. You can be victimized- stolen from or beaten right in front of a policeman, and unless you complain, nothing's done. Seriously. Cops here have been known to look the other way during stabbings and beatings for about ten U.S. dollars.

So the cousins who handed out the ass whoopins' went back to the foreigner and told him that the cousins in the hospital knew he'd paid them to do it, and that if he didn't pay them all five thousand pesos each, they were gonna file a complaint, and that he had to give *them* the money to give to 'em, because they also said that if he ever got anywhere near 'em again, they'd file a complaint. So he ended up shillin' out fifteen thousand pesos, and the ass whoopin' cousins skimmed three thousand each off the top and handed two grand each over to the ass-whooped cousins.

So other than that asshole- and I think he *was* an American- I've never heard of any foreigners here being physically hurt by the Filipinos. They hurt you in other ways.

You mean you haven't figured it out?

They take your money.

I know… I know… they can't take it if you don't give it to 'em. Just say no. You wait. They're the most sincere people, and they know exactly how to butter you up the right way, and they can tell once your guard is completely down, and then BAM! Out comes the need. Their problem? Their kid needs an antibiotic, they'll tell you. It's only one hundred pesos. That's just over two dollars.

Well, where you and I come from, if we know of a sick kid, and we know that we can help, what do we do?

Of course! We help.

Especially for such a small amount, right? Two dollars? Of course we're gonna give it to 'em. And they're so friendly, and we've just been talking to 'em for thirty minutes, and they've been telling us how much they love our country and blah blah blah.

Okay. Here're the facts! They probably don't even have a kid. And if they do? The kid probably isn't sick. They'll take your one hundred pesos and go out and buy a big 'ol bottle of rot gut Tanduay Rum, and them and three of their buddies'll sit around and get drunk and talk about the stupid, asshole foreigner that they scammed their drink money out of that day.

No shit. I'm not kidding.

Oh, and they refer to this activity as 'wise.' Beware that word. It's one of several they use in a different way than we do back home. Like the word 'slang.' When they hear you talk, they'll often say, "You are so slang!" and admonish you, like you've done something wrong. Well, what they're talkin' about is your accent. You have an accent. And remember that whole acceptance thing, or lack thereof? Your accent is different than theirs, so in the eyes of some of 'em, you *did* do something wrong by the way you pronounced your words.

And don't try tellin' 'em that slang is reference to a word that is indigenous to a location or subgroup, like ya'll in the southern U.S. or 'nigga' in the ghettos. You'll only confuse 'em with such facts.

Their minds are already made up. Accent is slang, and, by God, you are so slang!

Anyway, the word 'wise?' Same thing.

You and I know that the word 'wise' means, knowledgeable as the result of experience. And in our country, if we hear of someone being referred to as wise, we want to be around 'em. We want to learn from 'em.

Not here. Here, 'wise' means the ability to take advantage of others and not get caught until the advantage has been taken.

Seriously! And they brag about it! They view it as a trait worthy of having. And when they take a foreigner for their money, because they are so "wise," they don't see it for what it is. They lied to someone. They played on their heart strings to get what they wanted from them. They did whatever it took. Mission accomplished!

And the one that was taken advantage of? Well, you're just a fool for believin' it. You thought you were doin' so good in helpin' a sick kid. Well, it's your own damn fault you were took! You were probably just tryin' to make yourself look good anyway, they'll tell ya.

So. If you hear of someone bein' wise here? Run as far away as you can.

But remember. They're not all like that.

And don't beat yourself up about it if you decide to stay and you get suckered. Hell, I made the mistake of givin' to the Bajau once, and I had to move to the other side of town a month later.

Who are they? The Bajau? And that's pronounced Badge-ee-ow! Don't be so slang, Joe!

Oh, they're a local tribe of indigenous people. They're also known as the sea gypsies because of their lifestyle. The legend goes that they lost a battle with another tribe hundreds of years ago, and that their punishment for the loss was that they were never allowed to work again. Or live on the land.

So they live in all these huts out on the sea. They build 'em on log floats at low tide, and tie 'em down to giant chunks of coral and what-not, and they come in off the water to beg all day. The good Catholics give 'em hell and look down on 'em, because the majority of 'em are Muslim. Though a lot of 'em practice very primitive tribal religions and even voodoo and black magic.

And they make more damn money in a day beggin' than you or I do, I'll tell you that!

Just like back home. The beggars on the corners beggin' from the people on their way to work in the mornings are makin' a hell of a lot more money than the dumb asses on their way to work who give 'em money.

So anyway, I gave five pesos one day to this really cute little Bajau girl. She was about eight. Well, on my way home that afternoon, she and her sister were there. So I gave more.

The next day, there're ten kids waiting outside my apartel. That afternoon? Twenty! Because see, I kept givin'.

It got to where if I wanted to be able to get by, I had to take a ten pesos coin and throw it down the street, opposite the direction in which I was goin', and then run for it once they dispersed. I got tired of dealing with it- I mean there were fifty kids there waiting on me every time I went out after that- so I moved.

And once you're here for a while, you learn that the money you give 'em doesn't go to 'em anyway. They take it home and their fathers use it to buy rot got tuba or Tanduay or Red Horse.

So you've got to learn to say no. Even to the kids.

Listen. It breaks my heart, and I'll never understand it. But for some reason, too many of the people here mistake the kindness of the white foreigner for weakness. And they exploit it. It's like a game to 'em.

But you know, that seems to happen in any third world country, so you can't write it off as bein' exclusive to Philippine culture. It's an issue of socio-economics. Hell, read "The Good Earth," by Pearl Buck. Did you know she was the first woman to win a Nobel Prize in literature? And she was born right across the border from where I used to live in Virginia. Some wide spot in the road in West Virginia. Remember what I was talkin' about earlier? About perspective? Hell, folks back home write everyone from West Virginia off as dumb hillbillies, but Pearl Buck wasn't no dumb hillbilly!

Anyway, she wrote about it in her book, and all that was based on her own experiences. She was raised in China. Her parents were missionaries. Can you imagine her frustration? I mean, by all intents and purposes, and in every way *except* ethnicity, she was Chinese. Yet she spent the majority of her life having to deal with the ignorance thrown at her because of the color of her skin. The skin tax. The stares. The complete lack of acceptance, even though she was part of the culture. She knew the language, she knew the ways, she knew the traditions, but she couldn't change the color of her skin.

Anyway. Mistaking the white foreigner's kindness for weakness. Back to that.

I've been out before and I've had people- street vendors- tell me that my asawa was by the day before and bought a pop cola- that's like a really shitty, generic version of coke- and that they got to talkin' and that she forgot to pay 'em. "It's only eight pesos," they say, and give you those big puppy dog eyes. So you feel sorry for 'em. Tell 'em you're sorry on your asawa's behalf and then you give 'em eight pesos.

Then they go back and high-five their buddy and they laugh. They just took you for eight pesos, and they view it as if there's nothing wrong with it, because in their minds you're rich, and they think you should just give to 'em anyway. It's the worst entitlement mentality I've ever seen. They make the biggest welfare bums in America look like the hardest workin' men and women you'll ever meet.

Then that story spreads. Then you can't walk down the street without every street vendor givin' ya some bullshit story about how your asawa was there yesterday, or last week, and bought whatever the hell their sellin' and forgot to pay.

Listen to me. I get a beer in me and it gets a little hot, and all that reprogramming of my mind that I just told you about starts to undo itself. Everything I just said is negative, and derogatory toward a whole race of people. And that will only turn to hate, and racism, and then I'm no better than they are. But I'm just tryin' to help you understand the way things are here when you're a foreigner. It's for your own protection.

Life in the Philippines can be marvelous. But you've always got to keep in mind the fact that there's life in the Philippines as a Filipino, and then there's life in the Philippines as a foreigner. And the two lives can be worlds apart. Doesn't make it a bad thing, that's just how it is. And remember what I was sayin' about perspective? Look! Don't view it as bad. Just know it's how it is and learn how to live around it, and you can still enjoy your time here.

Most of the time.

So I've given myself a defense for this, by the way. Bein' approached with all their problems once they've buttered me up with a bit of friendly conversation. And I've done it to make sure I don't let it get me down and turn me into a hateful bastard.

It's a simple statement.

What's the statement?

It ain't my problem. That's the statement.

Now, if they're trying that 'sick kid' crap on me, I don't tell *them* it ain't my problem, because there is always that slight chance that they're tellin' the truth. And I do mean slight. But what I'll say is, "I'm so sorry to hear that, but I have my own family to take care of. But I will pray for your child, that God will bring his wonderful healings to its body and make it whole."

Now look, you've got to be sincere when you say it, and be sure to use the God thing.

Why?

Listen. This may be the last county on earth where the Catholic Church has a stranglehold on the government and the culture. Like I mentioned briefly earlier.

No, I'm serious. They do.

Yes! Even in the twenty-first century, there is a non-Islamic nation- a Christian nation- allowing the church to control their politics and their economy.

I'm sure there're some still in South America, too. Or Latin America.

But anyway, they take the whole God thing seriously, so not only do you seem sincere, as opposed to a shallow prick by simply saying, "It ain't my problem" when they're talkin' about a sick kid, but you remind them of the whole God concept, and they hesitate, just for a minute, and remember that, "Thou shall not lie and steal" thing.

And it works. And for a minute, they almost recognize you as a human being, and not an ATM machine. You can see the flash in their eyes. But only briefly.

But it keeps you from bein' taken, which would lead to bein' pissed off all the time, which leads to misery. What did Mark Twain say about anger? He said anger is an acid that can do more harm to the vessel in which it is stored than to anything on which it is poured. That's what he said.

I told you I read all the damn time.

The biggest danger, at least as I see it, is that in time your anger'll turn to hate. Life can be a sweet place to be, but not if you're angry and hateful. And life isn't about where you make it, it's about what you make of it, whether you're here or back in The States or in Finland. A nice little province of America as the locals might think of it.

Oh, look. Here we are.

Now, remember what I said. I only speak English in here, so don't ask me anything about what they're sayin'. If you need to know, I'll tell ya.

Hey, let's sit back there in the far corner. It's dark and cool back there, and people can't see us from the street.

That's another thing. You don't wanna be seen from the street when you go into a place to eat or have a drink. By the time you come out, they'll be lined up with their hands out. Not to mention how annoying it is with all the faces pressed up to the window like you're an exhibit at the D.C. zoo.

Oh! And you *especially* don't wanna be seen from the street in a place like *this*.

Why?

It's a little more than a waterin' hole.

What do you mean, what do I mean? Look around.

Yes!

Now you get it.

Pretty ain't they?

Hold on. Let me get a beer. Here comes the waitress.

One liter of Pilsen and two glasses, please. And Ice.

No. We don't speak your language. Sorry.

No. I don't want a girl. Just a beer and some ice.

Look at that cutie over there by the door. She's all of eighteen and one hour old, I bet.

Oh, they really are eighteen. Not much older though. The owner of this place is the chief of police- well, his wife runs it- but it's his money that keeps it goin'. But he can't afford the scandal of workin' underage girls in here.

That's one of the erroneous parts of the reputation of this place anyway. Oh, hell. Everyone in America thinks if you come to the Philippines that you come here to screw kids. That's the biggest bunch of bullshit I've ever heard. In all my time here, I've never seen any child sex tourists.

Listen, the people here wouldn't allow it. One thing that's sacred here is children.

There're many aspects to life here that I can appreciate more than back home. And one of 'em is the fact that the monsters back home- like the child rapists, the molesters, the abusers- they aren't here.

And you know that saying about how it takes a village to raise a child? Well, that's true here. You can see it. You might see a couple little kids, three or four years old, playin' around in the street, and at first you think, "Oh Jesus! Where're their parents?" Well, their parents might not be around, but every set of eyes in the vicinity- and as you've seen, there're people everywhere- are on those kids. And if you try to hurt 'em? Or abduct 'em? You'll have half a dozen machetes swinging at your head.

Oh, I know I said they weren't violent. Until you fuck with their kids. And that's true just about everywhere, isn't it?

Oh, here she is with our beer.

Excuse me, Miss?

Oh, the girl at the door thinks I'm guapo?

Tell her I think she's guapa, but I'm married.

Thank you.

Okay, now guapo, if you'll remember, means handsome. But what it really means for us is, "I think you are rich and I am going to tell you whatever I think I need to tell you to get your money." I mean, look at me. I'm forty years old and ugly as the ticks on that dog sleepin' over there in the corner. That pretty little thing, like so many of 'em, could be a model anywhere else in the world. What the hell would she want me for any reason other than my money?

Oh, I know. When I first got here I was actually naïve enough to believe I *was* guapo. But not anymore. Been here long enough to know I'm ugly again.

Okay, time for the story about that Island I was tellin' ya about. The one with the lightning.

What?

Oh, I know I've been sayin' I'd get to it all day, and I am now.

Remember what I said just a minute ago about there not being monsters here like back home? Well, there're different kinds of monsters here. And not the kind that comes in human form. And they're over there on that island.

I already asked you if you believed in Bigfoot, right? And you said you believe in the possibility, right?

Well. Keep that same open mind for this one. And at least be willin' to believe in the possibility of the truth of these things.

I can assure you.

They're real.

6

Here in the Green Room's where it all started, so this is the best place to tell it. Guess this was the arrow pointin' to the Isle of Kapre, as I've come to call it. I don't come here much anymore. Gotten away from these old stompin' grounds of mine. But I had to bring ya here for the story. The atmosphere of the place.

Back when I was livin' a life of ill repute, I used to come here a lot for the girls. And I used to work a bit, and this was always a good place to pick up some odd jobs. Jo Jo was a maggot, and because of that he had some maggoty connections. And that's what I needed at the time.

What kinda work?

I used to do contract work.

For who?

Well, certain interests. I can't really say the Philippine Army, even though Captain Morales, my boss, worked for them. He was using some of the men from his platoon for side jobs himself. And that's where I'd get my work.

Oh, it isn't legal. I mean, if they went by the rules it'd be the same as if some Army guys back home were using the government dime and weapons and troops to have private militias. I mean, almost all their laws here, especially within their military, are mirrored after ours.

But if you haven't noticed, laws here are really more like recommendations. Especially the damn traffic laws. As long as you don't have an accident you can pretty much do what you want. And even then, as long as no one gets hurt, no one's cited. I mean, you've seen the way they drive. I came up with the solution to their population problem once. Send over about ten thousand U.S. drivers. That would take care of it.

How?

Road rage of course.

No, they don't get that here. I've seen 'em run right into each other, 'cause they don't even look before entering an intersection. They just go. The attitude is that if someone's comin' they'll stop. Most of the time, yes. But not all the time.

But don't expect to see a fist fight when there's a fender bender. Remember, the people here are very passive. Physically. Now they'll aggress the hell outta your wallet. But when they have fender benders, they'll laugh it off and as long as no one's hurt, they just go on their way.

So, send over about ten thousand U.S. drivers, who do very much suffer from road rage, and I think in about six months the population would be under control here, because it would certainly be reduced.

Listen, I know that while I tell you about how life here is, and it seems like so much of it doesn't make sense, and even defies logic, you'll have to admit that a lot of it would be nice in our own countries. I mean, I know the 'structure' we have is required, and it's made us civilized, but wouldn't you agree that so much of that civility is strangulating?

I mean, just think about your damn car since we're talkin' about drivin'. You have to have a title. Then a registration. Then a license. And that little sticker that goes on your license plate. And then the one that goes on the windshield.

I mean seriously. If you get pulled over for a driving violation in The States, it's not just good enough that you have one proof of obeying one law. You have to have like, eight or ten different things to show you're obeying the eight or ten different laws in place making it legal for you to be on the road.

Oh, and don't forget about the damn insurance!

Okay, so back to Morales. Jo Jo's friend, the army captain.

He led a small team of mercenaries on the side.

Who did he go after?

Oh, whoever he was paid to go after.

Listen, you didn't hear it from me. But he made most of his money during election years. They'll tell you this place is a democracy, but it's not. It's a bunch of little dictatorships built on top of each other.

How's that work?

Like this.

It starts at the barangay level. That means neighborhood, remember. So there's a barangay captain. That's the first dictator. He answers to the mayor, who answers to the governor of the province, who answers to the senator or congressman, who answers to the president.

And they all want public office, because that's where the money's at.

Let's say the barangay needs the roads paved. The barungay Captain determines he needs five million pesos to do it. So he asks the Mayor for ten million.

Why ten million?

Because he knows the Mayor's gonna skim off the funds if they're approved, and he has to pad some in to skim himself.

No, I'm serious. And it's not a secret. The people here *know* this.

What?

Because they don't care. That's why they don't do anything about it. Apathy. They'll tell you they care, but you and I both know that if they cared enough, they'd do something about it. That's human nature. Only when they've had enough will they do anything. For now, guess they just haven't had enough yet.

So anyway, you get where I'm going, right? The amount requested goes up and up as you work your way up the chain. Once it gets approved, and the money starts workin' its way back down the chain, and everyone pads their pockets, the barangay Captain may or may not get what he needs, and he may or may not start the project. And more than likely, he won't, until just a few months before the next election so that it can look like he's doin' something for the people. Once the election is over, the construction stops.

Have you noticed all the half-finished public works projects as we've been out walkin' today? That's why. Don't worry. Some of 'em'll come a little closer to getting' finished next year when the elections roll around.

Sounds asinine to us right?

Oh, and they buy votes. The average vote costs four hundred pesos. That's about ten U.S. dollars.

So where does Morales come into this?

During the last election, more than two hundred people were murdered in this province alone.

Yes, I'm serious.

Who?

The candidates.

See, usually, whoever is the current office holder is part of a political dynasty. At least at these smaller levels. Hell, at the national level, they actually elect their celebrities. There are a few dynasties there too, though.

Why?

Because they like 'em.

Oh, I know that doesn't mean they can lead. Hell, I love Lady Gaga but I don't think I'd like her as a congress woman. But that's how they do things here. It defies logic. And then they wonder why, in the year of our lord that we're in, and while the rest of the world has done such things as travel to the moon and create the internet, the Philippines is still a third world nation.

Anyway. What did I tell you earlier about me digressing?

So, during elections, if there is a man or a woman from the crowd who actually *does* desire change, and can get the constituency to actually focus on platforms, and not popularity, and they start to gain some ground in the polls, one of the other candidates, and usually the dynasty member who is threatened, will have that person killed.

Oh, they do it in public. There'll be dozens of witnesses at times.

But no one says anything.

Seriously. When it comes to politics, the Philippines has a hell of a lot more in common with the old Iraq, or current Iran than democracies such as the U.S. and Canada. Yet they call themselves a democracy. I'm gonna have to call bullshit on that one, too.

Okay, so Morales.

Morales and his goon crew take part in political assassinations during election years.

Oh hell no! I never worked with him on any of that. Look, I did what I did for him, because I needed money. I came here with a fair amount, but it ran out, and I had to do something, so why not do what I was trained to do? I'd been an infantryman in the U.S. Army, so...

What did I do for him?

I helped him go after terrorists.

Oh yea, they have 'em here. And I knew it was just a game of cat and mouse anyway, and that no one was gonna get hurt. I mean, I never killed anyone, and I had lots of guns pointed at me, but hell, I doubt they were loaded.

What terrorist networks?

Oh, there are two radical Islamic groups and a communist group. The communists are the NPA- New People's Army. They've been around since '69. Started as Maoists. They go around where they're located and bully businesses out of some money- another tax so to say- so that they can eat, but it's not much. The U.S. considers them terrorists, but the local government no longer does and has actually been working with them peacefully. Tryin' to come to an agreement on stoppin' the bullshit.

I'll tell you how much of a real threat they are. Usually, when you hear anything about 'em, it's when you hear of a couple of their members coming down from the mountains and turnin' themselves in to local authorities because they're starvin' and they know that at least in jail, they'll eat.

Okay, then you have the Islamists. The first group is MILF. And man do I bet they wish they'd picked a better name. But what it stands for is Moro Islamic Liberation Front.

And finally, and the biggest of the three, is Abbu Sayyaf.

The Islamic groups want the same thing that every radical Islamic group the world over wants. Autonomy and land. They'd both been funded predominantly by Muammar Gaddafi, but I don't know who's been bank rollin' 'em ever since we killed him. Probably the C.I.A.

What?

Of course I believe that. Hell, if I didn't, I wouldn't have worked for Morales. It's all cat and mouse. Cat and mouse. Act as if you believe the lie, and no one gets hurt.

I like what Deep Throat said about the best way to hide the truth.

No. Not the Nixon Deep Throat. The Deep Throat from the old X Files show.

What did he say?

He said the best way to hide the truth is between two lies.

Anyway, one of the ways those groups *try* to make money is by kidnappin' westerners and holdin' 'em for ransom. Oh, it works with those stupid missionaries. Those churches always raise money from their damn near impoverished congregations who really should be givin' their money to their mortgage companies and utility companies. The groups'll hold 'em for a while, until the money stops, and then they turn 'em loose.

Morales was getting' paid, by somebody, for every Abu Sayyaf or MILF member he could arrest and bring in. I don't know how much, but he'd turned the whole thing into a little side business.

And that's where I came in.

Yes, that's right. I'd let 'em use me as bait.

Once Morales and his men had gotten intel that a couple guys were in the area lookin' for Joe's, I'd move in, make sure to be seen, and act drunk, making myself an easy target, and then they'd take me and Morales and his men would come save the day, and I'd get paid.

How much?

You're gonna laugh. But it was enough to get me through for a month or more back in those days.

Ten thousand pesos. About two hundred and fifty U.S. dollars.

Yes, I'm serious. I was allowing myself to get kidnapped by radical Islamic terrorists for two hundred and fifty dollars.

Hey, what were my options? I had no money. I was a disabled Iraq war vet, and when I went to the VA for help, all they wanted to do was throw me on every new pill their buddies at big-pharma were pumpin' out to see if they worked and if they could start releasing 'em to the general population so they could *really* make a profit. I couldn't find full time work back home, so I came here, and I'd blown through my savings. Hell. I didn't even have the money to fly back home in the event something would'a come up and I had to.

No, I don't do it anymore. Don't have to.

Why?

Oh, that's in the story. I get a little VA disability now. Not much. About a grand a month. But hey, that's enough to live here. And it keeps me from havin' to have empty WWII era rifles pointed in my face.

What's that?

I'll tell ya how I started getting' it. It's part of the story. I'd gotten a big lump of back pay, too. Almost two million pesos.

What's that?

Oh, it's gone.

Yes. That's why I'm livin' in that little concrete shack playing "Are you smarter than a third world peasant" with my neighbors.

What happened to it?

Well. That's part of the story. Stop rushin' me. I'm gonna tell it.

But I'm savin' my money. With the baby comin' and all. And I think we'll be moving up in the world soon.

Unless this monkey right here jumps back on my back and gets a hold of me good this time and won't let go. Here, let me order another bottle. My mouth's getting' dry from talkin'.

Damn, you're puttin' it away pretty quick, too. Better slow down or the monkey'll be on your back.

7

I came in here one night to get a girl. I was already drunk and I was horny, and I'd been worrying about the rent money. So I came to ask Jo Jo if he knew where Morales was hangin' out so I could hit 'im up for some work.

Well, I wasn't in here long. Before he could even answer my question, I see the hottest young thing ever! I mean, she makes this cutie over here by the door look like a dog. She was smokin'! I left Jo Jo in mid-sentence and went over to talk to her.

She told me her name was Julie, and she asked me if I wanted to go to a room. She's just one of many girls in this story, and I've forgotten most of their names. But not Julie's.

Because she was so damn hot! That's why.

I could tell by the way she pronounced her words that she'd already exhausted her full knowledge of the English language. No doubt Jo Jo had taught her how to say these few words when he hired her to prepare her to talk to foreigners.

Jo Jo wasn't dumb. He just screwed up and got caught stealin' from his sister, I guess. He was probably drunk, or he'd gotten too greedy and was overreaching, or both. And see, in their defense, they steal and cheat from each other too. Not just us.

Some defense, huh?

Anyway, back to Julie. I wrapped my arm around her small waist and led her down the dark, stingy hallway, lined by half a dozen dark and dirty, 8 feet by 8 feet rooms. Moans and groans were comin' from all of the rooms except one. I kicked the door to this room open (God, never touch anything back there, especially the door knobs) and led 'er inside. The room was dimly lit by a red bulb, like all of 'em.

"I love you, Joe. I love you, Joe," she said, whispering in my ear as I started licking her neck and undoing her bra under her shirt. Now remember, I knew this was all a facade. None of it was real. But still, I'd wished the new girls would've learned to cut the 'I love you' crap out earlier in their careers. No need to make it more obvious that it's all fake.

"I love you too, baby," I said, flattering her as I dropped her shirt and bra to the floor. She had wonderful, perky little breasts.

But when I heard the balot guy come by blowing his horn, I forgot Julie was even there. I love balot. Have you had any of those since you've been here? What is it, exactly?

It's a chicken fetus, boiled alive, only a few days before hatching. Doused with sea salt and drowned in native vinegar, it's awesome! It's a delicacy of Asia, and one of my favorite foods.

If what the Hindu believe about reincarnation is true, I'd sure hate to come back as a chicken in the Philippines. Let's see. When you're an egg, you got more than half a chance of being boiled alive as a balot. If you do make out of the egg stage alive, you'd better hope you're a hen. Otherwise, once you're a year or so old, it's off to the cockfights to fight until you're killed.

"I'm hungry. Wait here," I told Julie.

"Walla ko kasabo," she said, looking me in the eyes. 'I do not understand,' she was sayin' in Visayan.

"Gigatom kaayu ko!" I'd said. I'm hungry!

"I love you, Joe," she said, leaning in to kiss my chest, which was level with her face.

"No, really," I told her. "I'm freaking hungry!"

I remember covering her top with her shirt from the floor and then running outside as fast as I could to catch the balot guy.

So I catch him, and I'm out there eating balot, and Julie comes running up behind me yellin', "You pay me Joe!"

"Pay you for what?" I said, cracking the egg shell on the handlebars of the vendor's bike. He had his balot filled bucket sitting between his knees. "We didn't do anything."

"You pay me or I tell Jo Jo!" she said. She gave me her best angry face but hell, I thought it was cute.

"Look," I told her, and I couldn't stop giggling at her mean face while I rubbed salt on the egg with my fingertips before grabbing the bottle of vinegar to pour on top. Man, I just love the pieces of local chili peppers and spicy roots of various sorts they put in the vinegar for seasoning. "I know that out of the five hundred pesos that you charge, you only get three hundred. How about I give you two hundred and we call it even."

"I need money, Joe!" she said, still trying to make her pretty face look angry and failing. "I have baby!"

"Of course you do," I said. "So take the two hundred pesos and go home to your baby. Jo Jo will not make me give you anything otherwise."

Julie looked to the street. She didn't understand exactly what I'd said. I don't think. But she got the gist of it.

"Okay, Joe," she said with her head down, sounding defeated. But it was all an act. On the inside I knew she was happy because she got her cut without havin' to earn it.

Besides, she was really hot, and I knew I'd be back for her. Better to pay her and reserve her services for later than piss 'er off and have 'er go off and scheme out a way to take me for a ride later.

"Thanks Joe," she said, turning to see if Jo Jo was watching. He was nowhere in sight, so she hurried down the street and around a corner, off to spend her money as quickly as she could. If he'da seen it, he'da forced her to give 'im a cut. Oh, he's a bastard, Jo Jo.

So I paid for the balot and then headed back to the bar. Another drink or two with Jo Jo the pimp to remind him to hit Morales up for a job- I'd be broke again in less than a month unless I could secure more contract work- and I'd call it a night.

That's the first time I met her.

No, not Julie. Rose. The next woman in the story, and I guess you'd say the star.

"Pssst!"

The call had come from the alley. Looking that way, I saw a woman, covered from head to toe in a black burka, and she was motioning me toward her. Reluctantly, I headed her direction, looking all around, making sure no one was following. You always have to be conscious of a trap. And if I was gonna get kidnapped by anybody, I was gonna get paid for it, damn it.

"Yes?" I said, looking into her eyes. It was the only part of her I could see. Because of the burka, ya know. And though her eyes were black like everyone else's in the country. Hell, the continent. That's the thing that I find most amazing about Asia. There're 3.5 billion people here- literally more than half the world's surface population- and there's only one eye and hair color.

Black.

But her eyes seemed different. They were hypnotic. It was like looking into an abyss. Not that looked back at you, but that invited you to dive in.

"I need your help, Richards," she said, speaking better English than most people back in my part of Virginia. "I have work for you."

"What kind of work?" I asked. I immediately didn't trust her. But do I really trust anybody here?

No.

"I come to you for help. Abu Sayyaf has taken my sister. I need you to get her back," she said.

"Yeah right," I said. "Why would Abu Sayyaf kidnap another Muslim?" I asked her.

"Our father is in line for succession in the network," she said, looking around as she spoke, as if making sure that she wasn't being watched. I just viewed it as part of an act. "He is very unpopular because he wants to make peace with Philippine government and the West. Abu Sayyaf does not want this, so they take my sister."

"Why doesn't your father just resign from his post?" I asked her. I was still skeptical. Hell, I'd become a professional skeptic from all the things I'd been through by then.

"You know our ways," she said, and though she was already close, she stepped in even closer so as not to be overheard by any members of the sea of humanity that was making its way around us on the street. This allowed me to smell her, and I liked what I smelled. Aside from being paranoid, I was now curious. What was under that sheet, I thought.

"A woman is worthless in our system," she continued. "My father could care less what happens to my sister. He is more concerned with his ox which can plow a field. My sister cannot plow a field."

"You bring up a really good point," I said, rubbing the stubble on my chin and wishing I'd shaved that week. "If there were any truth to this, they would've kidnapped one of your brothers."

"I have no brothers," she said, her voice sounding as if it were making its way close to the pleading border.

"Forget it lady," I said, and then turned to leave.

"I pay you one million pesos," she said.

That got my attention.

"I'm not walkin' into your trap," I told her. "Get away from me, or I'll rip your veil off and French kiss you on the lips, right here in front of everyone. I can fight my way out of the fallout, but you'd be stoned." I turned quickly and sharply into the bar.

"My friend!" Jo Jo said from the table in the dark, back corner of the bar. Why, it's this very table as a matter of fact! "We drink more!" he yells.

"Yes, we drink more. 'O-how kaayu ko!" Visayan for 'I am very thirsty.'

I took up the glass on the table that Jo Jo had just filled to the brim, wondering just how many bottles Jo Jo'd put on my tab while I'd been away from the table, and drank while turning to face the street.

The girl was gone.

8

'Course I saw her again. I told ya she was the star of the story, right? Calm down. Hell, we have time. You'll find that pretty much is all you *have* here is time.

It's a blessing at first, but it'll drive ya crazy. You gotta have something to do. That's why I've taken to gardening so much. And readin'.

'Course gardening'll be a pain in the ass now that the vines are dead. I'll have to deal with all the damn stares while I'm harvestin' my string beans.

Have you seen those here? The string beans? Hell, they get four feet long if ya let 'em go to seed.

Hey! I have an idea!

I'll build a trellis. Put it about a foot inside the fence so they can't reach through to it and cut the vines! The vines'll be back in a month!

Hot damn! American ingenuity wins again!

For now.

Remember. You can never win this game, "Are you smarter than a third world peasant?" You can only hope to stay ahead.

Oh, I don't know what they'll do, but they'll do something.

Anyway, so Jo Jo hooked me up with Morales, and I ended up gettin' another job. Just in time too. My rent was due the next day, and when a foreigner tells a Filipino landlord that they don't have money, do you think for a minute they believe 'em?

Hell no! Because we all have that donkey that shits gold back in Foreign Land. Remember?

Anyway, I show up for Morales' little goon squad meeting. "Broke again, huh, Richards?" Captain Morales says when I walked in ten minutes late, like usual. I told him it cost money to live and I was out of it and then I took a seat beside private first class Sanchez. You know, in all my time here, I still find Asian people with Hispanic names a bit odd.

This place is certainly unique. I mean, think about it. The people, ethnically, are Asian. They have a Spanish history due to Spain's four hundred and thirty three year rule and occupation. One of their main languages is English, and their current societal culture and political structure is American. At least on the surface.

I think that's pretty damn fascinating. Like the whole only one eye and hair color among nearly four billion people thing.

"All that beer and all those whores get costly after a while, huh?" Morales said, teasing me so that all of his men could laugh at me.

"No one ever said the life of an alcoholic sex addict was easy, Sir," I said, choosing self-deprecation over self-defense. I'd learned by this time that Filipinos don't lose their cool, and if you lose yours, then you do just that. You lose. It's better to just laugh it off and change the subject.

"All right, men," Morales said, once he got tired of the cheap shots. "Same situation as usual. We've received reports of kidnappings in this area." While he spoke he pointed to a map with a long wand that looked like a car's radio antenna. Because it was a car's radio antenna. The location on the map was another nearby province.

"Richards, you walk down this street," Morales said, looking at me to make sure I was awake. Guess I'd been known to fall asleep, or pass out, during these briefings, but hell, they were all the same. Walk down the street, go to the bar, act drunk, get kidnapped, and try not to take it all too seriously and no one gets hurt.

"Our intel tells us," Morales continued, "the guys we want are hanging out in this bar on the corner. It's called 'Bottoms Up.'"

I'd been there- cold beer and hot women- and I told him so.

"Good," he said, trying to collapse the wand, and realizing it really was a car antenna himself. He threw it at the private who'd gotten it for him. Guess in some ways the U.S. Army and the Philippine Army really *are* similar. "We don't have to worry about you getting lost this time," he said.

"Unless I see some hotter girls on the way there," I told him. That time the men laughed *for* me, not *at* me.

"Let's go!" Captain Morales said, and then he led the way out into the street.

"You are not safe here, Joe," the beautiful Filipina lady said, leaning forward, acting as if she was licking my ear and like she didn't know me. "There are bad men here tonight, Richards. You must go."

"I'm safer here than I am most places back home," I said. Just like I'd told you earlier. This girl's name was Candy. Oh, I'll always remember her name. It's easy. She did this amazing trick with a lollipop.

Oh, I can't tell you about that. I'll get so damn sidetracked that I'll never finish the story.

But I'll tell you this. She'd obviously been doing it for too damn long, because when I met her, she was missing half 'er teeth.

What?

Oh, no. I didn't notice 'til I had her back in a short room. She was a smart one. She'd learned to smile without revealing it. She was missin' 'em on the left side of her mouth, so she'd always tilt her head to the left like Mariah Carey. I mean she could act.

What?

Oh, I read once that Mariah Carey thinks one side of her face is better than the other side, so in photo shoots that's the only side she'll allow to be photographed. Go Google images of 'er sometime and you'll see.

Anyway, it got on my nerves after a while. I mean, she was perfect! Looked like a model except for the damn teeth.

What's that?

Oh, I know. So many of 'em look like models don't they?

I told her I'd take her to a dentist and have her teeth fixed. She was so happy she started cryin'. Really. I tried to get her to set a date that we could go together, and she almost panicked and told me not to come with her, because when the dentist saw my white skin the price would jump up three or four times for the procedure.

Now mind you, I'd only been here a couple months by this time. Sure, I'd been taken by the girl who'd suckered me into takin' her whole damn village to the Chocolate Hills. But I was thinking, ya know? Those people were squatters. Dentists are professionals. There is *no way in hell* that an educated professional was gonna be so blatantly racist in *any* country on God's green earth.

Well, she was pretty convincing, and so I didn't go with her for the estimate. She went alone and came back and told me the dentist had told her he could fix her mouth for three thousand pesos. I'm thinking, Wow! Seventy five bucks! That would've to cost four times that in America. I love this place!

So a few days later, at appointment time, I wanna go with 'er. I was afraid that if I chucked over the three grand in cash, she'd get sidetracked at the mall on the way to the dentists and come back with lots of nice new clothes but still a messed up mouth. I didn't want that, so against her persistent insistence, I went with her.

We get to the dentist's office, and here's this old Filipino dentist sitting in an empty office, and he's all laid back in the patient's chair readin' the newspaper. He looks up and sees us, and says hello, and then gets out of the chair so Candy can lay down.

He starts talkin' to her in Visayan, and I asked her what he said, because I heard him say something about ten thousand pesos. She told me that he had asked her if I was her husband and that she'd said no, and then he'd asked if I were an American, and that she'd said yes and then he told her the price was gonna be ten thousand pesos.

Well, I got pissed and told him that she'd been here before and he'd told her three thousand. He turns around and says to me, with very little local accent at all, that if I were in America I'd pay the equivalency of ten grand for this, and that he knew that because he'd practiced dentistry in America for thirty years. He'd gone there after dental school through the help of some American Christian missionaries he'd met through his church who'd also paid for his dental school, and he'd retired a few years ago and had come back home.

I told him we weren't in America, and he said he knew, we were in the Philippines, and that's how it was, and that I was gonna pay American prices. I couldn't believe it. Then he went on and on about how we Americans come here and take advantage of the Filipinos because of the currency conversion, and that it wasn't fair and that I was gonna pay American prices.

I looked him dead in the eyes, and I asked him one question. I said, "The whole time you were in America, did *anyone* charge you a different price than they did anyone else because of the color of your skin or your nationality?"

"Of course not!" he said, and he nearly spit when he did, as if the question was absurd.

I said, "And why not?"

You know what he said? He said, "Because it was America. They don't do that there!"

And I said, "Exactly!"

Then he said, "You are not in America!" I mean he was *pissed*.

He looked at Candy and said something in Visayan. I didn't know the language at that time, but this whole experience is one of the reasons I wanted to learn. Figured knowin' what they were sayin' about me right in front of me might save me some money over time, and it has. I asked her what he'd said, and she said that he told her that I either had to pay ten grand, or he wasn't doin' the work. I grabbed her by the arm and pulled her up out of the chair and said, "Come on. Let's go!"

As we were leaving, I noticed that he had a cross with Jesus hanging on it just above his door, like most businesses and buildings and houses here. I turned around and said, "Are you a Christian?" while I was pointing at the cross, and he said, "Of course!"

I said, "No you're not!" and we left.

We'd been in a complex of medical professionals, and when we came to another dentist office, I gave Candy five grand and told her to go in there and get her work done and to come to the bar across the street and get me when she was done. She came over about a six beer buzz and two hours later with the prettiest teeth I'd ever seen and twenty five hundred pesos in change. She'd gotten it all done for twenty five hundred.

I'd learned that day that the educated professionals here can be just as hateful toward us foreigners as any squatter *ever* could. Maybe more. So much for thinking an education changed anything.

But think about it. The squatters are layin' around drinkin' tuba all day. They see us and they hope they can sucker some Red Horse or Tanduay money out of us with that whole 'sick kid' bullshit. If they can? Good. If not? Oh well. Back to the tuba and the hammock.

The educated professionals? Think about *them*. What's their day like?

Just like educated professionals back home. They get up early, they go bust their asses workin' all day, tryin' to pay their mortgages, their car payments, and their student loans. And then they look at us and they get livid!

Why?

Okay. I'll spell it out for ya. I get a little VA disability now. I've mentioned that already, and you'll get the details of how that all worked out later in the story. It's not much. About a grand a month. But that converts to about forty thousand pesos here, and that's more money than most doctors and lawyers in this country make. No kiddin'.

I told you we were savin'. And I saw you smirk when I did, like, 'yeah right, what's this poor bastard that sits around countin' blue slippers and readin' paperbacks with no covers all day have to be savin'?' And those paperbacks were sent here to be givin' out for free, too, by the way. But they cost me more than a damn used paperback back home at the ukay ukay. But what choice do I have? Kindle, I guess.

Anyway, think about it. You got these dentists and lawyers and engineers bustin' their asses all day, having nothin' to show for it because of their stupid personal debt they carry so they can appear to be someone they're not. They have that *very* much in common with the middle class the world over. And then they drive by on their lunch breaks and see you and me in here drinkin' cold beer and talkin' to beautiful women half our ages.

And they hate it!

But hey, it's not *my* fault. And I've never rubbed it in their faces. I can empathize for 'em. But I ain't lettin' 'em take it out on my wallet!

Just as I've come here to be able to live on what little *I* have, they can just as easily work abroad and save up their bigger salaries and come back later, just like that prick dentist did, so there's no need to take it out on me.

Ya know, something like ten percent of their people work abroad. They claim that coconuts and bananas are their most precious exports, but the fact is, their brightest and most valuable people are their most precious exports. There's not a thing here for 'em, so they work abroad to have a nice life. I knew several in the Army and in the various medical facilities I got locked up in. They were wonderful people. The salt of the earth. They'd gotten an education, they refused to accept poverty as their lifestyle, and they went to America to live better lives. And isn't that what America's all about? It's how we all got there at some point.

So anyway, back to Candy.

"Most of the time, yes. You are safe here," she said, taking my hand in hers and kissing it, sexy. She was makin' sure that any eyes watching- and there were indeed eyes watching it turned out- would never suspect her of warning me.

Candy didn't care about me or my safety, and I knew it. Even though I'd bought 'er a new grill that'd tripled her business for 'er in no time. But if I were taken and never seen again, she'd lose out on one of her regular income streams. Candy was nearly twenty five years old, much wiser than the 'I love you, I love you' type girls of eighteen and nineteen.

"So who are these bad guys?" I asked, naively. "Who should I be afraid of?"

Leaning in to nibble my ear, she whispered, "The two guys in the corner, in front of the C.R." That stands for comfort room. It's how they refer to the restrooms here in the Philippines. But trust me, most of 'em ain't that comfortable. Especially in the whore houses. Hell, the biggest rats I've ever seen on this whole damned green planet were in the C.R. here in the Green Room.

What's that?

You gotta piss?

Perfect time to tell ya that one then, huh?

Just hold it a minute, and then go piss at the chicken place next door. Won't do you any good though. Hell, the rats run through the walls of the whole complex. The whole city really.

Just make sure you never sit down in any C.R.'s while you're in public and you'll probably be fine. Even the women here pop a squat on their feet in the C.R.'s when they piss and keep a watchful eye for anything that might decide to come up through the bowl while they're there.

Okay, so back to the story.

"Only two of 'em?" I said.

Morales had told me earlier that he was gonna pay me a little different. Ten grand per abductor. And remember, that's in pesos, not dollars.

"There is another," she said. "I think. He is in room with girl. But I'm not sure if he is with them or if they are just friends. You should leave now while there are only two for sure." When she pulled away from me she made sure to look at me longingly, as if she'd just asked me if I wanted a throw.

"Could you go tell them you know me and that they need more man power? They *have* to have more friends somewhere."

"Buang kaayu ka!" she said, Visayan for 'you are very crazy.'

"Buang kaayu wak wak ko!" I said, informing her that I wasn't just crazy, but that I was a crazy ghost. That's the nickname given to me by my Philippine Army buddies due to my combination of daringness, my ability to move around undetected when necessary, and of course, for my whiteness.

"I warned you," Candy said, rising to leave as the man she'd spoken of joined his friends, his shirt sticking to his sweaty back. He was a sizable man for a Filipino. He stood nearly six feet tall and was a stocky one hundred and eighty pounds. He appeared to be middle aged. A mole on the right side of his chin had a protrusion of half a dozen hairs, six inches each in length.

A beautiful young Filipina girl of perhaps eighteen years old came down the hall behind him counting money. Hell, she may've been younger. This bar wasn't owned by any cops or anyone else who gave a shit about image.

I ordered another beer, noticing out of the corner of my eye that the men were looking at me and talking about me in hushed tones. I'd hoped that since I was alone they'd view me as an easy target. But I was worried that they were spending a little too much time sizing me up.

I know I'm forty, but that's far from old, and my fit, athletic build gives a hint that at some point in the past I *may* have been a soldier. At least an athlete. I'm only five feet, ten inches tall and one hundred and seventy pounds. Not big by American standards, but big here in the land of little brown people. And I'm still pretty fast. And strong.

When I'm sober.

Three beers and an hour later, the foxes still hadn't taken the bait. I was starting to get too buzzed to be effective. It didn't appear as if the terrorists were bringin' in reinforcements so I'd have to settle for thirty thousand pesos.

Time for the old drunken foreigner trick.

Rising to my feet, I staggered toward the videoke machine, exaggerating my level of intoxication. Like the mother killdeer bird back home, I wanted to appear wounded. Come across as an easy target. But I wasn't trying to lead 'em away from the nest. I was trying to lead 'em to it.

I intentionally fumbled around, hitting the wrong numbers on the machine a few times before finally hitting the right ones for the right song.

I started doin' a little drunk dance when the music came on, and I picked up the mike and started beltin' out the words, as badly as I could.

What song?

Oh, the very song they say you *never* want to sing in the Philippines. Unless you wanna get killed.

My Way, by Frank Sinatra.

You know, several people a year get killed in Manila alone singing that.

Why?

Well, I researched it once on Google, because I thought the whole "never sing Frank Sinatra in the Philippines unless you want stabbed" thing was like, an urban legend.

But it's true.

The reason is that Sinatra played the last show of his last tour here. The Filipinos took that as a tremendous compliment from the old crooner and put him on a pedestal forevermore. Story has it that he was so shook up when he sang My Way, that he mumbled and cried through the whole bit and the people took that as even *more* of a compliment.

Fact is, he was drunk off his ass.

Anyway, by the end of the first stanza when *I* sang it, actin' as drunk as 'ol Frankie 'imself, the three Abu Sayyaf members had seen and heard enough.

"Hey Joe, you are good dancer," hairy mole faced man said. All three of 'em approached me.

"Thanks man," I said, intentionally slurring my speech.

"Come with us. We buy you beer," one of the other men said, motioning to the front of the bar. I knew he was really motioning for the door. And I knew he was lying. Remember what I told you earlier? About bein' here five years, and ain't never a Filipino bought me a beer?

"Mabuti!" I said. That means 'good' in Tagalog, and it's one of the few words of the language I know. I didn't want them to know that I knew Visayan.

"Come here, Joe!" hairy mole faced man said, grabbing me by the upper arm and dragging me out of the bar once we'd reached the front. "Let's go for ride!"

He threw me into the mid size S.U.V. that was waiting. Its windows were tinted heavily with silver so that no one could see inside. Once

I was in the back seat, I was bookended by the other two men while hairy mole faced man raced to the driver's door, jumped in, started the ignition and began driving away.

All I could focus on was the driver's mole. The hair protruding from it was sticking halfway between the driver's seat and the passenger's seat, just bouncing up and down a couple feet above the vinyl like granddaddy long legs telling everyone where the hell the cows had gone. Why didn't he just cut that shit off with scissors?

"We take you to better bar, Joe," he said, smiling into the review at his buddies in the back seat. "Better girls. Cheaper beer."

"Great!" I said, but no longer acting drunk. "Can you do me a big favor though?"

"What favor, Joe?" the man to my right said, and he sounded nervous. I looked him in the eye and I could tell that he knew the jig was up.

"Could you get a few more of your friends to meet us there? I really need the money."

"You are mercenary!" the driver said, an accusation, not a question.

"Well, yeah," I said. "But I only get paid ten thousand pesos per abductor, and my rent is due. I'd like another ten to make sure I eat for the next month."

"Pag helum lang ba!" the man to my right screams, his native tongue for 'you shut the hell up!' and then he shoved the business end of a .9 mm pistol into my right temple.

I rolled my eyes and said, "Come on Kuya! (Visayan for 'brother')" You know you can't shoot me. You can't ransom off a dead guy."

And besides, I knew the gun wasn't even loaded.

"Unsa ako buhaton? (What do I do?)," the gunman asked to the driver.

"Throw him out!" hairy mole face man says, slamming on the brakes.

It was too late though. The red and blue lights of the Philippine Police vehicles exploded in the mirrors of the S.U.V. And thank God for that, 'cause if they'da thrown me out before Morales got there, I wouldn't've gotten paid.

As the three ass clowns in the car with me turned to look out the windows and assess their situation, I acted immediately, grabbing the wrist of the man holding the gun. I twisted it back hard and nearly broke it. The pistol fell to the floor of the back seat, and with my other hand I reached into the front seat and grabbed the driver by the hair of his chiny chin chin. I'd been wantin' to do that since I'd first laid eyes on it.

"You let me out, and I let you live," I said. "You give up easily, or not all of you get out of this car alive!"

I mean, I really needed the money. I couldn't let these guys get away.

The man to my left, the only one not in some sort of death grip- hell, I didn't see the need. He'd just sat there like a knot on a log the whole time. He opened the door to run but was pulled out at gunpoint when he did. Morales' men took over from there.

"Good work, Richards," Morales said, counting out thirty, one thousand pesos bills once I'd walked back to his truck. He had this way of staying safely out of view. Not because he was scared of gettin' hurt- Morales was pretty badass- but because he didn't want people to see him moonlighting. And not because they'd report him. Oh no. That wouldn't be so bad. He'd just get yelled at. Remember, people think differently here than you and I do.

If someone saw him, they'd blackmail him. They'd threaten to report him, or tell the people he hunted down unless he paid 'em. Morales didn't wanna add another person to the payroll just for the sake of keeping his payroll alive.

"Let us know when you're up for more," he tells me as he hands me the cash.

"Things got pretty hairy in there," I said, resisting the urge to laugh at my own pun. Morales just gave me a look that said *I smell bullshit.* "No. Really! They held a gun to my head," I said.

"They always hold a gun to your head, Pete," he says. "You know they're never loaded."

"Come on Raul. I'm broke. My rent's due." I pleaded with him. Using his first name. People are supposed to feel endeared by that shit. Warm and fuzzy. They'd taught me that the year I was a door to door stock salesman. But that only works where we come from, not here.

"Sorry Richards," he said, shaking his damn head like he really was, but I knew he wasn't. "I have my boss, and I take my orders from him just like my men do from me. I'd help you personally if I could, but I can't afford to give you that kind of money. Besides, you're a foreigner. You know you are rich."

"Well," I said, shoving the wad of cash into my front pants pocket and ignoring his comment. There was no use to acknowledge it, and as I've already explained to you, that great misconception that if you are white, you are rich, is a battle we'll never win. I mean, these people actually think that foreigners always keep at least a million pesos hidden away somewhere in our apartments. Not the sock drawer though. Any whore would know to look there the minute you passed out. But they think we've got it somewhere. I sure as hell would like to know where.

"Please let me know if anything comes up in the next week," I told him. "I know you don't believe it because of my skin tone, but I really need the money."

"Okay," Morales said. "Oh, someone came by looking for you yesterday."

"Let me guess," I said, stutter stepping. I'd been just about to leave. "Muslim chick. Black burka."

"No," Morales said. "White man. American. Said his name was John White. Do you know him?"

"I know him," I said. What I didn't say was how amazed I was that the man had made it this far in his quest to find me. "Did you tell him anything?"

"No. I don't care what you've done or haven't done back home. I need you here. I played dumb. Want a ride home?"

"No," I said, looking over my shoulder. "I'm goin' back to Bottoms Up and talk some more to an old friend."

"What's her name?"

"Candy."

"And you wonder why you never have any money."

Hey. I'd made a twenty five hundred pesos dental investment, and I just wanted to get some dividends.

In trade.

9

So who's John White?

Oh, I'll get to him. But not yet.

I wanna get back to the mystery woman in the burka first.

John can wait.

What's that?

Okay. Go piss, and I'll wait 'til ya get back. And mind those rats!

***

All better? Your eyeballs were startin' to float.

Oh, I'll have to go soon. And you know you will too, now that you've let the damn burst.

Okay, so one morning a couple days later, the mystery lady in the black burka was sittin' across the street from my apartment, hidden in one of the back corners of a small eatery. Just like we are here. People can walk by on the street, so blinded by the sun, they can't see you only ten feet back in the dark.

She was watchin' my apartment and probably thinkin' *does he sleep all day?* It was around 8:00 a.m. I'd say, and that's a late wake for here. As you've noticed already, this part of the world's located just a stone's throw above the equator- a stone thrown out of a passenger jet at 35,000 feet, but still, it's close- and anything that needs to get done outside of the safety of an air-conditioned room or one heavily armed with multiple electric fans needs to be done either before 8:00 a.m. or after 4:00 p.m. Otherwise, it ain't gettin' done.

And good luck sleepin' in anyway, with the gazillion roosters and all the street vendors goin' up and down the streets startin' at 5 a.m.

Isda! Isda! (Fish! Fish!)

Where was I?

Oh, I'd had company the night before.

The same time the mystery Muslim woman was sittin' across the street watchin' my apartment, the young woman in my bed was watchin' me sleep and listening to me snore beside her.

I wasn't awake, no, but I could tell you exactly what she did. They all do it, and I always find evidence of it once they're gone.

She got outta bed and went creepin' around the room. First she'd go through my dresser drawers in search of my wallet or a wad of cash. She'd slide the drawers in and out, real slow, alternating lookin' in the drawers and back at me to make sure I wasn't wakin' up. But remember, I already told you. You never keep your cash or wallet there, because that's *always* the first place they look. Hell, sometimes even when I'm awake I'll pretend to be asleep just to watch, so I know. But I really was asleep this time.

Refusing to leave empty handed, she put on her panties and shorts, slid her tee shirt over her head, and sneaked into my small kitchen. Opening my cupboards she would've been disappointed, because I never had much food in the house. Pork and beans, some canned Garbanzo beans, and a few packages of instant rice noodles were all I had there that time.

She found a plastic bag under the sink and filled it with what few food items I'd had. All I had to drink was San Miguel Light and a can of Sprite. At least she was kind enough to take the Sprite and leave me my beer.

One flight of stairs led to the street. On her way down she lost her footing and she let go of the bag in order to stick her arm out. Grab the wall and catch herself.

"Bah!" she would have said. Visayan expression for "shit!" or "damn!" The sound of canned food clangin' down the stairs is what woke me up.

"What the hell?" I said, startled awake. My first instinct was to do a quick roll to the left side of the bed, which I did, and I reached under and grabbed the .9 mm Beretta I kept hidden there. Somethin' I've always done since coming home from Iraq. I did a quick roll back, and it occurred to me that my bed was empty.

"Where'd that girl go?" I said, sitting up. I thought I'd had a girl there. I crept out of my small bedroom, business end of the pistol leading the way, and I looked for… hell, I hadn't even gotten her name. But I was lookin' for her.

A quick glance around the living room and kitchen- which was basically the same room, the space of the two areas separated by a worn couch that smelled like stale beer- revealed that she was gone

I put the gun away and went to the front door. I opened it just in time to see her place the last can of food in the plastic bag down there at the bottom of the steps and then run out the door and to the street.

The flimsy aluminum door, screened at the top, banged shut behind her. Dust from the smog of the street that had collected in the screen created a cloud of smoke. It reminded me of the small toadstools in the forests of my youth, back in America, that I'd loved to stomp on for the same effect. It's the little things like that that'll make ya homesick here. And they jump out at ya at times when you'd never expect 'em, and you make the connection instantly. It's really odd.

Just before opening the door and steppin' onto the street, I thought better of it. I realized I was completely naked. I turned and headed back up the stairs. I got dressed and made my way back out to the street to find breakfast. I knew the girl was long gone, whatever her name was, and what little food I'd had was gone with her, so it was breakfast out that day.

So I'm halfway across the street to the little eatery across from my apartment, and here comes mystery Muslim woman.

"You hungry, Joe?" She asks. "I treat you breakfast."

"You again?" I said. "What are you doin'? Stalkin' me?"

"Yes."

"An honest woman in the Philippines," I said, and trust me, I was really layin' on the sarcasm. "And you're off limits." My eyes went up and down her burka so she'd get the point.

"I know you are broke, and it looks now like you have no food either," she said, ignoring my sarcasm, but again, they take English literally here, 'cause that's how they learn it, so she probably hadn't gotten it anyway.

"You saw all that, did you?" I asked her.

"Yes," she said, smiling at me with her eyes. And man, did she have the most beautiful eyes. "You are lucky if she did not take what little money you *do* have."

"I've figured that one out," I said, chuckling lightly. "Never leave your wallet in your top drawer." And it's not a sock drawer here. Just a top drawer. Rarely here do people wear socks. Just flip flops.

"It gets hot now," she said, not interested in hearing a story she knew all too well. Different foreigner, same situation. "Let's go there," she said, pointing to the eatery from which she'd just emerged.

"Lead the way," I said. I didn't trust this woman, and I didn't want anyone I didn't trust behind me. She knew where I lived. What else did she know?

That's another thing about living here as a foreigner. You can move into a town with half a million people, and by the end of the week they all know where you live. Complete strangers will walk up to you on the street and tell you that they know where you live, and then tell you where you live to prove it, and then smile and walk away. You really have to be careful about givin' out any personal information. Always keep in mind, that anything you tell any of 'em, you're telling all of 'em, because they will pass word around in less than a week. I've never seen anything like it.

I followed her into the shade of the open walled eatery, ducking so as not to hit my head on the ceiling. After years of livin' down here you get used to ducking in stores and eateries, and while gettin' on and off jeepneys. That's those long bus lookin' things you've seen goin' up and down the streets spittin' out all that smog. All these things were built with short Asians in mind, not tall Westerners.

"I'll have two orders of chicken adobo and two cups of rice," I said to the old lady runnin' the small place as I passed the counter. The smile on her face revealed only one tooth. In America I would've viewed the smile as friendly- one that came from a grandmotherly type- but here in the Philippines, smiles like that one make me nervous. No clue how much she was jackin' up the price in her head. But I wasn't payin' this time, so I didn't care.

"I know you need money," mystery Muslim woman said as we sat down. Gettin' right to business. "Why you do not help me?"

As much as I'd heard it, and in spite of how many bad experiences I'd had with young Filipina ladies, I still found their broken, improperly spoken, and at times, hard to understand English cute. And she was no exception. I'd planned on actin' like a tough guy, but with her English and those eyes, I was turned to goo and I started giggling.

"I don't trust you," I said, leaning back in my chair, giving the old lady room as she sat my small dishes of food in front of me. The amount of food served was the standard serving size for the country, enough for the average Filipino, but we're nearly fifty percent larger than the average sized Filipino, so whenever I eat I always have to order at least two portions. Twice the chance for getting' screwed price wise, but I hate walkin' away hungry after I eat.

"You don't trust me? Yet you let trash like the whore who just stole your foods into your home? You have how many girls like that in your home every week?"

"Good point," I said. "But that's different."

"Why it's different? Because they give you sex and you give *them* money? Would you help me if I give you sex and *you* pay *me*?"

"How old are you?" I asked, looking up from my food. She seemed smart, even wise. And I mean according to the real definition of the word wise, not the Filipino usage of it. I wasn't unaccustomed to dealing with people like this here. Not that there're not plenty of smart people here. They just weren't to be found among the pimps, prostitutes and drunks I usually ran with. *My* kind of people at the time.

"I am going 24," she said, their way of saying 23.

"What's your name?"

"Rose."

"Would you really have sex with me if I help you?"

Didn't hurt to ask.

"You are typical foreigner!" she said. Catching her voice rising, she looked around the small room to make sure she'd not drawn attention. She hadn't. "You know it is against my customs! I am not typical Filipina girl!"

"Sorry," I said, seeing that I'd really offended her. "Really, I was joking. Char lang! ('Joke only' in Visayan). But hell, how many times had I heard that one? I'm the one that's different?

"Why you just not help me for the money? Or that it is right thing to do? You were soldier. I thought it was your job to protect the innocent?"

"Well," I said, drawing out the word and holding up a spoonful of rice with a piece of chicken on it, wondering if I'd contract food poisoning yet again for eating in a colunderia. "That's where you thought wrong," I told her. "After a while you just don't care so much about protecting people who couldn't give a rat's ass that you protect them."

"Then do it for the money, Joe! I know you need it."

"Okay, I'm sick of everyone calling me 'Joe!'" I said, dropping my spoon to my plate and looking her in the eyes. You know, eating here in the Philippines is so much like basic training in the U.S. Army, in the sense that the only eating utensil used is the spoon. In the Army, at basic training at least, it was for the purpose of eating with speed. Here in the Philippines, it boils down to poverty and multi-purposefulness. When you can only afford one utensil, buy the one that can be used in the most ways. "You can start off by calling me Richards," I told her.

"I know your name, Pete," she said, pushing her rice away like she wasn't hungry anymore. "If Richards is what you want, then I call you that."

"And how the hell do you know so much about me?" I asked her. That's before I knew that if you're a foreigner here that they chat about you like you're some kinda damn celebrity. And it freaks me the hell out. You never have privacy, and you figure out that you're always bein' watched, and that everyone watchin' is always comparin' notes. Like I mentioned already.

Go do some small talkin' with some dude on the corner. Just for five minutes. Then walk up a block and blend into the crowd and turn around and watch. Everyone'll come over and start high fivin' the bastard for having talked to you, and they'll all want to know what you said. Sometimes I'll just go say, "I like rice," over and over again and then leave, and look back and watch 'em tell everyone about how I said I like rice over and over again. Then for the next several days as I'm walking down the street, I'll hear people saying, "That foreigner really likes rice," as they point at me with their lips. That's how they do it here. They point with their lips. And that freaks me out too. Especially when they do that, "Americano! Americano!" thing and point with their lips. Looks like they wanna kiss you.

"It is none of your business how I know all your business," she said.

"Make it two million pesos!" I said, after that one.

"Bah!" she said, jolting upright. "Do you think I am rich? Do you know how hard it was for me to collect one million?"

"It sounds like a hard job, for that much money. Who knows how long it'll take? I might be getting' underpaid for only a million."

"It takes one week," she said. "I know the island where they take her. We charter boat. Go at night. We get her. We come back. All in one week."

"What island?" I asked, looking her in the eyes. I'd forgotten about my food.

"You know when we get there," she said, pulling her eyes away from my stare.

"You see," I said, looking down and shakin' my head. "You want me to trust you, and you don't even tell me where we're goin'? How do I know you aren't just settin' me up? Leading me into a trap of a hundred or more Abu Sayyaf members?"

"I give you hundred thousand today and the rest when we get back," she said, and she lifted her hand from below the table. She had a wad of cash wrapped up in a rubber band in it.

I looked at the money, and man, it was hard to resist. She knew she was in the driver's seat. The position of strength. She slid the money toward me and let it touch my fingertips.

"When do we leave?" I asked.

"Tonight."

I didn't know it at the time, but in a small eatery across the street, my old buddy John White was sittin' there watchin' everything. He'd told me later. Said when he saw me take the money he called me a sum-bitch and sipped his tea.

10

Who's John White?

Didn't you just ask that?

Oh, I'll tell ya, but we're still not there yet. I gotta tell the story in the right order, see. And where John comes in, he comes in with a bang.

Okay. So that night, I met Rose at the docks.

"Personally, I think we'll look more suspicious goin' out at night," I told her, followin' 'er down the dock. There was a small private boat tied at the end waitin' for us. I had my assault pack that I'd had in Iraq with me, and it was pretty full, but my hands were empty. I liked to travel light, no matter where I was goin', see. That's one of the first things ya learn in infantry school. The more ya take, the more it weighs.

"Less eyes at night," she said, holding her veil against her face, playin' tug of war with the wind. God how I love the sea breezes here. "Eyes cannot see in the dark. Most of them."

"Whatever," I said, stepping into the small boat. It had a two hundred horsepower outboard, and that's big for here, so I knew we were goin' out quite a ways. "Just remember. I'm in charge once we get there."

The boat's owner asked her where we were goin' in Visayan, and she handed him a wad'a cash and told 'im to go south by southwest until she told 'im to stop.

He looked at the wadda cash and shrugged; no problem. He seemed to have the same reaction to money that I did. He rattled off something in Visayan that I'm sure was, "Whatever you say, ma'am," and then sat down in his captain's chair.

I still didn't trust this woman. I kept my eyes on the sky the whole way out to sea and mentally mapped our travels by the constellations. I didn't have a GPS device, and I didn't need one. I'd been an infantryman. Don't know what you know about that, but we're a little different. We're the only specialty in the Army in which the man is the weapon. And the weapons systems. And once you learn it, it's hard to let go of it. And I don't think I'd ever want to anyway.

"Are you sure you know which island she's on?" I asked Rose, hungry for conversation after half an hour of silence. In that period of time the boat had traveled a pretty good distance, and I was gettin' nervous. I still wasn't so convinced I was really goin' after a young lady who'd been kidnapped by a bunch of tribal ass clowns. I was still leery of bein' set up.

"I am positive," she said, her black burka making her appear more like luggage in the seat beside me than a person.

"Do you know anyone on the island?" I asked, thinking of questions I *should* have asked before accepting the job. And I *would* have had I not been in such need of money. "Will we have friendly contacts if we need help?"

"No," she said. "We want to remain unseen by all eyes on the island."

I saw that she wasn't up for any mind altering conversation so I just sat back and shut up. That's something I miss about America too. Stimulating conversation. You won't find it here. They focus on the bare necessities, and I get that. They're still at that point with their civilization. They don't have the luxury of concerning themselves with what's goin' on in all the different parts of Foreign Land. They have to focus on getting their rice. Today. But I think until they start having *some* stimulating conversations about some of the things that don't take place right in front of 'em, that ain't gonna change.

Ignorance ain't so bliss when you're hungry.

The captain started nippin' on Tanduay, and as much as I wanted a drink, I wasn't gonna ask for a drink of that stuff. Talk about rot gut! They actually put formaldehyde in every bottle. I've drank it before, and I've always shit blood the next day.

I sat back and enjoyed the view, which even at night was beautiful. The moon was nearly full, and it *would* be in a few more nights. It glistened off the waters of the Philippine Sea like light off of tinsel on a Christmas tree.

The trip made me think of how I really should spend a little less time, or a lot less time really, in girly bars and more time island hoppin'. The country's made up of 7,107 islands. Unless the tide's in. Then it's more like 6,000 or something. If you spent just one day on each island, and then moved on to a different island the next day, it would take nearly twenty years to see the whole country. I find that astonishing. Not as astonishing as 3.6 billion people and only one hair color, but pretty astonishing.

And Indonesia? Just to the south and where we seemed to be heading? They have more than 17,000 islands! That same sightseeing trip- an island a day- would take you more than forty six years to visit all the islands of Indonesia!

Now *that* competes with the one hair and eye color deal.

There're so many islands in the Pacific Ocean. And I've heard some pretty damn amazing tales about some of 'em. There's the ones the U.S. used as a nuke testing ground after WWII. The Pacific proving grounds. More than two thousand islands stretching for about three thousand miles. Those are part of the Marshall Islands, and most people know about 'em. But what they *don't* know about are some of the other islands where they've done some other testing. Group behavior experiments, stuff like that.

I know this one guy, a foreigner living here in the Philippines, who claims to have taken part in some of the group behavior experiments. Claims he was one of the researchers. Something to do with takin' a bunch of natives who didn't have any concept of materialism or government. A peaceful group of people as he explained it. Very simple minded, but simple in how they lived too.

The tests involve introducing them to materialism and a very confining form of government. The study, according to this guy, is still ongoing, and it *has* been for a couple of generations.

Anyway, he said that what they've found is that the more the people have been made to want whatever their form of materialism is, and the more tightly they're governed- making it harder for them to achieve their wants- the society as a whole has become increasingly violent. He said it took less than ten years before they had their first war. And he *claims* that certain interests working within the U.S. Government not only run the tests, but use them as some sort of precursor for ways in which to control U.S. society.

Amazing story, huh? Don't know if I believe it or not. I mean, I already told you most foreigners here are crazy. But I also told you about my experience with that beautiful older lady on the car lot one hot summer day back in Virginia.

But there *was* something somewhat convincing about the guy.

His accent.

What kind was it?

That's the thing. He didn't have one. Think about that. Have you ever really heard someone that had no accent? Hell, you can tell I'm from south of the Mason Dixon line. More so with the more of this beer we drink. You can generally pin-point the British and the Germans, and most other parts of Foreign Land if you've traveled the world a bit. But this guy?

Plain vanilla.

What's that?

Maybe you're right? Maybe he *was* Canadian?

I don't know. But part of me wants to believe his story. And after you hear mine, you might agree that his is an easier story to believe.

At some point I fell asleep on the boat, and I don't know for how long. But when I woke up, Rose was arguing with the captain.

"Deli! Deli!" the captain was saying. Visayan for 'No! No!'

"Pag sure oie!" Rose said right back at 'im. 'Are you sure!'

"Wak wak kaayu!" the captain said. "Wak wak kaayu!"

Now I knew what the hell wak wak was because of the nickname the guys had given me for being stealthy and white. It meant ghost. I told you that, remember? And kaayu means 'very much.'

"Is he saying there're lots of ghosts on the island?" I asked Rose. I'd gotten up and made my way to the back of the boat. That's where the captain sits in boats over here. Right beside the motor. And he steers it with a bamboo stick tied to the outboard. They're ain't no steering wheels here, brother!

"Don't mind what he says," she said. She had her arms crossed over her chest, and her right leg was bouncing up and down over her left knee, so I could tell she was *high blood* as they call it. "He drinks too much!"

"What is he upset about? What are you upset about?"

"He refuses to dock at island so we can get off boat."

"What?"

"He turns around. He takes us to next island. He drops us there."

"How the *hell* do we get to the island we need to get to then?" I asked her, turning and looking back at the island behind us, watching it get smaller and not being happy about it. Lightning struck at a distant point, revealing mountains engulfed by clouds. The only clouds I'd seen the entire trip.

Remember the lightning I pointed out from back there at my house? Same place. Yeah, as far away as it is, you can most always see the lightning. It's always there.

"If close, we swim. If far, we make raft."

"Oh my God!" I said, turning to face her. "I can see your bill goin' up."

"Helum!" she said, and she was really angry when she said it. Helum means 'shut up!' in case you forgot.

The captain killed the ignition and let the boat drift to shore when we'd reached the island he'd taken us back to. You could smell the smoke from some dying fires, no doubt just within the tree line. That's the thing. Even with all these islands, there're people all over all of 'em. If you pushed all the islands together, the total land mass would be about the size of California, but the population is a full one third of the U.S.'s. They claim not to like bein' poor, but until they get that population under control, they've got no hope of any other way.

I thanked the captain as I jumped over the side of the boat to go ashore, and he said, "Hindi mabuti!" meaning, 'no good,' in Tagalog, while pointing in the direction of the island of interest. "Wak Wak kaayu!"

"Maybe a terrorist or two," I told him. "But no ghosts."

The captain closed his eyes, bowed his head and said a prayer and then crossed himself in good Catholic fashion. "May God protect you," he said in pretty good English before speeding away. Rose nearly fell in the water. She was still getting out of the boat when he ripped outta there, but I caught 'er.

"You're right," I told her. "He *has* had too much to drink."

#

"For big strong man, you do little work," she said, violently rowing with her makeshift paddle. I was sittin' across from 'er on the other end of the six feet long bamboo raft.

"I cut and tied all the logs," I said.

"Yes," she said, and even though it was dark, I could tell by the tone in her voice that she'd rolled her eyes when she'd said it. "All four of them."

"Isn't this how your culture operates anyway?" I said, chuckling. "I am the man. You are supposed to take care of me. Serve me always." And really, in many ways, I could have been talkin' about both of her cultures. Islam and Philippine.

"You are not Muslim and you are not my man!" she said, and her tone let me know that that was the end of *that* discussion.

For a couple of years over here, I thought I just sucked at initiating small talk. Took me a while to realize that they simply don't engage in it, like I've already told you. Their conversation is mostly necessity based. If they are hungry, they'll talk about being hungry and food. If they are tired, they'll talk about being tired and sleep. But to sit back and talk about the possibilities of life in outer space? If there'll be a cure for cancer in our lifetime?

Forget about it.

But again, I get it. They're not there yet. Three meals a day is still a struggle for most of 'em. Who's got time to consider the cosmos when your baby's cryin' 'cause it's hungry and there's no milk?

Remember what I said about ignorance? It ain't so bliss when you're hungry.

"So. Where exactly are we?" I asked, ignoring her wrath and buying more lazy time. I'd learned how to do that in the National Guard. Oh, the stories I have about that trip. They'll come later. As I tell ya about John White.

Oh, just wait, I'll get to him.

Back to Rose. I said, "We were already so far south. As long as that boat ride took, we should be in Indonesian waters by now."

"We are on border of Indonesia and Philippines," she said.

"So which country does this particular island belong to?" I asked, staring ahead at the island in question. Lightning was still striking intermittently toward the back of it, revealing the clouds and high mountains that were there. The mountains appeared to be twenty kilometers away from the beach toward which we were heading. Couldn't tell for sure because of the darkness and the distance, but I'd later find that that was a pretty accurate guess.

What's that?

Oh yes. We ended up goin' all the way back to the far side of the island. Back where the lightning was.

Boy, you just can't wait and let a man tell a tale, now can ya?

I'm gettin' to all of that.

And look. You need to be highly lit on this cheap beer when I do. Number one, so you'll be more likely to believe it, and letter B, so that if you call me out on it tomorrow and accuse me of bein' mentally insane, I can just say you were drunk and I didn't tell it like that at all.

So anyway, Rose told me that the island we were goin' to didn't belong to *either* country. Said neither *wanted* it.

"How do you explain that?" I said, turning my whole body to face her. "Everyone wants as much land as they can get."

"Shut up and row, Joe!"

"I said don't call me Joe!"

"You make me so high blood!"

"Whatever," I said. But we were gettin' pretty close, so I took up my oar and helped.

It was daybreak before we actually started to reach the beach. We'd spent more time in the motor boat that I'd realized. Guess I'd slept for quite a while. And it'd been slow rowin' from one island to the other.

So all of a sudden I hear Rose say, "Oh no."

"What?" I said, looking back. "Did you say something?"

And now *here* is where the story starts to get weird. I mean, *really* weird. This ain't no ordinary island, and things started getting' strange even before we stepped foot on it!

I asked her what she'd seen, and all of a sudden her mood changes. She goes from bein' this 'I don't want to talk to you, Joe' bitch, to acting like she's concerned about my wellbeing. She told me to lay down and rest. Close my eyes.

"What?" I said.

"Yes," she said. "Take a break. You've worked hard and will need rest. Sit on the boat and face me if you do not want to sleep. We talk. Just face me."

"Really?" I said, and I turned my body toward her. "So you're chatty all of a sudden?"

Rose looked past me, and I could tell she'd seen something. She'd later tell me what it was, and I'll tell you later in the story, but what I remember seeing wasn't anything like what she'd later claim she'd seen. But after what all we ran into- and I mean we ran into a lot of strange things on this island- I *did* believe her. Still do.

"Pick the topic." Rose said, panic in her voice. "I want to hear you talk. Tell me story about war."

"What's gotten into you?" I said. "I thought you were repulsed by me and my stories?"

"Talk damn it!"

And just as she'd yelled, I began to hear the most beautiful music I'd ever heard.

"Oh my God!" I said. "That sounds like Celine Deon!"

I turned around, and I saw what Rose had seen.

"She's beautiful!" I said, and I was completely mesmerized. There in the water, swimming around like a fish, was this beautiful blond bombshell! She had the face of an angel, with sea green eyes, high cheekbones, and her skin was white as snow. And that long blond hair. Man!

"Do you know how long it's been since I've screwed a white girl?" I said, and I started climbing out of the boat to go in the water.

"Don't look at her, Pete!" Rose yelled, poking me in the back with her oar. "It's not what you think. Cover your ears!"

"I love you," I said to the girl in the water, and I was ready to jump in.

"I warned you, Joe!" Rose said.

And that's the last thing I remember.

11

Next thing I know, I'm bein' woke up by havin' sand kicked in my face.

"Wake up," Rose said, leaning over, blocking the sun from my eyes. "It is past noon. You sleep long. We lose light."

"How many beers did I have last night?" I said, sitting up and grabbing my throbbing head and wonderin' how in *hell* that bump I felt got there. "Where did that hot blond go?"

I remembered her. I looked all around, holding my pounding head in one hand and shading my eyes from the sun with the other.

"What?" Rose said. "There is no blond. This is Asia!"

"There was a blond girl. She was beautiful."

"You had dream, Richards. You fall off boat and hit your head. I drag you to shore."

"Really?"

"Yes! Now get up! You waste time! My sister! She waits!"

At the time I'd believed her about fallin' outta the boat. But like I said she finally fessed up about the truth later. And I'll get there.

"Whatever," I said, and I got up. I was still rubbin' that knot. It reminded me a little too much of the time I'd been dropped on my head in airborne school. Yeah, the airborne instructor had done it on purpose, and I'd known it. He was tryin' to get me dropped from the class due to a concussion, but I'd stayed in, never complaining, and I'd really gotten a concussion from the fall.

The black hat, that's what you call instructors at airborne school, because they wear these black ball caps. He didn't like National Guardsmen being at airborne school, because we'd not go on to an airborne unit afterward. There aren't any National Guard Airborne units. He viewed it as if we were wasting an active Army guy's spot, and I get that. But he didn't have to drop me on my head like that.

"Which way?" I asked Rose, strapping my backpack on my back.

"We enter jungle," she said, walking toward the tree line. "We are seen too easily on the beach."

"Are you sure you were never in the Army?" She seemed pretty smart. She knew what she was doing.

"Shut up and walk," she said, hurrying into the jungle. With a scorching sun overhead, we both enjoyed the shade provided by the collection of banana, coconut and mango trees in the forest. The green fruit of the papaya trees hung in small bunches, looking like a bunch of footballs in a field bag, but without the bag. Papaya's my favorite. I let it get ripe and eat it, but most Filipinos actually eat it green. They cut it up and boil it in soups and what not. But I like it when it's blaze orange ripe! Like, five minutes before it goes to rot.

It didn't take but a minute or two for me to realize another way in which this island was different from the rest. There were no people. You couldn't smell smoke. And I'm talking about in a country, where on *any* shoreline, you can't look a hundred yards in either direction without seeing squatter shacks and nasty old worn clothes hangin' on laundry lines everywhere. But there was no sign of anyone on this island. And that made me nervous.

"So tell me about your sister," I said. I'd learned by now that she wasn't much of a talker, at least not with me, and it made me think that I was in for a long week, but I guess I was speakin' out of nervous energy more than anything myself.

"It does not matter," she said. "You do not care about anyone but yourself. Your own wants. You would not care about my sister."

"How can you say that?" I asked, ducking to avoid head butting a low hanging bunch of bananas. "You don't even know me."

"Foreigners all the same," she said, intentionally holding the limb of a juvenile Mango tree just a little longer than necessary as she made her way past and then releasing it at just the right moment to slap me across the face with it.

But I caught it.

"And you guys are always bitchin' that *we* stereotype *you*," I said, smirking at her failed attempt with the limb. "I just want to know that the person I'm saving is worth the trouble."

"The only thing worth it to you is the money!"

"Whatever," I said, slowing the pace. I was allowing the gap between us to grow in case she decided to slap me with another branch. I figured one bump on my head was enough for now, and I didn't want to hear any more of her opinions of me that were all based on the color of my skin. I hadn't come as far in accepting that crap back then as I have now, see.

***

"We rest," Rose said a while later. She'd gone much further than I would've expected her to be able to travel in one clip. I was impressed with her efforts so far.

"You seem quite motivated to get there," I said, sipping on water from a bottle I'd taken from my backpack. "She must mean a lot to you." I poured a bit of water into the palm of my hand and wiped it over the bump on my head. I'd gotten a throbbing headache by this point just beneath the bump.

"Wouldn't you hurry if it were your sister?" she said, accepting the bottle of water from me and sliding it under her veil.

"No," I said.

"How can you say that?" she said, lowering her head, taking a deep breath, then thrusting her head and the bottle back for another swig.

"That's one of the biggest differences between your world and mine," I said, taking the bottle back from her. I took another swig myself. "Family matters here in the Philippines. It's the most important aspect of your lives. And I have a lot of respect for your culture because of that. Family doesn't matter too much anymore in America."

"Do you find this naïve?" she said. She sounded prepared for my ridicule, but for the first time since I'd known her she also seemed interested in having a damn conversation. "That family matters to us?"

"No," I said, staring off into the jungle behind her. "That's perhaps what I respect most about your people and your culture. It used to be that way in my country. At least I'm told. I'm from generation X. Supposedly it mattered a generation or so before us."

"Gen… what?"

"Never mind," I said.

"Why it is not important now?" she asked, the rhythm of the rising and falling of her chest slowing as she caught her breath.

"I'm not sure," I said, looking down and shaking my head. "I don't think I can really pinpoint it."

"Why the people in your country all get divorce?" she asked. Divorce is non-existent here. I mean, they have it. But it's rare. Not more than half of all marriages like in The States.

"It seems as if marriage has become nothing more than an income stream for lawyers," I said, trying not to sound bitter, but not doing a very good job. "The more they can get a couple to fight while going through the divorce, the longer it takes, and the more money the lawyers make." And that's pretty much my take on it.

"Wouldn't that be hard on the children?" she said, listening intently. She knew I was being sincere with her, and she respected that and turned off the bitchometer.

"That's the worst part about it," I told her. "The kids are viewed as nothing more than pawns in a chess game. Each parent uses the kids against the other. No concern for how messed up they're making their lives. It's a form of child abuse really. But since the courts are involved, it's all legal. All's fair in love and war, and fucking up perfectly innocent children."

"You sound as if you've been through it?" she said, her voice still soft.

"Part of it," I said, looking up to meet her gaze. "I was married, but I don't have any kids. I always wanted 'em. I wanted 'em bad. My wife never did."

I found myself lost in her eyes again. I'd only made eye contact with her a few times, and I was starting to think that doing so might not be such a good idea. But I could only imagine how the rest of her might look. If only she weren't a slave to the veil and the burka, I remember thinking. Forced to cover the possibly beautiful face and body the creator had given her due to the deranged views of some religion.

"Why do you care?" I said, pulling my eyes away from hers. I knew I couldn't look into them too long. I might start believing in that great fable in which I'd once believed. Love. "Are you married?"

"No," she said.

"Why not?" I asked.

"I have not found right man," she said. Cookie cutter answer.

"Give me a break," I said, rising to my feet. "That's the oldest line in the book for, 'I'm gay.' Are you baklah (Visayan for gay)? I was trying to lighten the mood.

"No!" she said defensively. Failed again. "I have standards! Standards so high no man I meet yet meet them!"

"Oh, you're that great, huh?" I said, teasing her. "Got that much going on under that bed sheet huh?"

"I do not know why I talk to you, Richards," she said, rising to her feet. She strapped her backpack on and started stompin' off through the jungle again. I followed.

#

"We camp, here," she said, coming to a halt, and it was the first time she'd spoken to me since storming off two hours before. I hadn't even attempted to talk to 'er.

"Good with me," I said, dropping my pack to the ground. I was impressed that she'd been able to go for as long without a break in round two as she had in round one. I sat on the ground beside my pack, resting my back against the trunk of a banana tree. They're real soft ya know. Kinda let ya sink into 'em. Mother nature's Lazy Boy.

"I hope there're some freshwater streams on this island," I said, catching my breath. I'd just taken a big swig of water, and I was gonna run out soon. "I love coconut juice, but it gives me the shits if I drink too much of it."

"There will be streams for sure," she said, looking around, taking in our surroundings. It made me nervous the way she was doin' it. She was looking for someone. I could tell.

Or some*thing*.

We didn't know it, though I know now that Rose had suspected it, that was why she was lookin' around like that- but a small pair of eyes were watchin' us as we sat there sippin' water. It was watching from the safety of its home in the hollowed out, rotten bottom of a coconut tree stump twenty yards away. The eyes belonged to a creature that wasn't quite sure what to make of the beings that it considered to be trespassing on its land. I don't guess any more than I'd know what to make of it later.

Me- the tall white one- he'd seen my kind before, just in darker shades and much shorter. It was the other one that would've completely thrown him. The smaller one (but still much larger than him) covered entirely in a black garment.

And since he had no idea what to make of us, he- the patriarch of his family- would be sure to keep an eye on us and any of our activities until we were what he considered a safe distance away. I'd find that out later. He kept his beady little eyes on us.

The eyes of the duwende. And that's pronounced doo-win-dee.

What's a duwende?

Oh, just the magical Philippine dwarf.

12

Damn! You didn't have to spit your beer all over me!

Oh, I know it was an accident.

Sorry.

Just that whole 'easily activated startle reflex' thing I have because of my P.T.S.D. I wasn't expectin' it. But I guess you weren't expectin' this story to take a turn toward the paranormal, huh?

It already had anyway, with the chick in the water. The hot blond. I just haven't fully explained that yet, but I will.

What?

You wanna hear about the duwende first?

Well, okay. But now it's time to tell you about my friend John. See, you wanted to hear all about 'im and now that I'm ready to tell ya, you wanna hear about the duwende.

All in order, friend. All in order. Or none of it'll make any sense. Hell, a lot of it doesn't already.

What's that?

Oh yeah, most of the locals believe in this kinda stuff. They're very superstitious. They don't call it paranormal though. They call it aswang.

Okay, I'm gonna tell you about John now, because the whole time Rose and I were creepin' across the island, he'd been followin' us. Hell, like I've done told ya, he'd been followin' me for awhile. I just didn't know it at the time. And by tellin' ya who John is, I can introduce ya a little more to the world of the paranormal.

Or for the purposes of this story, the world of aswang.

Okay, so John's a weirdo. That's what most people who know him think anyway. He's a year older than me, but he looks much older. Lack of givin' a rat's ass about personal hygiene might have something to do with it. Matter-a-fact, the first day I met him, when I'd been assigned to work for 'im- he'd been my national guard unit's supply sergeant at the time- he explained to me that one of my duties was to remind him to take a bath every third day if he'd forgotten to.

His eyes look tired- all the time- like they'd seen things. Note what I'm sayin' here. The man doesn't look like he's *lived* things, but like his eyes have *seen* things. There's a difference, and I think in a few minutes you'll understand more of what I'm tryin' to say.

I worked with John almost every day for three months before our unit deployed to Iraq. He spoke very little to me the first couple of weeks- other than tellin' me to make sure he bathed every third day.

Once, after I'd been with him almost a week, he walked up to me, looked me square in the eyes, and said, "Your aura is completely fucked up." Then he went back to whatever he'd been doing.

I'd been diagnosed as bi-polar and manic before, but that's the first time I ever remember bein' diagnosed for a fucked up aura.

John liked to make me move boxes filled with supplies or simply filled with air to one side of a storage room, piling them neatly as I did, and then move 'em back the next day. It didn't make much sense to me. I asked him about it, and I remember he told me it was obvious that I'd never done much work for the government or I'd understand. I think I understood *that*.

Over time John began opening up, mostly by venting frustrations, and eventually let down whatever guard he'd seemed to have had in place, and I would go as far as to say that we had become friends by the time our unit deployed. Once in Iraq, he and I were both removed from supply- thank God for small favors- and we were made part of a convoy security platoon.

I saw little of John on convoy during the first half of the year. I was a gunner for one truck crew, which is also made up of a driver and a truck commander- that's the highest ranking person in the team who rides shotgun and sleeps most of the convoy. John was the commander of a different truck in our convoy, and I remember always wondering if it was his driver's job or his gunner's job to tell him to bath every third day in the event he'd forgotten.

About half way through the year, our gun truck teams started switchin' up. People were goin' home on leave, people were goin' home due to injury or illness, some people were losin' their minds in one way or another and were bein' placed into duties that didn't require leaving the green zone, and more importantly, being able to get their hands on a .50 cal with a virtually limitless supply of ammunition.

During this time, I ended up being John's gunner. We switched positions within the truck to avoid boredom, so sometimes I was the driver. Once or twice he even let me be the commander. I just wasn't allowed to talk on the radio so that our platoon leader, Lieutenant Bee, didn't know I was commanding the truck. And gettin' caught up on sleep. LT Bee loved to make everyone stay sleep deprived and miserable. And he particularly hated me.

Oh, I know it's not safe to be rollin' around in those huge gun trucks in a war zone all sleep deprived. Our unit only lost one man- which is one too many- while we were over there, and it's because he was gunnin' and his driver fell asleep at the wheel and the truck flipped. Dude got crushed to death. And I'm here to tell ya, if it weren't for assholes like LT Bee in charge, that would have *never* happened. We had an easy mission at that point in the war. Like I said, the war was over. We could've just done our jobs and come home, but LT Bee had to play all his little fuck fuck games. That's what they're called in the Army. At least in the infantry and other combat arms units. I think the Pog's- and that stands for "people other than grunts"- call it reindeer games.

But LT Bee was a class A prick! I'll tell ya that!

Various other team members were revolving in and out of our truck, and most of 'em kept to themselves. John had the reputation of 'weirdo' like I said, and frankly he made a lotta people nervous. He never made me nervous, though I often wondered just what in the hell he meant by my aura was fucked up.

Anyway, I remember our very first night out of the wire together as a team. I was drivin' that night, and as soon as we left the gate- I mean the very *instant* we get outside the wire- John settles down all cozy as you please in his seat and just conks out.

But he wasn't really asleep. It was like he was in a trance.

His eyes were kinda half shut and glazed, and you barely saw his chest rise, because he'd slowed his heart rate and breathing. It reminded me of the time an opossum had given birth under our back porch when I was a kid and then ran off and got hit by a car. The babies were just about weaned and when you'd see 'em out in the yard messin' around you could go pick 'em up by their tails and their eyes would gloss over while they played dead. And I mean they *really* looked dead. Well, that's what John looked like. Dead.

We were relatively safe outside the wire, and everyone knew it. I think the only people who still thought there was a war in Iraq at the time were the people back home watching television news who'd never been to Iraq, and who actually believed everything they see on the news, and I guess that was making the brass and the corporate sponsors happy. But still, I was just a bit leery of my truck's commander all opposuming out on me as soon as we left the wire. Mostly because of the poor visibility in the gun trucks. You could only see out your window and through your part of the windshield. I was completely blind to anything on the right side of the truck, and while my truck commander was playing opossum, so was he.

At least that's what I thought.

"Be extra vigilant around checkpoint seven," he said about ten minutes later when he came out of his trance. I'd written him off as play dead some time before, so when he spoke it startled me.

"What?" I said.

"Be extra vigilant around checkpoint seven," he said again.

"Okay," I said. And I said it the way people say it when they're being a smartass. You know, like when someone says something that makes no sense? Like this. "Ooooooo Kaaaaaaay?" Like a question.

John looks at me and says, "Have I ever told you your aura was completely fucked up?"

I looked at him and said, "Have you taken a shower in the last three days?" Then he goes to sleep. Real sleep, not that opossum stuff he'd been doing.

So, we get to checkpoint seven, no big deal- same old thing. A bunch of Iraqi Army guys layin' around on the sidewalk sleepin'. Yeah, real secure huh? But in that way, it really *was* like Vietnam. The more we did for 'em, the less they did for themselves. But I've been around enough to know that that's pretty much human nature. So it wasn't their fault. It was our fault for still bein' there. And you can see that shit here, like the people who consider themselves fortunate enough to sucker 'em a foreigner. Like the "orphanage" I told you about on Bohol. Why the hell *would* those people work if some dumbasses in Virginia're sendin' 'em more than ten times the average work wage?

Anyway, we start slow rollin' over all the speed bumps, and John sits up suddenly and yells something in Arabic, and he didn't even speak the language. I'm not sure what it was, but I went with the assumption of 'oh, shit!' At the same time, I see this Iraqi Army guy jump up and grab a huge stone and throw it through the windshield of one of the semi-tractor trailers we were escorting. The windshield shatters and glass goes everywhere. The driver was from Turkey, and the dumbass stops, gets out of his truck, and starts cussin' out the Iraqi.

See, most of the drivers of the trucks we secured were from Turkey and that really pissed off the Iraqis. They would ask us, 'You say you are here to help the Iraqi people, but you will not give us jobs? We can drive trucks!" And they had a point. I get it.

Our leaders, in their constant display of infinite wisdom, said the Iraqis couldn't be trusted with the information of where we were going and when. Our truck routes and times. But I have news for those leaders. Neither could the Turks or the Sri Lankans or any of the other third world peasants KBR was hiring and paying a whopping $400 a month to work 80 hours a week. Any of 'em would sell you out for five dollars. It's how most of 'em made most of their money. They'd befriend some Iraqi Army guys, text them what time our convoys were leavin' and where we were goin', and then they'd turn around and text their insurgent buddies, and they'd get five dollars, too.

Oh yeah. That's really how it worked. Look, those people were just looking for money to feed their families, just like people everywhere. I give the locals here a hard time for always scammin' foreigners, but before your heart turns to total ice, like mine, from having been here too long, your heart really does break when you see these poor bastards' kids runnin' around all dirty and hungry. That's why I get so infuriated with them though. Even when you try to give 'em a fair shake, and explain to 'em that if they'd just deal with you squarely, and don't try to fuck you over, they'll never have to worry about their kids goin' hungry again. But they just don't get it! Oh, sure, they act like they do, but that's part of the scam. It's all about makin' the most that they can off of you once and then fuck tomorrow.

I've tried the chicken and the egg analogy with 'em. No, not the one about which came first. That's bullshit. It's this one: If you have a chicken, and that chicken lays eggs, you can eat every day as long as you only eat the eggs. But if you get greedy and decide to have a big chicken dinner, you'll only eat once, because after that there is no more chicken and no more eggs.

You'd think they'd get that, with all the chickens around here, and that's why I use that specific analogy. But again, it seems to be a game for 'em. A challenge to see how much they can get from the foreigner one time so they can go around high fivin' their buddies.

I've known so many foreigners who've come here with mad cash in savings and tried to open businesses. Everything from restaurants to construction companies. And the reason all of 'em've failed is because of their employees. They've told me their employees would rather steal fifty dollars from 'em once than earn fifty dollars from 'em over and over and over and over.

The problem with that line of thinkin' is that tomorrow usually *does* come. And they can play the ignorant, uneducated peasant held captive by a corrupt government card all they want, but again, how many times do I have to say it, and how long do they have to live it?

Ignorance ain't so bliss when you're hungry.

So, anyway, back to Iraq. While we're yellin' at the Turk guy to get back in his truck and drive on, we start takin' sniper fire. This motivated the guy to get back in his truck and start drivin', and in no time we'd caught back up to the rest of the convoy.

"How did you know that was gonna happen?" I asked John.

"I have my ways," he said.

"How?"

"You wouldn't understand."

"Why? Because my aura's fucked up?"

"Something like that."

"You stink."

"You haven't reminded me to bath."

"I asked you about that."

"Not until we were already in the truck."

That's how our conversations always seemed to go. One liners-usually insults. But it was endearing.

***

Sleep deprivation is real, and it will kick your ass. Hell, it'll get ya killed. I already told you about that. And I already told you that prick LT Bee did his best to make sure we always had it. I think he wanted us to die so he could get our names tattooed on his arm and then sit around in bars cryin' about us for the rest of his life hopin' someone'd buy him drinks. No kiddin'.

One of the things sleep deprivation does is it screws with your dreams. Sometimes you might be awake and the things you think you're seein' appear to be a dream, even though you're awake. If that makes sense.

How did LT Bee make sure we were always sleep deprived?

He made sure that we were always workin'. Through his direct orders, we were always bein' forced to wake up and go to stupid classes on how to properly wrap a sprained ankle, or we were forced to go to a firing range to shoot a weapon, like the MK-19 grenade launcher, which was no longer allowed in theater anyway. It caused too much collateral damage. Sometimes he'd wake us up to go to the gym. The point is, the one thing he'd never do is just let us sleep.

"You're not sleeping, and it isn't a dream," John said, walking up behind me with a pudding cup in his hand this one time. It was about 4 a.m., and we were at some outpost in northern Iraq. Turkey was right across the Tigris River and you could see the western most portions of the Himalayas from where we were. We'd often stand there in the 130 degree heat of the afternoon sun and long for the snow atop the mountains. Supposedly, we were looking at where Noah's Ark had been found.

"Did you see him too?" I asked.

"Yeah, but no one else did, so don't say anything, or they'll send you to combat stress."

Combat stress was where they sent the crazies. They'd dope you up on half a dozen different trial drugs from the big pharmaceutical companies whose C.E.O.'s had gone to grad school with some general, and then they'd take your weapon and give you some shitty job inside the wire. And the drugs *really* made you go nuts. Benzodiazepines is what they'd give you. Real nasty shit.

Everyone would know you'd been to combat stress, because if you were outside your CHU, and that stands for company housing unit, you *had* to have your weapon. Civilians call it gun, but in the Army its weapon, because guns are cannons and howitzers, and don't you *dare* call a howitzer a tank, because every field artilleryman from here to the other side of earth will kick your ass. Anyway, the only people who didn't have weapons were the crazies and everyone would pick on 'em and that would make 'em even crazier. Hell, while we were in Iraq, some dude down in Baghdad went into combat stress and shot the place up. Killed five people. I think he was on his third deployment.

If you ended up goin' to combat stress because of the crazies, when you got home they'd come up with some bullshit you didn't really do and article 15 your ass to get you out without having to pay disability for having gone insane on their dime. But there's always a really high chance you're gonna do something stupid or illegal once they get ya on all their dugs anyway. Either way, they don't wanna deal with the fucked-upness that's caused on their watch. Easier to make you out as the bad guy- pre-existing conditions or whatever- and push you out and dust their hands of ya.

"Who the hell was it and where did he go?" I asked John. About the guy he said he'd seen too, but that no one else did.

"It's just an ancestor spirit."

"Is that like, a ghost?"

"Yeah."

"I've never seen one before."

"You have now."

"But he just walked around the corner here," I said, pointing down the long, empty hall. "And he's gone."

"Yeah, that's kinda what ghosts do. Go to bed. You have a few hours and you need the sleep. Trust me. There's shit around here you don't wanna see. And whatever you do, don't acknowledge them. They'll never leave you alone. They're attention whores."

"Roger that, big 'sarn," I said and then I went to bed.

***

John ended up leaving our team for about a week. Our leadership didn't really like him, because he was so weird, and they used him as a fill in for a neighboring unit who'd had too many guys go on leave at the same time.

One of the nights while John was out on mission with the other unit, and our unit was off, I'd been sitting up in the TOC hitting on some cute specialist that worked at the front desk. Okay, she wasn't *that* cute, but I'd been in Iraq for nine months, and she was one of only seven girls in our unit of a hundred and fifty soldiers. And I wasn't really flirting. I just missed talkin' to girls. I know that sounds weird, but it's one of the realities of a deployment. You miss things you'd never think could *be* missed. Like the dust flyin' off my screen door and reminding me of those mushroom puffs I'd mentioned earlier. It's the strangest things that make ya homesick.

What's that?

Oh, TOC. That stands for tactical operations center.

So, we're there in the office, and we keep hearin' the communications comin' across the main channel from the various convoys out on the road, when all of a sudden we hear, "Contact left!" come across the speakers.

"Who's that?" I asked what's-her-face. I've been back for so long now I can't even remember her name. I think it was Emily.

No, wait. Wasn't her. Emily really *was* cute.

"That's Bravo six eight," what's-her-face-said. "They just crossed the bridge into Mosul on their way back."

"Shit!" I said. "My T.C.'s with them tonight." And I was talking about John.

"Contact right!" another voice came across the scanner.

"They're really getting lit up," what's-her-face-said. "Sounds like an ambush!"

We listened to the radio. Someone came on and said something about seeing tracer rounds droppin' straight to the ground, about ten feet before hitting their gun truck. A few seconds later someone else made a similar statement. And you could hear amazement in these guys' voices. Me and what's-her-face just looked at each other, eyes wide and mouths open.

"Break! Break! Break!" came the voice of the unit's platoon leader. "Maintain radio silence, unless it's urgent!"

"What the hell's that all about?" I asked.

"Hell if I know," she said. "Sounds weird."

An hour later, the platoon that'd been out on the road and had gotten lit up came in and went into the little conference room off from the side of the office where me and what's-her-face were to have their post mission assessment. We went in to listen, which isn't uncommon, but we got ran outta the room by the platoon leader. Some chaplain, I could tell by the little cross patch he was wearing, was walking around the room like a holly roller on Wednesday evenin' with his hands up shouting, "Praise God-ah! Praise Jesus-ah!" I was able to get a glance at John before we left, and man, did he look like shit. He looked tired and worn out, and like he'd aged five years in one night!

I just assumed that all the missions he'd been goin' on were takin' their toll. I asked him later what had happened while they were out on the road that night, and he said he couldn't talk about it, and for me to mind my own fuckin' business. I told him to take a bath and pretty much forgot about it.

Until a month later.

***

We were about a month away from goin' home, and things were getting' stupid. Sure, we'd been lucky. *Really* lucky. We'd lost only one man, and that's one too many, the poor kid I told you about who died due to his driver's sleep deprivation. Other units who'd been there before us had it worse. They'd lost a lot.

Anyway, here at the end, we had all of these high rankin' fobbits-those are people who work on the F.O.B., or forward operating base-who never went outside the wire while we were there, who all of a sudden wanted to start goin' outside the wire. And I'll tell ya why. It was all so that when they got home they could say shit like, "I went outside the wire," or, "Man, this one time, when we were outside the wire…" or, when asked all the stupid questions civilians ask like, "Did you kill anybody? (that one takes the cake in *my* book)," they could say, "Listen. I've been outside the wire. And what happens outside the wire, stays outside the wire."

Anyway, this one night, on one of our very last missions before we came home, we had our brigade commander, Lt. Col. Jenkins (we called him Jerkin' with Jergens) in our convoy. He'd not been out all deployment. He had a non-combat M.O.S. - 46Q, public affairs specialist- and how in *hell* that made him the right guy to be in charge of a combat arms unit, I have no clue. But like we say in the Army, if it all made sense, we'd all be dead. And again, the real war was over, so I guess all in all it was okay.

I assumed at the time that this jerkin' to Jergens guy was some political post seeker who wanted to pad his campaign speeches with all the bullshit war awards they hand out like candy these days, like the bronze stars they give to anyone who's an E-7 or above. No kiddin'.

My grandfather, in WWII, had to fight his way from the asshole to the armpit of Europe to be given the bronze star, but now, if you're an E-7 who sits in a T.O.C. for nine months in Iraq, you get a bronze star on your way home.

Turns out I was right. This dip shit got out a year after we were back and ran for state senator in his home state of Iowa. He was handily beaten by a guy who'd taken part in the invasion in 2003, as a private, and who had NOT been awarded a bronze star. I loved hearing about that shit.

So, anyway. Back to this night.

I remember we had this kid named Corey Prine with us in the truck. I say kid, but he was in his mid-twenties. He had a really friendly, boyish face though, so he looked younger.

I liked Corey. He was a good guy, and we had a common enemy in our platoon leader, Lt. Bee. Everyone hated Lt. Bee. He was your typical Napoleonic complex sufferin', lower commissioned ass-hat who was pissed off at the world because no matter how much he wanted everyone to look up to him, they couldn't, because he was only five feet six. But for some reason, the prick had singled Corey and me out early in the deployment, so we always enjoyed being together in the truck, because we could bash Half Man all night. That's the nickname Corey and I'd given him. Half Man. Because he was so small.

Corey wanted to gun because he'd been drivin' a lot lately, and I didn't care, because I'd just been going through the motions a lot lately, and making sure to stay out of Lt. Bee's sight when I could. Seemed like every time he saw me he'd come up with some extra special stupid detail for me to do. I'd gotten good at keepin' to myself, but I knew it was takin' its toll. I'd find myself mumbling to myself a lot. Talkin' to people who weren't really there.

Or were they?

I let Corey gun, and I drove, and John T.C.'ed. We bashed Lt. Bee quite a bit as we drove through the city, but as always, the night was uneventful, and once we got out into the sparsely populated desert everyone started dozin' off. First John- and not one of those opossum sleeps, but a real one- and then Corey. I could hear 'em both snorin' through the headset.

Just before we started climbin' the hills in the mountainous part of the region, John bolts upright. And he's droolin'. I catch the movement out of the corner of my eye and I hear the weirdest grunt. Then something again in Arabic.

"Are you okay?" I asked him, looking over. And by the dim light of the communications system in the truck, I see his eyes rollin' into the back of his head, and I think, Oh shit! He's having a seizure! I'm just about to go on the mike and ask for the medic when Corey starts yelling, "Contact left! Contact left!"

I immediately look out the window to my left, and here comes tracer rounds from about a hundred meters away. I'm thinking, oh shit, here we are, a month before goin' home, nothing's happened all year, and now we're gonna get waxed!

But the strangest thing happened. All the rounds, about ten feet before hitting the truck, went straight down to the ground. I mean, like they'd hit a steal wall. But instead of bouncing back in the direction from which they'd come, they went straight down to the ground. I could see the dust jumpin' up eight feet high from the impact of the rounds.

By this time, Corey'd announced the contact over the communications system, like you're supposed to. Lt. Bee calls out for a S.A.L.T. report, like this was some kinda practice run in basic training.

What's a S.A.L.T. report?

Oh, that stands for size of enemy – activity of enemy- location of enemy- and time of enemy activity.

"Right now, you numb-nutted half fuck!" Corey yelled out over the radio. That became an instant classic, but it would cost Corey forty days of extra duty- which ended up being cut by twenty percent or so, because there wasn't forty days left in the deployment- and about ten thousand pushups, but he said it was worth every last one of 'em to get that Freudian slip off. Especially with a Lt. Col on convoy with us.

So I get on the mike and tell the Lt. we need a medic.

Everyone in the convoy's convinced someone got shot. We blow down the road about half a mile- the incoming rounds had ceased about quarter of a mile before this- and then we pull a wedge security stop. Our truck pulls into the center of the wedge, and the truck with the medic comes over to our side. All the gunners are pullin' three sixty security. I mean you could tell these guys knew what to do, and everyone was excited to *finally* be doing it.

The medic comes into our truck. "Who's hit?! Who's hit?!" he's screaming.

"No one's hit," John says, cool as a cucumber.

I look over at 'im, and he's perfectly fine. Except for the fact that he's seemed to have aged another year or two since we left the gate just a few hours before.

"What the fuck!" the medic yells. "Why the fuck did you call for a medic?!"

"He was having a seizure!" I yelled.

"Who?!" the medic yelled back.

"Sergeant White!"

John looked at me as if I was the most delusional man on earth. "I'm fine, Richards," he says, and then looks at the medic like he has no clue what I'm talking about.

"I'm gonna make sure Lt. has your ass, Richards!" the medic says just before leavin'. It was no secret to anyone that Lt. hated me, and I guess the medic, who sucked the Lt.'s ass any chance he got- a suck up that guy was, I'll tell ya- was gonna make sure he used this to his advantage.

Those twenty eight days or so of extra duty Corey Prine did? I did 'em with 'im.

All three of us, John, Corey and myself, were forced to go to a week-long combat stress class after that night. We'd been handed down a case of the crazies.

A damage assessment was done after the incident, and no bullet holes were found in our truck's side, or in the sides of any of the tractor trailers filled with supplies we'd been escorting. Our unit's translator asked the Turkish truck drivers who'd been close to us if they'd seen anything, and they verified our account. You could tell by their animation and the way they spoke. All excited like. They kept praisin' Allah, too, but Half Man ordered the translator to claim they said they'd seen nothing. Sure, I couldn't understand their words, but I'd understood their body language, and I could see it in their eyes.

The best part of the whole night though? Was when once everyone realized no one had been hit and everyone was okay, they started freakin' out about the brigade commander who was with us, and what he thought of the whole debacle. Turns out, when he *was* found, he was hiding in the very back of his gun truck, cryin', and he'd pissed his pants.

None of this ever came out in the media later during his political campaign, but word has it that his opponent had gotten the message passed around through the voting district using a system much like the old 'private news network' he'd learned all about while serving in the U.S. Army. Basically, word of mouth with no evidence leading back to the source. Rank might have its privileges, but so does having friends in low places.

The week long combat stress retreat was actually a nice change. They moved the three of us to private quarters over at the mental health clinic. It was great after having shared a room hardly larger than the size of the inside of our gun truck's cab with up to five other men at a time over the previous year.

Though we had private rooms at mental health, we didn't have doors. That was because there were sentries posted in the halls to make sure we didn't commit suicide. That was a real issue, and to my understanding, with the limited amount of time I allow myself to check in with "the world," it remains a big problem back home.

I got a story that'll break your heart about that too. And that's for later. Found out through John. It really tore me up. I'll get to it.

Anyway, I didn't need a door. I liked the space. And the schedule was light. We'd have breakfast at 8 a.m., and classes didn't start until 10 a.m. We'd found that Lt. Bee always screwin' with our sleep- always makin' us wake up in the middle of our designated sleep hours and such for stupid classes on stupid topics- was to our advantage, because we never had any problems that week switchin' our sleep patterns from day to night. We'd never developed any consistent sleep patterns.

Our instructor was this really nice and sincere Captain. Captain Norris was the name. I remember because he looked nothin' like Chuck Norris. He seemed a little light in the combat boots if you know what I mean, but he brought a sense of peace and serenity with him that we'd been missing.

The week went by quickly- I think mostly because we weren't miserable during the time- and nothing of significance really happened.

Until the end.

On the second half of the last day, Captain "not Chuck" Norris brought in a chaplain to talk about God and all that stuff. I'd learned to tune that whole religion thing out a long time ago, and there's a reason for it- mom was Catholic, dad was Baptist, I was forced to be both as a child, so now I'm bi-polar and agnostic- but out of respect for those who're into that kinda stuff, I always keep my mouth shut and my views to myself and just let 'em talk.

Anyway, when the chaplain walked in, I thought that he looked familiar. When I saw him look our way, and I noticed John slink down into his seat, I was able to pin him. He was the chaplain that'd been screamin' "praise Jesus-ah!" and all that the night after John's other convoy got lit up. They'd been on convoy together.

I knew John hated organized religion as much as me. He told me once that he was a spiritualist, and when I mistakenly took that to mean that he was very spiritual, and asked if he was of Christian belief, he went off on me, yet explained what he meant- it put me in the mind of Native American shamanism- and then he told me my aura was fucked up.

The chaplain pointed John out, yelling, "You were there! You were there!"

The chaplain starts his spiel with a word of prayer. Then he launches in on what would've been the wildest of tales, had I not recently lived through a similar tale myself. He told us of having gone out on a convoy security mission the previous month (he was a Major, and no doubt had wanted to leave the wire at least once before going home so he could have his 'war stories'), and coming under an 'attack of biblical proportions,' yet, of how not a single round or blast hit any of their trucks or gunners. It was a 'miracle of biblical proportions.'

"We were a-takin' rounds from all sides and all angles-ah," the chaplain said, describing a night that sounded all too familiar to me. "Yet not-a-one-of-em hit us-ah! It was as if the shield of God-ah had been placed upon us-ah! Jesus Christ-ah was ridin' shotgun with us on that convoy that night-ah. Praise Jesus-ah!"

After his presentation, which I thought was gonna go all the way 'til Sunday- if it wasn't Sunday already, hell, you lose track of days on a deployment- he came up to John and shook his hand and asked him how he'd been since that night of Christ-like miracles.

"Been okay, Sir," is all John said.

"You don't look like you've been okay, son," the chaplain said. "You been sick, boy?"

"A little under the weather, Sir," John said.

"Well praise God-ah, it's good to see ya again, son," the chaplain said, and then he went around the room asking everybody if they were friends with Jesus.

"Why didn't you tell him it happened again?" I asked John.

"You ask too many questions, Richards!" he said. "Where's Prine? Let's go to chow."

And that was that.

We never really talked about it again. I tried, but John never wanted to. I tried to talk to Corey about it, but he'd closed himself off pretty tight by this point in the deployment. He kept to himself a lot, too, but he'd let it out that his wife back home in Virginia'd run off with some guy she worked with at the bank. Corey admitted to me once that he didn't miss her so much, but that she'd taken their son. The kid was only three months old when we'd deployed, and Corey had a strong feeling that he was never gonna see 'im again. He told me that if that were the case, he didn't see it as if life was much worth livin'. He was really tore up about the thing.

It didn't help that when that little prick Lt. Bee'd caught wind of it that he made things worse by teasin' Corey about it every chance he got. Corey was goin' off about it one day, talkin' about his wife runnin' off with the little faggot from down at the bank. Half Man comes up and slaps 'im on the back and says, "must not be too much of a faggot, Prine, if he's layin' the pipe to your wife!"

It's a good thing Corey hadn't completely lost his mind by this point, or I believe he'da shot the little prick right there.

I never had kids, and thank God for that, as messed up as I was myself when I got back from 'Raq, but I could really empathize with Corey and all the other soldiers this was happenin' to. But I thought he was just blowing smoke with that whole life not worth livin' crap. Corey was a strong kid, and he had a good head on his shoulders. I was sure that barring some freak event, or unless he got hooked on the drugs they throw at ya for havin' the crazies or something, he'd never kill himself. Not Corey. That's what I was thinkin'.

I thought I'd talk to John about that night on convoy, and the night he'd been out on the other convoy when the 'shield of God,' as the preacher man had called it, had descended upon us for our protection once we got home. But I never saw myself goin' into the hospital. When we got home, John and the majority of the rest of our unit went one way, and me and half a dozen other 'broke dicks' as we're called in the Army once we get hurt, went off to that terrible, terrible warehouse for broken soldiers that they call warrior transition battalions to get medical treatment and therapy, and addicted to every fuckin' drug they could throw at us.

So. That's who John is.

And now, here he was again. Hadn't seen 'im for three years, and I'd never planned on seeing 'im again, but while I'm getting' spied on by some two feet tall magical munchkin, John's only a couple clicks behind me, trackin' me down like a wild animal.

Again, I didn't know it at the time, but I soon would.

Remember I told you he comes in with a bang?

Just wait.

But for now, it's *my* turn to go piss. Grab us another beer.

13

No rats! Thank, God!

Now, where was I?

Oh yes. The duwende. Nasty little trolls.

So Rose and I are just chillin' ya know. The sun was goin' down and I was happy that we'd finally established a dialogue.

"How long it has been since you visit your country?" she asked me. She was breakin' up small sticks to make a fire. She was careful not to use too many, because she knew that the fire or the smoke it would create would be a dead giveaway of our location. Remember, I'd already noticed that the girl knew what she was doing.

"I haven't been back for three years," I said, and I started to help her. "I have no reason to go back."

"What of your parents?" she said, pulling a lighter from her pack, igniting the outer furry edge of a piece of coconut shell on the bottom of the pile of sticks.

"Dead," I told her. Not really the truth, but I'd already learned not to give too much private information away by this time. They just use it against you to take advantage of you when they can. The one you give it to might not, but remember, they chat like crazy. Someone somewhere will use it. It's not that you can't always trust the person you're talkin' to as much as you can't trust who they might know that you don't.

"Did you love your parents?"

"Of course I did," I said. "What the hell kinda question is that?"

"So you DO have the ability to love someone other than yourself?"

"What is it with you!?" I said. "Every time we *almost* start to become friends, you get defensive."

"I just know your kind too well," she said, fanning the growing flames of the fire she'd just lit. Once they caught, she reached into her pack again, this time pulling out a sealed package of dried fish. Those are small fish, the size of large minnows, dried in the sun and cured in salt. They could be eaten as is, but she preferred them slightly warmed over an open flame. They sound gross, but they're actually good. Like the balot I told you about earlier. I think most of the native food here is an acquired taste.

"*My* kind?" I said, rolling my eyes. "How about *your* kind? A bunch of damn opportunists if opportunists ever existed!"

"You only associate with the lowest of the low, Richards," she said, bringing up a point that was spot on. "If ever you get out of the girly bars, away from the pimps, you would see many of my kind are very good."

"Yeah, well, maybe you'd see that there were many of my kind that is very good too, if your kind didn't make it so easy to come here and go crazy with beer and sex."

"That is not our fault," she said, poking a thin stick through the body of a dried fish and then holding it over the flame. She offered me the pack of fish. "Perhaps your kind should not exploit my kind."

"Thank you," I said, taking the fish. I was pretty damn hungry by this point. "You guys exploit yourselves. When you tell your children to run up to us with their hands out and say, 'Hey Joe, give me money,' while you sit back and laugh, and most of your women spread their legs upon the sight of white skin, how do you say that *we* are exploiting *you*?"

"You find what it is that you look for Richards."

That was simple, yet very profound. But I didn't want to give her the point, so I kept going.

"How do you know I wasn't looking for better when I first got here?"

"What were you looking for?" she asked, speaking with her mouth half full.

"You'll just laugh at me and insult me if I tell you," I said, sticking the tail of a fish into my mouth. That's my favorite part. They're crunchy, like a potato chip.

"I will not laugh or insult you if you do not insult my people," she said.

"I came here in hopes of having what I couldn't have in *my* country. A family." I paused between bites, waiting for an insult. I felt like kickin' myself in the ass, too, for having been honest about that. That really was a big part of the reason I'd come here.

"And then?" she said, the Filipino way of saying, 'finish the story; tell me more.'

"And then it didn't work out," I said, handing her the head of a fish. That seemed to be her favorite part. I love the tails, but I don't eat the heads.

"Were you looking for wife in girly bars?" she asked, placing the head of the fish I'd given her underneath her burka. I almost smiled, seeing the garment move up and down after she did and hearing the crunching of the fish's skull underneath. And I gotta tell ya, I was still curious as hell as to what she had goin' on under that bed sheet.

"There you go again," I said, standing up and walking away just a bit. I was afraid to get too friendly with her. And I knew I faced danger by getting lost in her eyes. She'd have me wrapped, even though I had no clue what the rest of 'er looked like.

"I am not insulting," she said, digging into the bag for another dried fish. "I am just asking you to look at where you may have made mistake."

"Okay," I said, sitting back down. I mean, she kept comin' up with a lotta good points. You *do* get what you look for, and you ain't gonna find a good little Catholic girl workin' in the bars. Not that I was lookin' for a Catholic, but you know what I mean. Most likely, any girl you end up with here *will* be a Catholic though. My wife that's not really my wife's a Catholic. "That's fair."

"What of your ex-wife? Where is she?"

"Last I heard, still in Virginia. Still happily remarried."

"She remarried? Who?"

"Another prick lawyer and the father of her children," I said. "She's a lawyer."

"What?" she said, stopping mid chew, her eyes meeting mine. "I thought she never want baby?"

"Well, and as we'd say in my country, the insult to the injury is that she not only has one, but she has three."

"How that happen? Why she change her mind?"

"Look," I said, thinking of how to keep it as simple as possible. I didn't want to go into how for all the years that my ex-wife and I'd been married, she'd always been embarrassed because I was a teacher and she was a lawyer. Any time we'd go to those fake dinner parties, all her asshole friends would always say, 'Oh, look, it's the teacher,' and laugh at me. Hell, the year I'd taken off from teaching to try to make it as a stock broker? That was her doin'. Yes, she really was that embarrassed to be married to a penny ante teacher.

But I knew Rose wouldn't understand when I told her I'd been a teacher. She'd say she thought I was a soldier in the Army, and I'd have to explain about the whole National Guard thing, and it would take forever and bring back too many bad memories.

"I was in Iraq for a year," I told her. "I came home at the end of that year, and she was three months pregnant."

"And then?"

"And then I left the bitch!"

"Who is father?"

"Some asshole lawyer. I told you. I really don't want to talk about it, Rose."

"I see," she said. She let a respectful silence pass and then said, "shame to your wife and to lawyer fuck!" She sounded genuinely pissed, and even though her words were out of order, it was really the first time I'd heard her cuss, and that's probably why the words were out of order, and I couldn't help but laugh.

"Why you make me fun?" she asked.

"I'm not," I told her. "I think it's cute how you cuss."

"This is common in your country?" she said, remembering now that she had dried fish in her hand, and she started eating again. "To cheat your spouse and get divorce?"

"Too common," I said, taking another fish from the small pack and nibbling on it. "Especially in military families it seems. They say that distance makes the heart grow fonder, but there's something about proximity that people find attractive."

"What?" she said, and she'd stopped chewing instantly. I should've known that one would throw her. That whole English learned and taken literally thing.

"Never mind," I said. The easy way out.

"So no one from any culture is perfect," she said, rolling the top of the pack of fish closed and putting it back in her backpack. I took note that she was making sure to be prepared for a possible quick getaway. That's the thing about learning to stay vigilant in the military. You can never turn that shit off. The shrinks back home gave me a pill for it, or four, can't remember just what all the pills they gave me were for, but they called this 'hyper-vigilance' and they said it was a bad thing and that I needed to be medicated for it.

Hey, I'll agree that the nightmares I have sometimes and the bouts of insomnia are bad, but I'm not so convinced being hyper-vigilant is. Especially in the world we've come to live in today, and especially when you're a lone white foreigner in a place where everyone is always sizin' you up as an A.T.M. machine. Again, the Filipinos are not violent by nature, but you never know when someone might feel a little froggy and decide to jump. That can happen in *any* country. Plus, there *was* the kinda work I was doin'. Like on this island.

"You are correct," I said. "The different cultures of the world are all so different in so many ways, but so similar in many others. People take advantage of other people. People lie. People end up disappointed. People don't get what they want, or can't find what makes them happy."

"I am sorry for what happen to you, Richards," she said. She truly was, and I could hear it in her voice.

"Thank you," I said. "So what about you? I know nothing about you?

"I never have husband," she said, looking down at the ground.

"Boy friend?" I asked.

"Some," she said, "But they all want only one thing."

"How do you know that's all they wanted? I mean, sure, all guys want sex. It's a very important part of any relationship. But perhaps they wanted more, and you didn't stick around long enough to find out?"

"For the guys I was with, it was the most important thing to them. The sex. I did not give it so they go away. If it were not the most important thing they would have stayed."

"You mean, you're a virgin?" I said, looking around as if someone else had spoken the words. It had been so long since I'd even heard the "V" word, especially here.

Now mind you, the Philippines probably have one of the highest rates of virginity outside of marriage of any country in the world. But again, I wasn't hangin' around with the good little Catholic girls. I was hanging out with the dirty little Catholic girls.

"Yes. I am virgin." she said, voice stoic.

"A twenty three year old virgin?"

"Yes," she said, and now she was getting high blood again. "How many times I must tell you?!"

"That's just odd. I guess maybe, because you're Muslim. Those traditions."

I was speaking out loud and I shouldn't have been, because she didn't like my thoughts.

"I do not do what I do because of religious beliefs or cultural reasons," she said. "I do it because of *my* beliefs and *my* reasons."

"Wow," I said. "And why exactly *is* it you believe this way? What *are* your reasons?"

"I see so many lives in my country ruined because of sex," she said, her tone firm. "Everyone seems to do it, but no one is safe.

"The Catholic Church, the ruler of the majority of our people, more influential to them than our government, has convinced our people that birth control is a form of abortion, not prevention. That is why our people will not use condom or pill. The result is that families have a dozen children who are born into poverty and never leave it. They go along the streets, collecting plastic to sell for five pesos per kilo, or begging from the foreigners. Half goes to the rice for the family to eat and their father's Red Horse or Tanduay or tuba, and the other half goes to the offering plate at the mass that is held every hour on the hour.

"This is what you don't understand, Richards. You think we are opportunists because our children beg from foreigner in the street. The foreigner knows when his next meal is. We do not. Parents do not laugh when their children begs because it is funny. They laugh because they are embarrassed, but they need the money."

She was really on a roll, and as you could probably tell by everything I've told you about the place so far, you can see that she was right on the money. She was giving me the view from the other side of the desk, as we'd say in teaching.

"It gets old when you have to deal with it all the damn time," I said. "I mean every goddamn time you go down the street, some kid comes up callin' ya Joe and askin' for money."

"It gets old to hear your baby cry because she has no rice to eat or milk to drink," Rose said.

"How does that have anything to do with us taking advantage of you?" I asked.

"The little girl you turn away who begs? In ten years you will pay her for her body. And she only sells it because she has learned that is the only way you will pay," she said.

"We foreigners didn't tell you guys to have all those babies," I said, remembering a time or two when I'd told a beggar girl to come back and see me in ten years, thinking it was funny. Didn't seem so funny now. Rose took all the humor out of that, but I didn't want the old heart to start thawing out again. I told you before, I used to empathize, and I ended up going broke tryin' to help. And they just viewed my kindness as weakness and took advantage anyway. But I guess there've been times I've gone a little past self-protection to pure asshole. And that's *not* excusable.

"And you bring up another major difference between our countries that has always fascinated me," I said, keeping at her. "The Catholic Church. They allow contraception in America. They know that we are an educated, fiscally advanced nation. If we cannot afford to have babies, we don't have them. Most of the people anyway. The church knows that we wouldn't listen to 'em if they told us not to use birth control. Catholics in America would even defect the faith if they were expected to live by such an asinine rule. It's an old belief system that doesn't hold up in an advanced society."

"Why the difference?" she asked. "Same church?"

"We have a saying in my country," I said, slowing my speech. I was calming back down. "Follow the money trail. It will lead you to the answer."

"I do not understand."

So much for being a swami.

"You've already explained it, really," I said, nodding at her. "Here, the more beggars in the streets, the more pesos in the basket at mass. In my country, charity begins at home. If there're four mouths to feed, instead of only two, then instead of giving one hundred dollars to the offering at mass, you give only fifty."

"I see," she said. "So the church says what it needs to say in different countries and different cultures to make the most it can make?"

"Exactly! They do the same thing in Mexico and South American nations that they do here. It would take two to three generations to turn this country around, make it an advanced society economically. It all starts with education, the most important form being sex education, in the current state you guys are in. You *must* get your population under control or there is no hope for anything other than poverty."

"I did not realize the church is so bad," she said, looking down, as if questioning anything she'd ever believed. And this took me, because she was a Muslim. Why had she thought highly of the Catholic Church?

Remember. Hyper-vigilance.

"It isn't just the church," I said "The corporations do it too. In many ways, they've become the churches of my country. They've taken away the right to pray in schools, and they've taken away the right to have the ten commandments posted in courthouses, but it still says, 'In God We Trust' on the almighty dollar bill."

"And then?"

"Listen, if you go to the grocery store in America, generally, the more bulk in which you buy any product, the less you pay for each unit of the product. Like grams per pesos?" I paused, making sure she was following. Her head nod confirmed that she was.

"Okay, I've noticed here, you guys are terrible at math and think only of today. I'm not insulting," I said, noticing her body stiffen under her burka. "I'm just stating facts. You guys learn all that language and Catholicism in your schools, but very little about mathematics, science, world cultures. Even your own country's history. That whole 'hey Joe' thing?"

"What?"

"I'll explain later. It goes back to World War Two. Anyway, the corporations know that you guys are only buying products for today, because the typical Filipino only has enough money for today, *if* he's lucky. So they set the system up to profit from you should you attempt to be responsible and plan for the future."

I couldn't see her face because of the burka, but I could tell by the way she tilted her head to the side and was squinting that I'd lost her.

"Like, if you buy a 100 gram box of crackers at ten pesos, you pay ten centavos per gram," I said. "However, if you buy a 240 gram box of crackers, instead of paying twenty four pesos or less, you pay twenty eight pesos. That means you are actually paying more to buy in bulk."

"I see," she said. "I've never thought of it that way."

"Of course you haven't," I said. "None of you do. You think you're doin' somethin' good because it'll last you more days. That's another day you can worry less about your struggle. And the corporations, most of 'em admittedly American, laugh all the way to the bank."

"So it isn't just the Catholic church?" she said, her voice soft.

"No," I said. "It's anyone who stands to make a buck off of your plight."

"Do the corporations do this to the people in your country?"

"Oh yes. Just in a different way," I said.

"And then?"

"They do it by brainwashing us through marketing and advertising. They convince everyone they need all these material things to be whole. A big car, a big house, a pool in the back yard. The banks lend us money to purchase all these things, because we wouldn't have the money to buy them otherwise. Next thing ya know, you're a slave to the bankers, at interest, for the rest of your life. You can never get ahead." I looked down and laughed. "And you guys see all these things in our movies and music videos and think that we're all rich. If you only knew how enslaved the American people really were. And the stress that comes with it.

"You see," I said. "I guess we really are the same in so many ways. The actions taken by those who benefit from taking advantage, how they do it I guess, may be different. But the result is always the same. The people at the top get richer, be they a corrupt barangay captain in the Philippines, or a corporate C.E.O. in America, and the people at the bottom get stuck in a rut and can't get out."

"I am tired now. I sleep," she said, and she sounded depressed. She moved away from the fire and lay on the ground.

"Me too," I said, moving away from the fire in the opposite direction. I used my backpack as a pillow, and I was soon asleep.

***

What's that? What's any of this long winded conversation have to do with the magical dwarves I told ya about? The duwende?

Well, nothing really. I was just tryin' to show you that Rose had lightened up by this point in our journey, and it's good, because I needed her to give a little bit of a shit about me, with all that happened next and everything.

What happened next?

The duwende happened next.

14

"Oh, I have to pee!" I said, waking from a deep sleep. The ground was hard, but I'd been able to sleep anyway, because I was so tired.

Other than when Rose'd knocked me out, I'd not slept in more than a day, since we'd been up all night the night before getting' to the island. Well, I guess I snoozed for a bit there too, huh?

What's that?

Oh yeah. She'd knocked me out with her ore. She only told me I'd fallen out of the boat and hit my head. You'll hear why she did it here in a minute.

Anyway, I know that when I sleep deeply that I snore really loud, and I was in such a deep sleep that I almost didn't wake up in time to avoid pissin' myself.

"Oh, oh, oh, I have to pee!" I said again, hoppin' past Rose. She was sound asleep on the ground. The embers from our small fire were now gone, and man was it dark.

I went about twenty yards past her and took a piss, and it felt good. I went back and had no problems fallin' right back to sleep. Woke myself up a couple times with my own snorin, but I was soon enough out for the count again.

"Oh, I have to pee!" I said, waking again from a deep sleep again! "I just went, damn it!" I didn't know how long I'd been out, but not long enough.

Once again I crept past Rose, still asleep on the ground, and I went back to where I'd gone the time before on the rotten stump of this old coconut tree. I undid my fly, pulled out my manhood and…

…nothing.

Nothin would come out.

"What?" I said, confused at first, but then scared. "I have to freakin' pee!"

Had I developed a serious health problem? Contracted an S.T.D.? I'd been dodgin' *that* bullet for quite a while. Maybe the train had finally arrived at the station, was what I was thinkin'.

I began jumpin' up and down, tryin' to shake it loose. I was afraid my bladder was gonna burst, so I just kept jumpin'. Higher and higher- harder and harder. Moaning loudly, and then…

…CRUNCH!

Something took a bite outta my right calf!

"Owe! Shit!" I yelled. I hobbled a few yards away and fell to the ground. All the ruckus woke up Rose, and she came over to see what was wrong.

"Something bit me!" I said, feeling her draw near me in the dark.

"Let me see," she said, shining the small flashlight she'd brought with her, and that until now, I hadn't known she had, on my leg.

"What the hell?" I said when I saw the bite. "That looks like. Like… little human teeth marks!"

"And there's plenty more where that came from if you don't shut the hell up!" I heard a voice shout. It was the duwende. He was standing at my feet. 'Course at the time I didn't know that's what he was. He looked like an ugly little troll to me. And the sumbitch was wearing a fucking crown!

"King!" Rose said. She sounded more like she was admonishing him than she sounded surprised to see him. I'd learn later that she hadn't been. "Why did you do this?"

"He is too very loud!" he said. "I kill him if he does not go away!"

"Really?" I said, too pissed off and in too much pain to think about how irrational I might be acting in the face of such an illogical and perhaps dangerous situation. "I'm gonna stomp on your little midget ass!"

I got up to kick his little troll ass. I mean he made Half Man look like Hulk Hogan. And once I'd gotten to my feet and I looked back down at him, I saw that where before there had only been one dwarf, there now stood at least thirty! They were dressed like circus clowns and munchkins and oompa loompas. As ridiculous as they looked, the little bastards had me outnumbered.

"Let me introduce you to all the king's men!" the duwende who'd bitten me said. "Just bring it, you Ogre!" And then they all broke down into karate stances.

***

What's that?

You're having a hard time believin' this?

How the hell do you think *I* felt? I was *there*!

Look, you don't have to believe me. Like I said, I wasn't comfortable gettin' to this whole part of the story until I could tell you were half lit anyway, so if ya call me out on it tomorrow I could claim you'd been drunk. Looks like you're a bit past half drunk now though.

All right. Go on and piss. I'll tell ya what happened next when ya get back.

Watch for those rats now. They can smell the beer on your breath. And they seem to love beer here. Brings 'em outta the walls.

Oh, I'm just messin' with ya. Go on now and get back here. I'll get us another beer.

***

Okay, you ready to hear the rest?

Still don't believe me?

Just wait. It gets even more unbelievable.

***

"Rose?" I said, taking a seat. The combination of the pain in my calf and the astonishment of the realization of what I saw kinda took the fight outta me. "What the hell is going on here?"

"Let me handle this," she said, turning toward the king. "Why did you do this?" she asked him. He made her look tall, and she was barely five feet even.

"He is too very much loud! He wakes my family! I have pregnant wife. She cannot sleep. My babies cannot sleep!"

"What is it?" I heard a small voice say. I looked over at the coconut stump I'd pissed on and realized there was a small door at the base of it. Right where I'd pissed. A small creature that looked like it'd just arrived from the North Pole was sticking its little head out, and it poked me with a tiny little index finger.

"It is a human, you dumb ass," another duwende said, drawing up beside this one in the doorway. This one wore a hat like a joker on a poker card. His face did not wear a smile. It wore a twisted, permanent snarl, revealing fangs like a vampire, yet he didn't have any other teeth in his head. Just those damn fangs.

"It is so large. So very pale," Santa's helper said. "What is wrong with it?"

"Nothing's wrong with me you little bastard!" I said. I was using both hands to hold my bleeding calf. It was really throbbing by this point. "Except the fact that your little rat friend over there bit me!"

"Do not call King rat!" the joker said, and then the little sumbitch came out and bit me on the forearm and then ran off before I could reach around and get a hold of him with my other hand.

"We do not want trouble," Rose said, talking to the king. "We go many kilometers today. We simply rest for the night."

"*Your* rest disturbs *my* rest," the king said. "Rest somewhere else!"

"If I could, I'd piss on both of you right now," I said to the two little people who'd been inspecting me. They were starting to sneak back out of the house. The tree stump, rather. "Back the hell up!" This drew laughter from the king's court.

"King has cursed your bladder," Santa's helper said. "You cannot pee on us. You cannot pee at all!"

More laughs from the large crowd of small creatures.

"We will transfer for the night if you lift the curse," Rose said.

"I lift the curse when you have transferred!" the king said. "Why he is so big? So... pale? And you. So black and hidden?"

"We are humans," she said. "He is from a place very far away. That is why he is tall and pale. I have beliefs that force me to cover myself in garments."

"Do not lie to King," he said, peering into her eyes. "I know many things, and I know lies."

"I am sorry, your majesty," she said, taking a knee and bowing before him. I didn't know what the hell he was accusing her of lyin' about, but I could see she sure didn't wanna argue with 'im. But I *did* notice. Hyper-vigilance.

"You go now," the king said with the wave of a small hand. "My men accompany you. When you are far enough away, I lift curse."

"Thank you, your majesty," Rose said. And then she helped me get up and start moving.

"What did he mean, 'don't lie to him?'" I asked her as we started limping away. "What were you lying about?"

"Never mind what he says," she said, whispering in my ear. "They always play so many tricks. Like the one he plays on you. We move. Then you pee."

"Stop your lies, female!" the king yelled from behind us. "I hear whispers! Nothing escapes me in my court!"

We hobbled back over to our backpacks, escorted by about a dozen of the little bastards, got our things all together, and kept goin'.

"This is good enough!" the Joker said, two hundred yards away from our original camp site.

"What?" I said, turning around, but seeing that no one was there but Rose. The duwende had vanished, as if they'd never been there, and hot piss ran down my leg as if I'd never been potty trained.

"Aw shit!" I said, thrusting my hips backward and bending over in an attempt to divert the stream. I couldn't get my junk out of my pants quick enough. Rose laughed, though I could tell that she was tryin' not to.

"Real funny!" I said. I turned away from her and relaxed as I pissed like I'd never pissed before. And man, did it feel good.

When I was done, and it took a really long time for me to get done, I hobbled over to Rose and sat down beside her. She'd pulled some leaves off of a nearby tree while I was pissin', and she was rollin' 'em up in her hands, squeezin' the juice out of 'em.

"Get my first aid kit outta my backpack," I said as I sat down beside her. "I need stitches. Get me the small bottle of alcohol and my sewing kit."

Rose laughed.

"Why are you laughing?" I said, and I was getting angry again. "You think this is funny?"

"For big soldier you cry like little girl," she said, giggling. I could see the smile in her eyes. It soothed me a bit, but I kept tellin' myself that I *had* to stop lookin' in her eyes. That was leading me somewhere dangerous, fast.

"What *is* that crap?" I said, watching her crush and crumble the leaves and stems from the tree she'd been mulling in her small hands.

"Mulunggay," she said. "The miracle tree. Good for everything."

"What?" I said. "Get my damn kit!"

"Relax," she said, grabbing my hands with one of hers, moving them away from the wound. With the other, she squeezed the juice from the Mulunggay leaves onto the bite. It instantly stopped bleeding. The pain vanished. Like magic.

"Woah!" I said, too amazed to remain angry. "What the…"

"You are typical foreigner," she said. "In your country, you get hurt, you run to hospital. You get shots. You get stitches. You take many tablets. How much that costs you?"

Man, what a point she had. And what excessive damage have all those meds done to my former society? Hell, what did they do to *me* after I'd gotten hooked on everything through the Army and the VA? People are always talkin' about the zombie apocalypse. Hell, it's here! At least in America. Everyone seems to be on somethin'.

"Oh, this would have been about a three hundred dollar emergency room bill," I said. "Roughly thirteen thousand pesos. Then my health insurance premium would have gone up. IF I weren't covered by the VA that is, and this wouldn't be, because it's not service connected, and how *dare* I actually need to use my damn health insurance I pay an arm and a leg for, huh?"

"What?" she asked. I could tell I'd utterly confused her.

"Never mind," I said. "What the hell is that?"

"I told you! Malunggay!"

"No," I said, shaking my head. "I mean, how does it work?"

"I do not know," she said. "Only that it does. It stops the bleeding and pain. It will prevent infection. You will heal much faster our way than your way. And it is good to eat in soup. Especially if you have high blood."

"You should eat some then," I told her.

"Helum!" she said. Remember, that means shut up. "I mean high blood pressure, not pissed on!"

"That would be pissed off," I corrected her. "Anyway, what were those… those… things back there?"

"Duwende."

"Duwende? You mean the magical Philippine dwarves?"

"You have heard of them?"

"Of course I've heard of them. I've been here for years. I've heard of all your superstition garbage; duwende, wak wak, kapre, all of it. But I thought it was all bullshit."

"In many places, superstition," she said, squeezing the last of the juice onto the wound. Already the swelling was decreasing, and the pain had stopped. "Here, very real."

"Oh, hell!" I said, skepticism heavy in my tone in spite of everything I'd seen.

"You see with your own eyes and still you do not believe?" she said, as if she'd read my mind. She was finally taking the first aid kit out of my backpack. She unraveled a roll of gauze and began wrapping it around my calf.

"There's gotta be a better explanation," I said. "They were just a bunch of midgets! Inbred midgets! They never get off this island so they've interbred. That explains the chromosomal defects; their height and deformed faces." I was looking for anything to help me from facing unpleasant facts. The American way, no?

"You are wrong," she said, securing the butterfly snap.

"Yeah, well then if everything back there was real, then what the hell was the little troll that bit me talking about? When he told you not to lie?" Time to call her out on this.

"I tell you," she said, putting the kit back in my backpack, zipping it up. "They play many pranks and tell many lies. You cannot believe them."

"I'm starting to wonder just how much I can believe *you*," I said, poking my injured calf with a finger, amazed that the pain really *was* gone. "Something has seemed fishy about this from the start. Why are we really here?"

"We are here to find my sister," she said. "You know that."

"Who *are* you," I said, unwilling to let her off the hook. "Who are you really?"

"I am Rose! And I am tired! We sleep now! Watch where you pee next time!"

She got up and walked away from me, ten yards or so, and laid down. She turned her back to me, but only faked sleep. I could tell. She kept peekin' over to see if I was asleep yet.

I watched her as she laid there. It was still pitch dark, and I could barely make her out. Her burka provided the perfect camouflage in the night. I made a mental note to be less open with her. My suspicions, which had previously been dying down, especially after it seemed like she was finally opening up, were once again rising.

I laid back on the ground now too, even more tired from the adrenaline rush I'd gotten from the recent events. I fell asleep quickly, and I'm sure once more began to snore.

If I'd stayed awake only a minute more, I'da heard Rose whisper, "Good night, Pete. I'd tell you the truth if I could. But you'd never believe it."

15

What was the truth?

Damn. Even after all this beer, and as relaxed as it's made us, you still just can't wait to hear the story the way it's meant to be told, can ya?

I'm gettin' there. All in due time, my friend. All in due, time.

Now, just for the purposes of wettin' your appetite, imagine if you will- a young, beautiful maiden. Only days away from turning eighteen. Come on now. As many of these beautiful young things as you've seen while we've been out today? It ain't hard.

Now, imagine if you will- this maiden's bein' held captive, in this large castle. Kinda like beauty and the beast. But trust me, this ain't Disney. This is real. This is happening right on the Isle of Kapre.

What's a Kapre?

Okay, I'll go ahead and prime ya for that, too.

Remember I asked you when we sat down for our first drink if you believed in Bigfoot? And you told me you believed in the *possibility* of Bigfoot?

Well, good. Because that means you'll also believe in the possibility of Kapre.

I'm tellin' ya what it is. Just sit back and listen.

A Kapre is the Philippine version of Sasquatch.

Yes, I'm serious. I didn't know either 'til I got here. I started hearin' about it and didn't pay any attention. Just figured it was another of their superstitions. But after I made it off that island I researched it a little bit. Man, I found some amazing things.

What's that?

Well, *one* is that every major civilization on earth has a Sasquatch type creature in their folklore. Here, it's Kapre, back home it's Bigfoot. In China, they have the Yeren. In Australia, it's the Yowie. In Nepal, it's the Yeti. We all know him mostly as the Abominable Snowman. The list goes on and on. They got Sasquatch type creatures all over Africa. Got 'em all over Europe.

What?

That's exactly what I thought! That the story just spread with world travelers. But my research shows- and don't you just love how anyone who uses Google these days can claim to do research? But my research shows that many of these stories existed long before world travel. And you know? Some of those places, especially in Africa, are so remote they've still never seen a white man.

Okay. So, there. I kinda got ahead of myself telling you what the Kapre is.

Well, wait a minute. Not exactly.

What I mean is, he's a little different than Bigfoot.

Well, for one thing, the North American Sasquatch wants to be left the hell alone and wants nothing to do with people.

Kapre?

Not so much.

He's a cocksman. A womanizer. A playboy. He's always out kidnappin' these young, beautiful Filipina women and takin' 'em off to his castle to be his mistresses.

His castle?

Oh, that's where it gets even weirder. I mean, it's cool that you believe in the possibility of these types of creatures, but with the Kapre, you also need to believe in the possibility of alternate dimensions.

Why?

Because that's where his castle is. That's why.

Oh, they call him the big hairy man of the tree, because he's often seen coming and going out of the tree tops, but that's just where his portals are.

What portals?

The portals to get back to the other side where his castle is.

No, I don't expect you to believe any of this.

But it's true.

So anyway, imagine if you will, that while Rose and I are layin' there sleepin', there's this beautiful young girl, Rose's sister, stuck in the castle with this big hairy man.

Oh, except in his castle, he wouldn't be a big hairy man.

Why not?

Part of the legend. Another way in which he's different from Bigfoot. He sheds his big hairy man skin on the other side, and they say he's quite attractive there. Jet black hair. Olive skin. Long nose as they say around here, which would mean a Westerner's nose.

I can still see it now in my mind's eye, and I had some of this confirmed by Rose's sister later. She'd be sitting there at the end of a long dining table, her favorite foods before her; chicken feet adobo, green mango pieces with vinegar, pork soup and rice. In spite of this, she'd be slouching, and though hungry, she'd have no desire to eat. Bein' held against her will would've taken her appetite.

"Why do you refuse to eat, my princess?" the tall, dark, handsome man seated at the other end of the table would say. "Is it not your favorite?"

Oh, and in my mind's eye, I envision him looking like a young Pierce Bronson. Not all the way back to the Remington Steele Pierce Brosnan. He was a pussy. But just a little past that. The 'For Your Eyes Only' James Bond Pierce Brosnan. He was pretty badass.

"I want to go home," she'd say, her voice soft and trembling. "I want to go back to my family."

"Soon we will make our own family," he'd say, and his tone would be all smooth, and there'd be no threat in his voice. But it would be all pervy, too, because she wouldn't be eighteen for a few more days. "You are beautiful. We will have beautiful children."

"I am still a child myself," she'd say, pleading. "I am only seventeen."

"That is why for now you are my princess," he'd say, tryin' to reason with her, but sounding even pervier. "You will be eighteen soon. A woman. It is then that I will make you my queen."

"I don't want to marry you," she'd say, lookin' up. Now, she wouldn't like looking at him too much, for the same reasons I had to make sure I wasn't looking into her big sister's eyes too much. Because he *was* handsome, and it made it hard to hate him. "I do not love you," she'd tell him, tryin' to convince herself not to fall in love with him. Because he is so guapo, ya know. I mean, Pierce Brosnan.

"You can learn to love me," he'd said.

"I can never learn to love you," she'd say, and she'd look down again before she started to.

"Why is that?" he'd ask, and he'd tell her he'd change anything about himself for her love.

"I know what you really are," she'd say, looking up, but only with her eyes.

Rage would flare in his eyes. He'd get up and leave her alone at the dining table in the long dining hall. And all of this would have been happening daily since he took her from the beach where she'd been collecting pebbles.

She'd hear the great door of the castle slam. She'd cover her ears, knowing what was coming next. She'd shudder in fear and disgust at the sound of the mighty beast's scream.

What's that? You like that narrative?

I should be a writer?

I love to read books, but to write one?

Who's got time for that?

And I didn't completely create the narrative. I kinda put together pieces of what I'd find out later. The loud scream woke us up the next morning, too. The morning after we'd run into the duwende.

The scream?

Well, I couldn't swear to it- though I promise you, I can swear to the rest of this story- but I swore I heard a loud scream, far off in the distance. And it's what woke us up. That and all the birds that'd been roostin' in the trees all around us. They heard it too, and their wings sounded like machine guns as they took off. No way I could'a slept in if I'da wanted to after that.

***

"Get up," Rose says, coming over and kicking my injured leg. But not where the bite was, thank God. She kicked me in the thigh.

"I'm awake," I said, sitting up, noticing the sun just making its way above the horizon. "What a freaky dream," I told her. "Like the blond. What is it about this place?" Starting to rise, I stopped, wincing. "Ah!" I said, feeling the pain in my calf, realizing it hadn't been a dream.

I reached down to feel the gauze, and a small amount of blood and green juice had come through and dried on the outside off it. The bleeding had stopped, and infection wasn't setting in, but it had swollen up on me a bit while I'd slept.

"It would hurt much worse if it were not for the Malunggay," Rose said, a bit of sympathy in her voice, and thank God for that. Made it a little better since she'd just kicked me and all. "We move now. We eat as we go." She handed me a ripe banana she'd plucked from the tree beside us, and off we went.

"So what is your plan now, Richards?" she asked me, about twenty minutes into our day's journey.

"What do you mean, what is my plan?" I said. Though favoring my hurt leg we were still makin' good time, and I was favoring it more in *fear* that it would hurt, not because it actually *did* hurt. I was amazed at how well the leaves from that magic tree were working. "We find your sister and then we get off this island," I told her.

"And then?"

"I go back home," I said. "Home as in my apartment."

"You plan ever to go back to your country?"

"No," I said. "Maybe to visit, but I've got no plans for that even. No time soon."

"So you spend the rest of your life drinking and screwing here in Philippines?"

"Most of it, I guess," I said, following her, yet making sure to stay far enough behind her that she couldn't slap me with any limbs, as easy as it was to piss'er off'n all.

"Why you are not scared to get kidnapped?" she said, pausing for a moment, turning to face me.

"Why do you want to know so much about me?" I said, making mental note not to stare into her eyes again. Hard to break habit, you know, but I knew I was gonna have to with her. "It's obvious you don't care for me. And you've told me so little about yourself."

"You are just odd," she said, turning and beginning to move forward again. "It seems you have no fear."

"I'd be scared if there were reason to be scared," I said. "Abu Sayyaf is no threat to me. I mean, no offense to your father's little gang of hooligans, but…"

"Oh, you are so tough guy are you?" cynicism in her voice.

"No," I said. "What I mean is they really aren't a threat to anyone."

"We sit here," she said, dropping her pack. "We eat more now. You explain what you mean."

"Okay," I said, dropping my backpack and sitting across from her. I leaned back against a banana tree, propping the foot of my injured leg on my back pack after taking a bottle of water from it. "Did you know that there are only between five hundred and a thousand members in their entire group?"

"And then?"

"And then, if the Philippine government really wanted them gone, they'd come down here and make pretty short business of 'em."

"Then why don't they?" she asked, curious.

"Because *my* government gives *your* government millions of dollars every year in aid for your military, because the threat exists. For helping out in the war on terror. If Abu Sayyaf was to disappear, and the MILF and the NPA, and there was no more threat, then the money would stop."

"You believe this?" she said, taking the pack of dried fish out of her backpack. She offered me first choice. I could tell she was starting to like me again.

For now.

"Thanks," I said, taking a fish. "I *do* believe it. I mean, look. It took more than ten years to find Osama Bin Laden. He was safely hidden in Pakistan for at least the last six of those years. His compound was right beside a Pakistani Army training center. The Pakistani government knew he was there. However, we were giving them billions of dollars a year to build up their military as long as they were supposedly helping us fight terror. They didn't turn him in, because they didn't want the money to stop."

"So you think our government plays charades with your government for money?" she said, chewing on a fish now.

"Yeah," I said. "But our government plays a part as well."

"What part is that?"

"Look," I said, looking her deep in the eyes- those beautiful black eyes- even though I knew it was dangerous. "I love my country. I fought for it in war and I would do so again if necessary. But I do not trust my government."

"What does your lack of trust for your government have to do with Abu Sayyaf or the Philippines?"

"It's all about control of the people. And fear is a pretty damn good control mechanism. A generation ago, before they used the terrorists to scare the hell out of the American people, they used the communists."

"Like NPA," she said.

"Yes. But it was the communist regime of the former Soviet Union."

"Who?" she asked, and I had to remember that all she'd know about was the Philippines and the U.S. Had to explain it to her in a way she'd understand.

"Have you heard of Russia?" I asked her.

"That is in America?" she asked, a common answer for these parts.

"No," I said. "But it *is* in Foreign Land. And once upon a time, Russia and many of the other provinces that surround it in that part of Foreign Land- we call it Eastern Europe- were united. And they posed a great threat to the democracies of the world."

"Like the U.S. and the Philippines?" she said.

"Exactly!" I told her, though she wasn't exactly right. I just didn't have the heart, nor want to take the time to explain to her that the Philippines was not a true democracy, rather a bunch of dictatorships built on top of each other through familial political dynasties. I mean, she'd know *that*. She's *from* here. But she wouldn't understand that, that's not how a true democracy is supposed to work.

"So anyway," I kept going, "back then, democracy was good, and communism was bad. And there was always this perceived threat that the communists were going to lob nuclear weapons over onto the democracies any given minute. That was the message my government sent to the people to keep 'em scared, so they would give the government a blank check to do whatever the hell they wanted to do, all under the flag of protecting them from communism."

"The threat was not real?" She asked.

"For a while it was," I told her. "But somewhere in the 1950's or so, maybe a little later, it was no longer real. The Soviet economy was collapsing, and the only reason they were able to hide the fact that it *was* for so long was because they were such a controlled society. Very little world news got in, and only the news they fabricated and wanted out, got out. Our government knew it though, but by this time they'd been given permission by the American people to do whatever the hell they wanted to do to protect them from the communists, and the government didn't wanna relinquish that power."

"So for a long time, your government controlled your people with an untruth?"

"Yes," I said. "And they do it now with the concept of terrorism."

"I see," she said, and pulled another fish out of the pack. "Why your government wants to control your people. You do not sound as free as you claim to be if this is true."

"A mighty wheel cannot turn without the spokes," I said. "All those working class Americans represent the spokes in the great wheel of America. If all the spokes were to leave the wheel, the wheel would no longer turn. It would collapse without the spokes to hold it up."

"I see," she said, drawing the words out. I could tell that even though I'd spoken figuratively, she still understood.

"So we have this arm of our government called the State Department," I continued, since she was following. "They're constantly putting out travel advisories and warnings. It is ironic to me that the most 'dangerous countries in the world,' according to *them*, are those where our dollar is worth so much more. Where you can come and live for next to nothing. Like here in the Philippines."

"They scare your people? So you do not come?"

"Yes. Not as much so we won't come *here*, but so that we won't leave *there*. The machine needs the spokes to turn the wheel."

"How you know so much?" she asked, taking a drink from her water bottle.

"I learned, as a soldier, to pay attention to detail- no matter how small. At first, in training, it kept you outta trouble. You made sure your uniform was always worn correctly, nothing out of place, or you would be punished with many, many pushups.

"Then, in combat, paying attention to detail kept you alive. For instance, if you were doing convoy security, like we did, you'd drive by the same piles of garbage in the city streets of Iraq, day after day. By paying attention to detail, you might notice one day that part of a pile had been disturbed. Something was not the same as it was the day before. Maybe an old tire had been moved. Dug up out of the pile and then replaced. Sittin' a little bit higher than it always had been before."

"And then?"

"And then you look closer and you see a wire sticking out from where the insurgents had come by and planted a bomb there. By noticing the small change, you stop your truck before you run it over and get blown up."

"Oh," she said, screwing the cap back on her empty water bottle.

"So I just pay attention to all details. I've figured some things out. Knowing history helps as well. You know, I taught history in high school all those years. My gut told me the whole time that a good bit of it wasn't accurate, but it's what the powers that be wanted going into the textbooks. You know, they say that those who win wars are the ones who write the history books."

"And then?"

"For instance," I said, "during the threat of communism after world war two, this one joker, McCarthy. A senator. He started labeling anyone he didn't like as a communist. They were put on trial. Even if they were not a communist or a communist sympathizer, which none of them were, their reputations and careers were ruined. Even others, who knew that the people he'd labeled were innocent, would not speak out for them in fear *they* would be labeled next. Hell, President Truman knew he was full of shit, and that the people he'd labeled were innocent. And he didn't even *like* the guy. But he wouldn't speak out against him. It was all kinda like the witch trials, which were earlier in my nation's history."

"Witch trials?" she said, lost again.

"Yes," I said, realizing I'd just entered the land of way too much information. "I won't go into that," I said. "But I'll give you another example. Have you ever heard of the Philippine Uprising?"

"No," she said.

"Have you ever heard of the Philippine-American war?"

"Of course," she said. "Everyone has."

"Very few Americans have," I said.

"Why not?" She asked. "I thought Americano know so much?"

"We know what we're *taught*," I told her. "What we're told to believe. The Philippine Uprising? The Philippine-American war? Same thing, different names."

"Why different names?"

"Different interests. We were occupying you guys after the Spanish American war, just as we did Cuba."

"Where?" she asked.

"It's a small country off the coast of Florida. They'd been a Spanish colony just like you guys. That's where the Spanish American War actually started, and we just ran Spain out of the Philippines for the hell of it while we were ending their position as a dominant world player militarily.

"So after we run Spain out, we stick around and start taking all your natural resources. Your people told us to leave, and we said, fuck you, we're takin' all your shit. Then your people came at us with guns and said, no, fuck you, leave. There were a couple skirmishes, and we didn't view it as worth the trouble of another war, so we left. You guys really ran us out."

"I know this already," she said.

"Well, here you call it the Philippine-American war. And really, short lived as it was, that's what it was. But we call it an uprising. See, an uprising is when people who are beneath you and don't know their place get outta line."

"That is insulting!" she said.

"Well, the powers that be in my country decided it might be insulting to know that the world's new power player got run off some islands by a bunch of natives with weapons barely more effective than spears." I could see the light of understanding gleam in her eyes.

"My point is that my government, and their use of the media machine for spin, is one big fear factory. They control the masses through fear. The fear in our modern times is terrorism and terrorist networks. We always need an enemy to support our own defense buildup and we always need a monster to be afraid of to control our people."

"So you do not think Abu Sayyaf is a real threat?"

"Not one of significance. If they were, we'd send in a few Army Rangers or Navy Seals and wipe 'em out in a day or two. We haven't done it yet, have we? I mean, sure. We have some "trainers" over here, but that's just for show. Justify the money we send. Add to the façade."

"The what?"

"Façade. That means show. Or Act."

"Why is it in your government's interest to send my government all that money for military buildup?" she asked, lost on this point. "Wouldn't the money be better spent in your country?"

"You scratch my back, I'll scratch yours," I said. "What that means," knowing she was about to say, 'and then?' again, or 'huh?' "is that you help me, I'll help you."

"I do not follow. You talk in riddles." So much for thinking I had it covered.

"The main reason we wanted to route the Japs during World War Two was to take control of the Pacific Ocean for commerce purposes," I said. "That is why we liberated your country from them in 1945. We already controlled the Atlantic, and we had since we'd defeated the British in the War of 1812. We knew the Asian markets would boom at some point and we wanted to be able to get merchant vessels through both Oceans with the lowest cost and least amount of problems as possible."

"But I thought the Japanese attacked your harbor?" And I was impressed that she'd known about that.

"They did, but we knew it was coming."

"And your country did nothing?" she said, astonished.

"No," I said, bringing my right fist into the palm of my left hand. "Our *government* did nothing. By allowing the attack, it would pull us into the war. And I'm not so convinced that our government didn't know that we were gonna be attacked on September 11'th, and that they allowed it to pull us into the wars in the Middle East."

"You really think these things you say?"

"Yes," I said. And I've already told you about the mystery woman I'd met in Virginia the summer I was peddlin' investments. "Why do you think I live *here* instead of *there*?"

"You seem more crazy than I thought."

"Ha!" I said, throwing my head back. "Now you sound like all my friends in America. And those bastards at the VA. They think the same. I'm just crazy. What they call a conspiracy theorist."

"You talk of these things with them?"

"Some of 'em. I think they call me crazy right around the time they realize that what I'm saying makes sense. It's their self-defense mechanism. Keeps 'em from believing what they want to believe, because it goes against everything they've already been taught and currently believe. That scares the hell out of people."

"I can understand that," she said. "Some of these things you say are scary. People like to think they are free, but you make it sound as if they are not as free as they believe themselves to be."

"Exactly!" I said, pounding my fist into my hand again. "The shackles of slavery have been replaced with debt and fear. The masses are in so many ways still enslaved, they've just been brainwashed to think a certain way so they don't see it. They do not see the world around them as it truly exists. They see it the way their government and the corporations who fund their government want them to see it. Kind of like you guys and the Catholic Church. And Hollywood."

"Hollywood?" she said.

"Yeah. You know. That whole *all white people are rich* thing?"

"But you are so very rich," she said. And I felt like I'd just wasted twenty minutes of air time. "Back to the control of the Pacific," she said. "My country?"

"Oh yeah," I said. "We pass in and out of the South China Sea, the Philippines Sea and the Southwest Pacific- all of the waters off of your coast- as free and easily as we want. If you were to look at tolls we might pay fees for crossing, you would find that the amount would be many times what we give you in military aid. Your government picks up the nickels and dimes we throw at 'em, all in the name of being allies, not realizing they're steppin' over dollars to do it!"

"I see," she said. "Like you explain yesterday with the cost of products in our stores. You think you are getting a better deal by buying in bulk, when in fact you are being taken advantage of. Your government gives my government money for military aid for free merchant shipping through our waters."

"Exactly! There's hope for you yet, kiddo!"

"Bah!" she said. "Hope for me? I do not need hope from you!" She stood and put her backpack on. God, it really didn't take much to get her goin'.

"So high blood again, huh?" I said, getting up to follow her.

"There is little hope for you," she said, walking in the same direction we'd been traveling. "You know so much, yet still so little."

"What do you mean?" I asked. It was *my* turn to be confused.

"For a smart man, you have so many girls here take you for fool. They rob you blind!"

"It's not my fault," I said. "You Filipinas are the world's best liars. You've been doing it for generations! I just haven't been here long enough to learn all of your dirty little tricks yet."

She turned and tried to slap the shit outta me. I caught her by the wrist, just as her hand was about to make contact with my face.

"Don't try that again, Rose!" I told her. "I like you, but not that much."

And before I knew what was comin', she slapped me on the other side of the face with her other hand.

"You claim you are smart enough to figure out the world's strongest government!" she said. "But you cannot out smart Filipina with grade school education?"

She had a point, and the slap brought it home.

"You are not as smart at you think. You are fool!"

And then she turned and kept marchin' through the jungle. I followed her, and I hated how much the truth hurt.

17

Want more beer?

Think we should take a break? Walk some of it off?

No? You wanna keep hearin' the story?

Okay. Well, let's switch over to water.

What? More beer? But…

Well, it's your call. But I'm tellin' ya. You think this stuff gives ya a buzz and makes ya have to piss twice as much as what you're used to, wait 'til tomorrow. Talk about a hangover!

But hey, it's your call. I'll wave her… oh never mind. Here she comes with a cold bottle and another bowl of ice now.

Okay, so where was I?

Did I say something about water?

Oh yes. Water.

***

"Water!" I said, fist pumping the air as I came to the edge of a stream. It was flowin' fast, and there was a waterfall of about twelve feet in height twenty yards upstream. "We camp here tonight," I said, taking my backpack off and pulling out the empty water bottles to fill 'em up.

"Okay," Rose said, kneeling to do the same.

I filled an empty bottle with water from the stream and drank it quickly. Rarely had water tasted so good. I mean, you will *sweat* out in these jungles. After drinking another half bottle, I undid the gauze on my leg and stepped into the stream to rinse my wound.

"Let me," Rose said, drawing up beside me and moving my hands away from it. "You sit."

I did as she said, watching her. As she got into the stream, she cared not in the least that her burka was getting wet.

"Maybe you and I should spend some time together after all this is over," I told her.

"I could not tolerate you." She said. "I will pay you, and you will go."

"There you go again," I said, no longer so relaxed.

"You would be defensive too if all you heard was insults about your people," she said, rising, deciding that she'd rinsed the wound enough. She began filling her empty water bottles, taking care of herself. Seemed to forget all about me.

"Oh, so when you lump me together with all those 'foreigners' you aren't doing the same?" I said and then I drank more water.

"If you did not act the same as other foreigners, I would not say so. I do not act like the geros you associate with, so why you compare me?" Gero here means whore.

"I wasn't comparin' you to geros. Just other Filipinas," I said, refilling my bottle for a third time.

"You would find we are all different if you just look to see it," she said. Her bottles now full and back in her backpack, she placed it on her back. "We go back, away from the stream so we cannot hear the water. If danger comes we will never know it."

"Are you sure you were never in the military?" I said, grabbing my backpack and rising as well.

"I might not have the education you have, Richards. I might not know where Cuba or Russia is, but I am smart. It is common sense to move away from the sound of the water."

"You *are* smart," I said. "And it *is* common sense. But I've found few here who have both traits."

She turned, her hand pulled back, ready to slap. But she did not.

"Uh-huh?" I said. "You claim to be so civilized, yet your first instinct is physical violence. Tell me more about how you are different?"

"Go to sleep, Richards. It gets dark. Tomorrow is another day. We go very far."

"Are we not gonna eat any fish?"

"I am not hungry," she said, digging the pack of fish out of her pack, tossing it at me. "You make me so high blood. I cannot eat!"

She walked away from the creek, and I followed her. Forty yards away we could hear it no more. She laid on the ground, and I leaned against a banana tree, nibbling on fish from the pack. I stared at her. I liked that she could think. I liked how she *did* think. And those eyes…

"Ah, the rest of 'er's probably dog ass ugly," I mumbled as I laid down myself. It wasn't loud, but loud enough for her to hear it I guess. As I shut my eyes, a small rock hit me in the back.

"Ow!" I said, looking back toward her.

"You will never know how the rest of me looks!" she said, rolling back over.

Boy, was she wrong. I'd soon see everything. And I'm not just talkin' tits and ass. I'm talkin' about seeing everything.

The truth!

Don't understand what I'm sayin'?

Oh, you will.

***

"Damn it!" I said, sitting up in total darkness. The pain in my leg was getting' worse, keeping me from sleep. I thought maybe I should wake Rose. Have her put some more of that magic tree juice on it.

I crawled over to where she'd been asleep. I didn't try to stand and walk over, because it was too dark to see, and my eyes hadn't adjusted to the darkness yet. I mean, when you get out here in these jungles, away from artificial light? Good luck tryin' to find your ass with both hands.

Anyway, I got there and I saw that she was gone. I felt around for her, and my eyes adjusted to where I could see just a little, in spite of the asshole blackness of night, but she was not there.

"What the…?" I said, rising to my feet, catching movement out of the corner of my eye. Looking over I saw a lady. And it wasn't Rose. No ma'am, no sir! And she wasn't all in black. This woman was dressed all in white, and she appeared to be glowing. Kinda like swamp fire back home. And she was motioning for me to come toward her.

I followed, reluctantly. And not only was she glowing, but she seemed to drift above the ground. She stopped once, looking back to make sure I was following her, then she just kept goin'. I'm not sure if it's that my eyes hadn't fully adjusted to the dark, or if they were playin' tricks on me, but it appeared as if she had no face!

She led me to the stream, and I watched in awe as she appeared to walk on water. She began walking upstream, toward the falls, motioning again for me to follow. I did, but from the bank.

I kept looking around for Rose, but I didn't see her. I knew in my heart that she hadn't left me though. She might not've liked me, but she needed me to get her sister back. How I wished she could be here now to see what I was seein'.

This lady in white, or white lady, whichever ya wanna call 'er, led me all the way up to the falls, and when we got there, she simply disappeared. It was as if she'd vanished into the moonlight, becoming a cloud white mist.

The moon's light shone on a large pool of water below the falls, the jungle's canopy broken here by the lack of trees. In the center of the pool, I finally saw her; Rose. But I now saw *all* of her, burka gone, bathing in the moonlight.

I kneeled behind a rock and watched. Her back was to me. She stood, knee deep, cupping water in one hand, and then pouring it over the opposite shoulder. Then she would switch hands, do the same.

Her hair, long and black as the night that surrounded her, hung to the top of her butt. It was longer than that of most of the Filipina women. I love long hair; the longer the better. And hers was the most beautiful I'd ever seen.

The mist that had recently been in the form of a woman rolled gently over her shoulders, causing her to turn, as if she'd felt it, like a hand caressing her skin, and this allowed the moon to shine on her body in such a way that, from my vantage point, her body's outline broke free of the night behind it, revealing the most perfectly formed set of breasts and the most perfect ass I'd ever seen.

Her breasts were set high, pointing upward, as if her nipples were commanding the moon to shine on them. She had a perfect, heart shaped ass that looked like I could cup one cheek perfectly in each hand. Why in *hell* she'd been hiding a package like that from the world with a black bed sheet was beyond me.

"Oh, my God," I said, a whisper, feeling myself beginning to swell. "I have to get outta here. I can't let 'er catch me watchin' her like this." I mean, I liked what I saw, but I'm not a voyeur.

I began to rise, to my feet that is, but hesitated. She turned and began moving toward me. She walked out of the water, just to the edge of the bank and then kneeled in prayer.

I watched her arms fold over those perfectly formed, handful and a half sized breasts. I saw her grab something dangling from her neck, something glimmering in the moonlight.

It was a crucifix! At the end of a rosary! A Roman Catholic rosary!

"Hail Mary, full of grace, the Lord is with thee…" she said, beginning the prayer.

***

Well a 'course she was Catholic! I couldn't spell it out for ya any plainer than that, could I?

I was thinkin' the same thing. She'd been lyin' about everything!

A 'course I wanted to know why, and yes, I was worried.

I confronted her all right.

Okay, okay. Drink your beer and listen!

***

While she was deep in prayer, and certainly not facing West toward Mecca while she was, I snuck back to our camp spot and laid down. But I'll be damned if I slept a wink the whole night. I tell ya, only two days on this mission and the sleep deprivation was startin' to crawl in on me like it hadn't since I'd been in Iraq.

"Did you sleep well?" I said the next morning, seeing her eyes open. I'd been staring at her since the daylight broke.

"You wake before me?" she said, sitting up, surprised.

"Strange, huh?" I said. "The lazy foreigner wakin' up before the jungle girl."

"I am not jungle girl," she said, grabbing another stone and tossing it toward me. I completely ignored the act, letting the stone hit me in the chest. It didn't hurt.

"I don't know what you are?"

"What do you mean by that?"

"Nothing," I said, picking up a banana by my side. I'd picked a few from a low hanging bunch close by while she was sleeping. I'd already eaten two. "Eat this," I said, tossing it to her.

She peeled the banana from the bottom and ate it. They're actually much easier to peel that way, and that's how most people where bananas come from do it. I think the whole peeling it from the top thing was a marketing ploy by western corporations once upon a time. Before she was finished I was up and standing, backpack on, hovering over her.

"You are in such a hurry today?" she said, swallowing the last bite.

"Yeah," I said. "I want to get this behind me. Finish the mission and get home."

We took off and we walked for hours, not even stopping for lunch before either of us spoke. It was finally her who did.

"Why you are so quiet today?" she said, breathing hard from the pace. The sun was now directly overhead. The trees, only intermittent here and mostly banana, provided only broken shade. We'd left the taller mango trees behind. We were in a huge banana grove, and we were starting to really make it closer to the mountain on the back side of the island. Even though there wasn't a cloud in the sky where we were, you could look up and see the clouds and lightning above the mountain. You could actually even start to make out the rain up there from where we were. And it looked like something- something resembling a radio antennae or a cell tower, which I knew could *not* be either- was sticking up in the dead center of the mountain.

"I don't feel like talkin'," I said.

"That is strange for you. Foreigners love to hear themselves talk."

"So, you always get high blood with me when I group all the Filipinos together but you can do it to foreigners?" I said, stopping and turning to face her. "By the way. I'm not a foreigner. I'm an American damn it! There are nearly two hundred countries on this big 'ol earth, and only *one* of 'em's America!"

"So you *can* talk?" she said. And you could hear the smile in her voice when she spoke. I'd lost my cool, and remember, you never wanna show that here, or anywhere else in Asia, because they consider it a victory. As classless as the place might seem to us, *they* consider nothing more classless than losing your temper.

"What do you want to talk about?" I said, sarcasm as thick as the humidity around us.

"It is up to you," she said, a common phrase of her countrymen when asked almost anything for which they have no opinion.

"Why don't we talk about something I saw last night?"

Rose hesitated. To her knowledge, I'd been sleeping the entire time she'd been away from me to take a bath. I was still there sleeping when she'd returned. Or so she thought.

"What did you see?" she asked, hesitant still.

"Well," I said, looking down and scratching my chin. I was being dramatic. O.A. as they call it. That stands for Over Acting. "I *might* have seen a ghost."

"A ghost?" she said, and I could hear relief in her voice. I know what she'd suspected me of seeing, and I was just setting her up to drop that on her later. "What ghost?"

"I'm not sure," I said, kneeling and taking water out of my backpack. She did the same. "I woke up because... because it felt like someone was starin' at me." And when isn't someone staring at you here? Remember the whole vines thing? But I didn't say that.

"And then?"

"And then I looked over and I saw this lady, all in white; glowing white. She motioned for me."

"What did you do?"

I looked at her, not sure if I wanted to reveal all that I knew just yet. Perhaps further investigation was in order. If I showed all my cards now, I couldn't play any of 'em later.

"It doesn't matter," I said, rising, having put the bottle back in my backpack. "It was probably a dream."

I started walking.

"It was no dream," she said, getting up and following me. She'd never told me exactly where we were goin'. I was instinctively heading in the direction of the mountain at the back of the island. It's almost as if I could feel it calling me. "You saw white lady!"

"White lady?" I said, stopping and turning to face her. "More of that Philippine superstition crap?"

"It is not superstition," she said, sounding more nervous than defensive. "It is aswang! There are many white lady on our islands. They are ghosts of young Filipinas who were raped and killed by the Japanese soldiers in the war."

"Whatever," I said, turning and beginning to move forward again. But I felt a chill run up my spine like a finger, because I knew I'd seen exactly what she was telling me I'd seen.

"You see with your own eyes yet you do not believe?" she said, taking nearly two quick steps to my one in order to keep up. My wounded calf didn't seem to slow me. My ire toward her overpowered the pain.

"So you are saying I should believe everything I see?" I said, not facing her.

"Yes," she said and then hesitated. "Well, not all but most." Now I knew I had her.

"What about the blond?" I said, stopping again. "I know I saw her." You tried to convince me that was a dream. Why aren't you trying to convince me the white lady was a dream?

"You did see her," she said "The blond."

"How much of what you've told me is real and how much isn't?" I said.

"Most is true but some is not," she said. "I did not tell you all. You would not have come if you knew the truth."

"What is the truth, Rose?" I said, drawing close to her. "If that's even your name. And aren't you supposed to pray five times a day? I've not seen you pray *once* since we've gotten here." Well, except for the night before, but I wasn't gonna reveal that yet.

"Yes," she said, stammering. "I pray now."

She dropped to her knees. Looking up, she saw the look of disbelief on my face. She lowered herself more, sitting on top of both her shins, bowing to kiss the ground.

"Um, you're facing east," I said.

"What?" she said, looking up.

"Mecca is to the west. You know, the place you face when you pray five times a day?"

"Oh," she said, doing a one eighty on her knees, and bowing again to kiss the ground.

"Get up," I said, grabbing her by the arm and pulling her to her feet. "I saw more than a ghost last night."

"Don't touch me!" she said, slapping me, now aware I'd seen all. I was getting really tired of getting slapped.

"You bitch!" I said, grabbing her veil, violently pulling it off, revealing her face.

And it was the most beautiful face I'd ever seen.

18

What'd she look like? Well, I'd imagine she'd look even better after all this beer.

Seriously though. You know that lead singer chick for the Pussycat Dolls? Nicole Schwarzenegger?

Oh, I know that's not her name. That's Arnold's. It's just the beer talkin'. It not only inhibits my judgment, but it also inhibits my sense of humor.

Well, Rose was the spittin' image of her. Except with a cute little pug nose. Hell, I can't hear a Pussycat Dolls' song anymore without rememberin' Rose. Man, she sure was beautiful.

So anyway. On with the story.

***

"Don't even talk to me," I said, marching onward.

"You need to listen to me," she said, pleading, now wearing only shorts and a tee shirt. Since the jig was up she was more than happy to ditch the burka. And I knew that later, after I'd cooled off and stood to look at 'er again, I'd be happy about it, too. I mean she was really pleasing to the eyes.

"What is this? A set up? Did you bring me on a wild goose chase? For... I still don't know what reason? Do you have some of your friends out here waiting? Gonna kidnap me for real? Ransom?"

"You are not worth ransom, Pete," she said, marching right on my heels. "I know your country does not care for you and does not want you back. They are done with you."

"Oh!" I said, and I turned and faced her. "You know so much, huh? I'm so worthless. So now you just wanna use me up and throw me away, too?"

"No," she said, grabbing my wrist with a small, dark brown hand. "I need help to get my sister back. I knew you were mercenary. I knew your reputation. You were the only one I could come to."

"If this is true, why not go to the Army? The police?"

"They not come to this island," she said. "No one comes to this island. Remember? Not even the man who brings us in boat comes to this island."

"Why?" I asked, my head and eyes rolling toward the sky. "What is it with this island?"

"It is haunted!" she said, and she almost started crying, and I could tell it was because of true terror. "You know what we have seen so far. Duwende. White lady. The blond you saw was mermaid. If I had let you jump in the water she would have killed you. You see her for beautiful woman, because you are a man. But I am woman. I see her for what she is."

Now you know all about the hot blond. And why Rose put me out with her boat oar.

"There is more here we have not seen," she continued. "People are scared to come here. This is why neither my country nor Indonesia claims the land. It is cursed!"

She was so taken after telling me all of this that she sat down. Tears were coming, but she wasn't sobbing. She did shiver though.

"So, Abu Sayyaf kidnapped your sister and brought her to a haunted island? So no one would come get her?" I knelt down beside her and softened up a bit. I'm good with readin' people- well, except whores- and I could tell she was tellin' the truth.

And to be honest with you? I spent a lotta time here ignorin' what I was readin' from the whores. Like Rose'd pointed out. We find what it is we go lookin' for, and I wasn't necessarily lookin' for honest conversation with the whores, now was I?

"The truth is my sister was not taken by Abu Sayyaf," she said.

"Then who took her?"

"She was taken by Kapre."

"Kapre?" I said, incredulous. "Your version of Sasquatch?"

"Sas, wa, what?" she struggled with the word.

"Bigfoot!" I said, and I could tell that she was still lost. She didn't recognize that either. "Never mind. Kapre. A big hairy guy that lives in the top of a big tree, in a big castle on the other side of our dimension. He took your sister?"

"Yes!" she said, excited. "You know him?"

"You expect me to believe that your little sister is being held by some sort of monster, like beauty and the beast, in some castle we can't even see?"

"Yes," she said, sounding more excited.

"I have been fooled by hookers and whores, my ex-wife, my own government and society, but if you think, for one second, I am going to be fooled with this bullshit story, think again brown sugar!"

"I do not lie to you, Pete! I need your help. I had nowhere else to go."

The light sound of music coming from the bottom of a steep decline off to one side of us caught our attention. I hadn't noticed it until just now.

"What is that?" I asked, heading to the edge of the knoll to look over the hill. The sun was setting. It would be dark soon. Remember, down here on the equator you get twelve hours of daylight twelve hours of dark. So it's not that it was so late.

"A bar!" I said. And man, was I ready for a drink! I felt like I'd discovered a pot of gold at the end of a rainbow. This was all before I'd met the princess I tried to introduce you to, and anytime I got high blood, I went for a drink, instead of countin' things.

"Do not go there!" Rose said. "This island is haunted! The things you see are not as they appear. It is all traps!"

"You're a trap," I said, beginning to walk down the hill. I could feel my mouth start to water as I went. I hadn't had a drink in three days, and mind you, this was at a point in my life when I pretty much had the equivalency of an I.V. bag filled with alcohol needled into my arm.

"Don't go!" she said. "It is not safe!"

"I need a drink," I said. "I'll be back later." I walked down the hill and toward the music.

As I walked, the music grew louder and the light of day grew dimmer. By the time I could see the lights from the place- oil lamps- it was dark.

There were tiki torches burning outside the small hut that passed as what may have been the only bar on this island. There were a few men inside the place, far in the back. Unless you haven't noticed, the far back corners seem to be the most popular places to sit here. I guess everyone's hidin' from a woman or three.

When I got to the door, someone that I hadn't noticed was sittin' there, and he stood up to greet me.

"Hey, Pete," he said. I knew the voice, but I had to squint to make out the face by the dim light of the torches.

"John?" I said.

And remember I told you a while back that he comes into the story with a bang?

WHACK!!!

He punched me in the face and I went straight to the ground.

***

Let's get another bottle for the rest of the story. Hell, it may be a couple more bottles before I'm done.

Oh, look at these guys. Guess this corner isn't dark enough or far enough back. Here they come to sell us peanuts. And watch, they'll pass everyone else in this bar to get to us.

Why? Do you really have to ask that? Why, it's because we're rich!

You know, if I were the other Filipinos around here, I'd be a little offended by this, too, wouldn't you?

Because every time it happens, it's as if to say, 'hey all you Filipino men sittin' in here drinkin'. You poor bastards aren't worth my time. I know you don't have money, and so what if you might want to buy my peanuts. White guys first!'

Here, let me handle this.

"Deli! Deli! Walla kaune ko mu-neet!" (No! No! I don't eat peanuts).

And look, out comes the hand. We don't want any peanuts, but we should just give them money anyway.

"Howah!" (Go away!)

I hate to be rude like that, but most of the time it's all that works. Remember, they'll always confuse your kindness for weakness.

Look at 'em go. Pass up every other man in here. Ya know, those peanuts only cost five pesos, and you know how good they go with beer. I bet half the men in here would'a bought some had they been asked.

Tell ya the truth, I wanted some, but part of being able to live here is not buying stuff off of the street venders.

No, not just so you don't get ripped off, I mean, that's part of it. But also because they all talk. If you were to buy peanuts off that guy, he'd tell everyone, and they'd tell everyone, and by the end of the week, word would be around that you were an easy sell, and you wouldn't be able to walk down the street without 'em trippin' ya up every other step. They'd be runnin' right underneath your feet, everywhere you went. Tryin' to sell ya something.

When you're new in any town, it takes a month or so of saying no, and saying it loud and meaning it, before word gets around. But it *will* get around, and they'll leave ya alone. For the most part.

What's that? Why did John punch me in the face?

Well, I guess he was pissed. Havin' to come all the way to the other side of planet earth to find me. Ah, I'll get back to it and tell it in order.

Here she comes now with our beer.

***

"Nice nap?" John said, hovering over me when I came to.

"What the hell was *that* for?" I said, starting to rise. John helped me up and walked me to a small table just inside the hut.

"Pick a reason, asshole."

"It's nice to see you too, John," I said, sitting down and then motioning for the barmaid in the darkness. She came, glass and jug in hand. They only served one kind of drink, so there was no need to take our order, and I bet you can guess what it was.

"What *is* this stuff?" John asked, pouring a little into the glass and taking a sip. They only give you one glass unless you ask for more. That's part of the drinking culture here. One man drinks a glass of booze, and while he's doing so, his partner or partners talk. When the glass is empty it gets passed on to the next guy. That's kinda sentimental I think, but it would drive me batty if I was really in the mood to knock 'em back.

"Tuba."

"Tuba? Like the instrument?"

"Yeah," I said, pouring some more from the jug into the glass. "It's coconut wine. Be careful. Only one glass and you'll have the shits for a day. And it doesn't take much to get ya drunk. The stuff's like prison squeeze back home."

"Speaking of back home," John said, picking the glass up for a sip. But I guess he'd thought over what I'd just told him, because he placed it back on the table. "You're free to come home anytime you want now."

"What?" I said, taking the glass from him and chugging. I had no desire to go back home. And after all I'd been through with Rose, I wanted to get drunk.

"Well," John said, drawing out the word. "You *were* AWOL when you just left and didn't tell *anyone* where you were going."

"They were gonna discharge me for havin' the crazies," I told him. "They'd already started the process, and I'd done everything I needed to do. The paperwork was in the system. I didn't need to waste my time hangin' around, getting' worse off than I was, while the paper pushers took their sweet ass time. It was my life, John! You know how slow they roll."

"They *did* discharge you. And in spite of your AWOL it was honorable. Not a medical discharge, which you could've gotten, had you stuck around and fought for it, but it *was* honorable. But you don't know how damn close you came to being other than honorably discharged for desertion."

"So."

"So you have no idea how much I went to bat for you! And I saved your ass! You would've been a felon. A wanted man. And you wouldn't've gotten any VA benefits," he said.

"How did you…"

"Friends in high places," he said. Guess you make a few of those when you're in a long time, and John had been in for about twenty years. "It helps too that the federal government's being sued by a bunch of veteran's rights groups for doing tests on us we didn't even know were being done. They aren't up for more ripples if they can avoid them."

"What kind of tests?" I took another sip of tuba. I knew I'd pay for it tomorrow, but I hadn't had a drink in days, and I was already starting to catch a buzz.

"Remember that time you and I were walking across post in Mosul in the middle of the night? The explosion?"

"Yeah, the mortar that went off just on the other side of that building that would've killed us if the building hadn't been there."

How could I forget? We'd been walking back to our CHU from one of Half Man's stupid classes- I think this one was on why the flag is flown backward in times of war, and that's because that's how it faced back during Revolution times when the flag bearer rushed forward into battle- and we'd been talking about how we'd gotten used to all the mortars. Our first couple of months in theater, one could hit a mile away and we'd hide under our beds. But by this point, we'd been there so long that one could go off a hundred meters away, and we wouldn't even look up from whatever the hell we were doing in acknowledgement.

But that one wasn't a hundred meters away. Or at least it didn't sound like it. It sounded like it was twenty meters away. Man, did we break the land speed record for near middle aged guys in combat boots that night!

"It wasn't a mortar, Pete. It was a controlled blast at the airfield. An I.E.D. detonation. It was just a huge I.E.D., so it sounded like it was closer than it was."

See, here's what he was talkin' about. A lot of times, if we found an I.E.D. out on the road that E.O.D. (explosive ordnance disposal) thought they could safely retrieve and bring back to base, they would. They'd study it to see what kind of detonating device it had, how it worked, and what we needed to do to block the signals so that this type of I.E.D. couldn't explode on us. By this point in the war, which again, was really an occupation, we could even tell who'd made the I.E.D. and we'd know where to send an infantry unit for a raid.

"What? They always announced over the base wide intercom that there was gonna be a controlled blast two minutes beforehand so we wouldn't freak out?"

"Exactly," John said, takin' his first sip of the rot-gut wine to wash down the bitter memories. "Well," he said, continuing his story after a tight grimace. "Turns out, a couple generals in D.C. got to thinking."

And you just *know* it's gonna end bad just from those words.

"Yeah?"

"Well, these generals decide, 'hey, if *we* know there's going to be a controlled blast because of the announcement, any insurgents in the area will know, too. They could lob in some mortars and no one would think anything of it. If someone got hurt, there might not be a sense of urgency to respond, because everyone would think it was a joke. It kind of makes sense."

"So, they stopped announcing the controlled blasts?" I said taking another sip. "And they just had the blasts?"

"Yeah. For about thirty days. Remember that combat stress place we were all going to before we came back? Talking to all those shrinks so we wouldn't kill each other?"

"Sure. Where we spent a week with Captain "not Chuck" Norris?"

"Well, they're the reason they finally started announcing the controlled blasts again. They saw a three hundred percent increase in traffic, because everyone's stress levels went through the roof."

"Yeah, I remember at one of those places down in Bagdad some dude went in with an M-4 and killed like, five people."

"That was during the same time period."

"You didn't have to punch me, you know."

"I know," John said, laughing. "It was pretty fun though. You had it coming, all the shit I've gone through for you."

"How did you even find me?"

"Remember that bullshit. You smoked a joint or something with one of your students?"

"Yeah," I said, shaking my head. What a bunch of bullshit that was. Long story short, I'd been teaching again for a few months after I'd gotten out of the Army hospital. They'd gotten me a job with the Troops to Teachers program. It's a pretty good gig, where they try to transition wounded warriors out of the military and into teaching. Since I'd already been a teacher before Iraq, I was a shoe in.

I was teaching in the Grays Harbor School system. It's just a little south of where I'd been in the Army hospital at Fort Lewis. Everything was goin' well at first. But then I'd gotten full bore addicted to all of the crack I'd been gettin' for my injuries.

I told you about that already. About bein' freaking hospitalized for six months at least. But I guess I didn't tell ya why.

It was due to a damn hernia I'd gotten on one of Lt. Bee's forced P.T. tests. The ones he made us take every two weeks, even though we were in a damn combat zone! Guess he ran out of stupid classes to make us take to fuck with our sleep, so he implemented the P.T. tests about half way through the deployment. And even though I'd never scored less than perfect on one in my career, I still had to take 'em too. I was tired. I was aging. My body'd just worn the hell out, and things started breakin'. And after I'd gotten the hernia? The bastard wouldn't even let me seek medical treatment!

And then, all the damage to the lower back from all the body armor.

Anyway, it was always so cold and rainy in Grays Harbor, and weather like that ain't good for chronic pain, I'll tell ya that! I'd double and sometimes triple up on my meds, and I was runnin' out of 'em before they were due to be renewed. It didn't help that by this point I'd also started takin' 'em recreationally, mind ya.

Anway, I'd run out this one time, and my back was killin' me. I was on my feet all day. Teaching. I didn't just hand out worksheets and sit at my desk and IM with my buddy up the hall teaching Algebra, like half the teachers do these days, just tryin' to get the kids ready for the big fill in the bubbles test at the end of the year that determines teacher's job security more than whether or not the kids had learned anything. I actually taught. I was up on my feet, walkin' around. Lecturing. Listening.

And it killed my back.

So I'm out of meds, my back is killin' me, and I'm approached by one of the local herb smokers, and she asks me if I wanna get high. She was high at the time. Anyway, I did. Well, I guess she thought it was cool to get stoned with a teacher, so she told all her friends, and you know how that goes. So a week later I'm sittin' in a small Podunk police station, surrounded by three cops.

They asked me if I'd smoked up with this girl, and I said yeah. Story she'd given 'em was that I'd had the pot and gave it to her, and I said yeah, sure. I'm sure the girl was in trouble and sayin' just about anything. I felt bad for her, and I was a maggot to've done it. I mean, she was already a stoner. That wasn't my fault. I didn't get 'er on the stuff. She was already on it. I should've drawn the line though. Smoke with another adult? Okay. Smoke with someone under age? Not okay.

So then they start makin' all these accusations that I'd fucked her. And that was total bullshit, and they knew it. But they were using the allegations as leverage.

Why?

Because it was a huge drug area. Meth labs and pills everywhere. I mean, that close to an Army medical facility, of *course* there were pills everywhere. Here's something that doesn't make vets look too good, and it's something the folks back home don't wanna hear, but a lotta vets who're being given a hell of a lot of drugs and who've been able to avoid gettin' hooked, are supplementing their incomes by selling them. No kiddin'.

I know a guy that was getting one thousand vicodin pills a month, and he wasn't takin' *any* of 'em. You know what he was selling 'em for? Three dollars! And he was still undercutting the street value by almost half! Basically it'd become his job. He was a dealer. And the VA was givin' him all of his product.

Oh, he'd been hurt and at one point needed it, but the thing is, as was the case for me too, is that once you get to the point where you don't really need the meds anymore, they just keep pushin' 'em down your throat. Like they want you to stay high or something. I've often wondered if it's because they view a stoned vet as a placated vet.

So anyway, they wanted to use the false allegations that I'd fucked some kid as leverage against me to get me to wear wires and go into known meth lab houses and get people busted. Be a nark.

I pleaded with them to simply charge me with the crime I'd committed. Contributing to a minor. It was like, six months probation and a one hundred dollar fine. Hell, from what I've heard, marijuana is legal to smoke in Washington State now, anyway. Soon enough, I'm sure it'll be legal everywhere. But more than anything, I knew that maybe the whole incident would end up getting me off to some rehab somewhere so I could get off all the shit they had me on. I'd never had a problem with any drugs before coming back from Iraq. I mean, I smoked the occasional herb in college, but who didn't? And hell, alcohol does more damage to any people in any society than marijuana *ever* has. Take a look around here, especially.

But they didn't wanna do that. They wanted to turn me into their little bitch. And after having been Lt. Bee's little bitch in Iraq, I was not going to put up with being anyone's little bitch anymore. Let me tell you something. If you've never had Stockholm Syndrome, you don't want it. You become some asshole's puppet on a string. You forget how to think for yourself. Hell, not to mention, I hadn't lived through a goddamn war to come home and get snuffed out by a pill head because I'd narked his buddy out.

So anyway, John tells me he catches wind that I'd gotten my ass in a sling over a joint, and he calls up some of his law enforcement buddies. They had a video from a security camera at L.A.X. of me entering the gate to board a plane. That's the last anyone had seen of me.

"But how did you know I'd come here, though?" I asked him. "To this particular island? There're more than seven thousand islands down here."

"I have my ways," he said, and that was the first time that I'd remembered all that shit from Iraq. Him opposomin' out on us on mission. Being able to see *my* sleep deprivation hallucinations too, because according to him, they weren't hallucinations. They were spirits. Ancestor spirits he called 'em."

"Amazing!"

"Don't be too amazed," he said. "I've had a watcher spirit on you for a long time. It took *him* awhile to find you. He had to have some very interesting conversations with some other watcher spirits. Seemed he was lied to quite a bit before he got the truth."

Hell, even the spirits, I thought.

"You know," I said. "You never really told me how any of that works. I wanted to talk to you about all that once we got back from Iraq, but I got sent off to that warehouse for broken soldiers."

"It's called astral projection. You'd never understand, and you'd never believe it anyway," he said.

"You know," I told him. "At the time, I probably wouldn't have. But I've seen some things lately. Things right here on this island. I believe now, John. Listen, there's…"

"Can I get you another drink?" the voice came from behind John. He turned to see the barmaid. She started rubbing his shoulders.

"No thanks," he said, closing his eyes in relaxation. "But that feels really good."

"I give you full body massage for five hundred pesos," she whispered in his ear.

"It's been a long week," he said. "That's tempting." He placed a hand on her leg. She was very petite, like most of 'em, and she'd be a liar if she was gonna claim to be eighteen. She was sixteen at most.

"Um, John?" I said. Suddenly I had another reason to get his attention. I'd noticed something.

"What happens way down here in the South Pacific stays way down here in the South Pacific, right Pete?"

"Um, John?"

"What?"

"Adam's apple," I said, pointing to the barmaid.

"Oh my God!" John said, pushing the barmaid back in disgust. "You're baklah!"

Baklah are Philippine crossdressers. Many take supplements to grow breasts. With Philippine men being so small, it's not hard for them to pass as women, and some Baklah can be very hard to identify until it's almost too late. This was one of those times.

"And you are so very handsome," the baklah said, stepping forward, rubbing John's shoulders again.

"Get off!" he said, and jumped out of his seat. He'd only been in the Philippines for a few weeks, but he'd already found out all about the baklah. They are very aggressive. They don't take 'no' for an answer. I guess that's part of their culture already, but when you throw the whole sexual deviant part in there, it makes it extra creepy.

"Get back," John said, now standing behind me, like I was some kind of shield. The baklah just tossed its hair over its shoulder and rolled its eyes and stomped back behind the bar. Now, notice I say 'it' instead of 'he.' That's because if you *really* wanna piss off a baklah, and possibly get knifed, call it a 'he.' They prefer 'she' but they sure ain't no she, so I use the term 'it.'

"That was close," John said. "I almost fell for that one. My God, I'd come even closer one night in Manila. Hate that place. Good thing you were here. And this wine is super strong."

Yeah, John, I'm thinking. Blame the wine.

"After that right hook I should've just let you have your little tranny surprise," I said, and we both laughed.

"So tell me about this work you do here," John said. "I've heard bits and pieces of it from people I've been talking to while tracking you down."

"Who did you talk to?"

"Several people," John said, dumping the rest of the wine in the glass onto the earthen floor and sitting back down. "Some fat guy named Jo Jo gave me the most information. Trust me. That guy is no friend of yours."

"I know," I said. "He usually has hot girls though. He rips me off all the time, charging me for beers I don't buy, but I'm always too buzzed and happy to realize it 'til the next day. That prick would throw his own mother under the bus for a bottle of Red Horse. His sister owns the place, and I bet he's stealing from her."

"He was telling me you let people kidnap you? And that the Philippine Army pays you for it?"

"It isn't the Army, really," I said, beginning to explain. "It's just a few guys within the Army. It's like a sideline job for a captain I know. I help him, he helps me."

"Well," John said, shaking his head in disbelief. "You don't have to do it anymore. You have money now."

"I have money? Where?" And boy did I laugh at that one. Sounded like he'd taken after the locals.

"Here," John said, pulling an ATM card out of his wallet, sliding it across the table. "Your pin is one, two, four, three. Get online and change it."

"This is a First National Bank card. In my name. How did.. what…"

"Ok, first of all," John said, waving one hand. "Since you were able to get an honorable discharge, you get monthly pay from the Veterans Affairs for your psychological disabilities. They put it into that account every month."

"What is my psychological disability?"

"P.T.S.D. Like the rest of us."

"Oh."

"And don't get too excited. Obama passed some law right around the time you left stating that if you'd deployed, you automatically qualified for P.T.S.D. Great, right? Monthly income."

"Yeah, I guess," I said.

"Wrong," he said. "He came back a couple years later and made a law stating that if you were above a certain percentage of crazy, you can no longer own a firearm."

"Really? What's the rating?"

"It doesn't matter, because you don't cut mustard. You're over it. You're nuts according to the U.S. government. You ever *do* come back, kiss hunting goodbye. Unless you wanna get locked up for the unlawful possession of a firearm."

"Wow! Seriously?" I'd had an M-4, a .50 cal., and for the first half of the deployment a MK-19 grenade launcher in Iraq, and my government was all *for* that. But now I can't go squirrel hunting with a .22 long rifle? Man, things were really changin' back home, I guess.

"Yup," he said. "But anyway. You got some back pay and your money's been piling up each month, so you're not broke anymore. Stop putting your neck out there doing stupid shit like allowing hooligans to take you for mid-night joy rides."

"How much money is in here?" I asked, looking at the card and trying to remember the last time I'd used one.

"Somewhere around fifty grand," John said. Once upon a time, that wasn't a whole lot of money. Here, that was like two million pesos.

"That's like, two million pesos!" I said.

"Hey, I take care of my troops," he said, and he poured another glass of tuba. I think more out of boredom than anything. Plus he felt safe seeing the baklah still behind the bar. "It's just a pain in the ass I had to come all the way down here to do it this time."

"I'm glad you did." I said.

We both took shots in silence.

"Hey," I said, all of a sudden in a pretty damn good mood. I mean, sure, my leg was throbbing and I'd just found out Rose had been lying to me this whole time. But I'd also just found out that technically, and relatively, I was a millionaire. Plus I had a really good buzz goin' by this time. "How's Corey doing? Corey Prine?"

John chugged another glass and coughed. Then he refilled, chugged again, and almost gagged. I didn't like the feeling seeing this gave me. There was something he didn't want to tell me.

"You never heard, huh?" He said.

"I never hear about anything, John. I stay offline."

"Corey's dead."

"Oh my God! How? When?"

"Suicide. About a year ago."

"Not Corey! No way!"

"Yup!" John said. "Got back and his wife and kid were gone. He couldn't find work. He'd gone to the VA, and I guess he'd gotten hooked on all the benzos. He'd gotten in trouble for damn hear beating a man to death. Some asshole giving him shit at the D.M.V. or something.

"Anyway, he was facing ten years in the slammer. They'd locked him up, inpatient ya know, and got him on even more drugs. Trial shit that no one could even really describe. Then when he was detoxing from all of it, he'd taken a rifle one cold winter night and went out into town and started shootin' the place up."

"No way!" I said. I couldn't believe what I was hearing. "That does *not* sound like Corey!"

"It wasn't Corey," John said. "It was the drugs. You and I both know that. We knew that kid as well as anybody."

"And then he killed himself."

"It's what they say," John said.

"You don't believe it?"

"Do I believe he put the gun to his head and pulled the trigger? Oh yeah. I believe that. Do I believe he killed himself? No."

"I don't get ya?"

"His wife killed him," John said. "She took his kid and wouldn't even tell him where they were.

"The system killed him. They were threatening to throw him in jail for not paying child support for which he had no income to pay, for a kid he couldn't see.

"The doctors killed him. They'd gotten him hooked on psychotropic medications that made him do things he would have never done otherwise, like beat the living hell out of someone and go on a shooting spree. He was facing jail for all these things. The little part inside of Corey that *was* Corey saw only one way out. And he took it."

"Wow." And I mumbled the word. It was all I could say. John was right. I have no doubt in my mind that if Corey'd gone back to The States after the war, and he would have had his son with him every day, he would've been fine. Sure, he would've had problems. Especially after the way Half Man had treated him. I mean, that little prick sure liked to pick on Corey and me. But Corey would've gotten past all that in time. But when his wife took his kid and the dominos just started falling from there... well.

John was right. *That's* what killed him.

"So, you wanna go back to The States with me?" John asked, pulling me out of my thoughts.

"Fuck no," I said.

"Why not? You aren't one of America's most wanted anymore. You're not AWOL and they never even charged you in that stupid pot shit you got yourself into."

"They didn't?" I asked.

"No," he said. "They issued a warrant for contributing, but withdrew it a couple days later. They were busy enough with all the Grundy murders, and they knew the shit was on its way to becoming legal anyway. Guess they picked which battles to fight."

Ted Grundy. The Serial Street murders. Now *there's* a story for ya. While I was teaching in Grays Harbor County there was a lunatic the whole time living out on the far end of the county in Ocean Shores. The news of the murders was just breaking around the time I left.

"Did they ever catch that guy?" I asked.

"Oh yeah," he said. "Caught him, tried him, and convicted him of over a hundred murders."

"Holy shit," I said. "Guess he'll never see the light of day again, huh?"

"He's already out."

"What?"

"He escaped from the Federal Prison in Federal Way, just south of Seattle. Went down to pay his old neighbors a visit. They'd testified against him in court. He killed everyone on his street except two families. Two single moms and their kids. Turns out they got away, but no one knows where the hell they are. They say at one time or another, this Grundy guy had dated both women. At different times, of course."

"Damn," I said. "Some of my kids were afraid to come to school while all that shit was goin' on."

"They'll never catch that guy if he doesn't want 'em to," John said. "But hey. You should come back. You've got a little bit of money in the bank. Head back to Virginia. Get a job. Get out of these jungles and the whore bars I'm told you spend way too much time in."

"I'm not going back, John. I can't handle the lies, the brainwashing. I mean, I was closer to forty than thirty when we went to Iraq, and while I was there, I realized that most of what I'd ever thought about how things were was total bullshit."

"Still hung up on all that, huh? No weapons of mass destruction. The Iraqi people being no threat to us. Just accept it, Pete. You have to if you ever want to move on."

"I'd rather stay here."

"And drink and screw yourself to death? Why not at least get a nice girl while you're here? Settle down with her and live like a king? You can afford to now. You get a grand every month. Not much back home, and you'd have to get a job if you went back, but if you'd sober up, you could live well over here on that."

"I've tried the girls here," I said. "Seems like they all just wanna take advantage of you. Or their family forces them to use you for their own selfish wants. You know how that works here. All the alleged stereotypes about the Philippines back home? Most of 'em are true."

"They aren't all like that, Pete. It's just like back home. We have our scammers. And a good many of 'em work in D.C. Give ya a diagnosis so you can get a check, then come back two years later and take away your second amendment rights because of the diagnosis.

"You just have to find the right girl. Hasn't there been *anyone* who seemed different?"

"Well, there was this one girl…" I paused, thinking about Rose. But I was thinking about Muslim Rose. Not Catholic Rose.

Oh shit! Rose!

"We have to go, John. I'll explain the rest on the way, but a girl's waiting on me about half a click from here."

"Ah, she might be the one," John said, smiling and rising.

"That's what I thought at one time," I said. "But wait till I explain the story she's told me. Biggest lie I've heard down here yet. But there may be some truth to *some* of it. There's been some strange shit goin' on. That's what I was tryin' to talk to you about before you almost got kissed by the he-she. I'll fill ya in on the way up the hill."

We left the small hut, entering the darkness, not realizing that the establishment's only other customers, the three beings who'd been sitting in the back had risen to leave as well. I say three beings, because they sure as hell weren't human. They were all bent, twisted and deformed, and they followed us out into the darkness.

19

What were they?

They were I need another beer is what they were. Damn this shit's done gone to my head.

Look. It's gettin' dark out on the street.

This is one hell of a whopper, isn't it? I bet when we came in here and sat down you thought you were gonna hear a buncha locker room talk. Like I was just gonna go on and on about all the hot women I've done down here, huh? Never thought you'd be in for a doozy like this, huh?

What's that?

Oh, the three things that followed us out of the bar? They're called sigbin. And man, aside from ugly, they stink like hell. I'd just assumed the bar we were in had stunk, but turns out it was these things.

What are they? They're one of the damned oddest paranormal creatures you could ever imagine. Excuse me. Aswang, as it's called in the Philippines. But you get me.

They stand on two legs, like a man, but they bend over at the waist and stick their heads between their legs. That's just how they're made. And they have the face and head of a rat. And big, long rat tails that they can use like a whip.

And they eat people!

What did we do? Well, let me tell ya what we did…

***

"So who's this girl we're meeting up with?" John asked, following me through the darkness. It reminded me of the night in Iraq that I thought we'd almost been blown up by a mortar that I now knew was not a mortar. "And what the hell are you guys doing on this island?"

"Her name's Rose," I said, feeling my way through the darkness. The top of the hill was outlined by the moonlight, silhouetted. "Just another girl that's suckered me. She's led me out here on a wild goose chase, I do believe. Her story is bigger than WMD's in Iraq, too."

"And you fell for it?" he said. "Let me guess. She has a nice ass."

"What was that?" I said, stopping and turning. I'd heard something behind us.

"I said, and you fell for it?"

"No," I said, lowering my voice. "Not that. I heard something behind us. I think we're being followed."

We stood motionless and listened. Sure enough we heard the scurrying of leaves behind us.

"We *are* being followed," John said.

"What are your orders, sergeant?"

"Cut that shit out, Pete. Those days are gone."

"Well, what should we do, John?"

"Let's wait. Hide. See who it is. It's probably the baklah."

We hid behind the thick trunks of two different banana trees that were straddling the game trail we'd been following. As we waited, the sound got louder. Finally, we saw them. Ten yards away and in the darkness. And we could smell 'em. It was still too dark to make out specifics, but we could make out the outlines of their bodies, and we could tell that something wasn't right.

"What the…" John whispered as he looked at whatever they were. They appeared to be men, but they were walking backward, bent over at the wastes, their heads between their legs. Like I told ya.

I rubbed my eyes. I couldn't figure out what it was I was lookin' at. One more oddity on this odd little island. Curiosity drew me back to the trail.

"Pete!" John said. "Get back!"

Kneeling down as the first of the three beings got within arm's length, I peered into the eyes, the beady little rat eyes, of the creature.

And it hissed at me!

"Ah!" I yelled, and I fell back on my ass.

The creature let out a loud, ear piercing screech, just like a damn rat, and it pounced on top of me, sinking its teeth into my calf. The one that hadn't already been bitten yet at least, but now both of my legs had been bitten by creatures I'd never seen and could not have ever imagined to be real.

"Come on," John said, grabbing me under the armpits, pulling hard. The creature simply clamped its jaws down harder, causing me to scream louder. The other two creatures jumped on John, knocking him backward. He let go of me and fell. Those bastards sunk their teeth into him, too. One on each leg.

About that time, here comes something else running up the trail, right at us. "Hi Yah!" It screamed, having jumped upon reaching us and coming down hard with a kick to the small of the back of the creature attempting to make its dinner out of my leg. The sigbin screeched again, letting go of my leg. I was able to roll quickly out of the trail and away from the sigbin.

"Get behind it!" the baklah said. That's who'd come down the trail and kicked the sigbin. "They can't see you if you are behind them. They are very slow. Just move around in slow circles so he cannot lay eyes on you."

I did as the baklah said, on my hands and knees, as my new injury kept me from standing. The baklah was right. It seemed to be working.

"Hi Yah!" the baklah screamed again. This time he'd done an acrobat type jump and had come down in a split, landing a heel on the backs of both sigbins feasting on John's legs. The beasts screamed in pain and let go.

"Get behind them," the baklah ordered John, just as he had me. "I take care of them."

John also did as he was ordered, crawling around on his hands and knees behind the sigbins.

The baklah stood tall however, well, for a guy that was five feet tall, and every time the beasts turned, he would kick them in the face and punch them in the back, quickly jumping out of their view after he had. It took only two attacks on all three creatures before they decided they would not feast here tonight. They slowly began making their way back down the hill, limping, having been badly beaten by the lightning fast baklah.

"What the hell *were* those things?" John asked, catching his breath, and holding both of his throbbing legs.

"I have no idea," I said, both hands on my new injury. Because at that time, I hadn't.

"Sigbin," said the baklah, fixing his hair.

"Sigbin?" John and I said, clueless.

"Yes," the baklah said, pulling a tube of lipstick out of his skin-tight miniskirt. "Very bad creature. They eat people. Thanks to God they are slow and stupid."

"How the hell did you do…" I began. "I saw that kick. That was awesome."

"I am not just baklah. I am ninja!"

I forgot to mention that baklah are very delusional. Most of them think of themselves as soon to be discovered celebrities. But I had to give this one some credit. He was at least ninja-esque. And as you can see, I'd decided to start calling it a he. The least I could do for it… er… him saving my ass.

"How old are you?" John asked.

"Sixteen," he said, and I knew it.

"So you are a sixteen year old, cross dressing, Filipino ninja?" John said through a grimace, the pain in his legs growing stronger.

"Yes," the baklah said, replacing his lipstick. "A hot and sexy one!" he added, while bending over and grabbing John.

"Hey now!" John said, drawing back his right hand. It was balled into a fist.

"I'd listen to him," I told the baklah. "He's got a hell of a right."

"I only help you," the baklah said, grabbing John around the waist, helping him up.

"What is going on here?" a woman's voice came from above us. It was Rose. She was standing on the hill above the trail.

"We were just getting our asses kicked by some really big sewer rats, before being saved by a sixteen year old, cross dressing ninja," John said. "Who are you?"

"That's Rose," I said, and she came down the hill to give us a hand.

"I see I was right about one thing," John said, checking out her ass as she bent over to help me up. We all limped our way back to the little makeshift camp Rose had set up on the hill above the trail. What a ragtag group we'd become.

**

Back at the bivouac, Rose squeezed fresh malunggay juice onto my new wound. The baklah leaned over John and did the same.

"What is your name, baklah?" John asked our new friend.

"My name is June," the baklah said. "Like the month."

"My name is John. And what the hell are you putting on my leg?"

"Let him do it, John," I said, my pain already subsiding because of the juice from the leaves of the magic tree. "I've had it before. It stops the bleeding, reduces the pain and prevents infection. Tomorrow you'll forget you've been bitten. For the most part."

"Ok," John said, throwing an untrusting glance June's way.

"So, tell me more about these sigbin," John said. You could see the grimace he'd had on his face disappearing as the juice on his bites eased the pain.

"Just one of many creatures on this island," Rose said. "Monsters."

"That's the story I was about to tell you, John," I said. "I've been recruited, this time, to chase scary monsters. Find the one at the end of the rainbow, some big Sasquatch or Bigfoot or something, that's holding the beautiful young maiden hostage. Rescue the damsel in distress and then we all go home."

"Kapre," June said, now wrapping gauze that Rose had taken from my backpack and given to him around John's leg.

"Kapre?" John said, looking at June for the first time in a friendly manner. He'd let his guard down.

"I know his place," June said, not batting an eye.

"How do you know it?" Rose asked. She was finished wrapping my leg and she turned to face June.

"He takes my sister."

"What?" Rose said, eyes wide.

"We come here when I am young," June said. "We flee Abu Sayyaf on our island."

"Did you not know the place was haunted?" I asked.

"Yes," June said, placing the butterfly clip on the gauze on John's leg to hold it. He switched to the other leg and began wrapping it as he talked. "My father did not believe the superstitions. So he bring us here. My mother tried to warn him."

"And then?" Rose said.

"And then, we begin to see strange creatures. We see that the stories are true. We decide to leave, but Kapre. He takes my sister. She was very beautiful. I was only eight years old at the time."

"Did you go after her?" John asked.

"Don't tell me you believe this crap, John." I said. In spite of everything I'd already seen, I did not believe that there was a big hairy man somewhere in a tree, taking all these beautiful, young Filipina women captive. Bigfoot's first cousin twice removed my ass! "This is all part of the set up. This guy is probably Rose's brother, out here playing a part in this scheme."

"Now you see sigbin and you *still* do not believe?" Rose said to me, standing quickly and walking over to June and John. "And then?" she said, looking at June.

"And then we go after her. We find his big tree, but we cannot get in. He sends out tikbalang."

"Sends out what?" John and I said together.

"Tikbalang," Rose said, facing John. I don't think she addressed me, because she knew I was going to doubt whatever explanation she gave. And at the time, she was right. "It is a creature, like a man, but has head and hooves of a horse. It is sentry for Kapre!"

"Like the headless horseman in reverse," I said, laughing. "But instead, it's the horse headed man."

Even John cast me a dirty look. I rolled my eyes and decided to let them tell their tales if John wanted to listen.

"The tikbalang has magical powers," Rose said. "He make you think things and see things that are not there."

"Yes," June said. "He make my parents think my sister is there, calling for them. They walk off cliff. Bounce off rocks to their death. They fall in sea below."

"What did he do to you?" John asked, mesmerized.

"Nothing. I hide. He did not see me."

"He makes you orphan at young age," Rose said, placing her arm around June's shoulder.

"Yes," he said, putting his head down and enjoying the affection. Baklahs are so melodramatic. Or, like I told you earlier, what they call here in the Philippines, O.A.

"Then how have you survived on your own this long?" I asked after giving June a little time to be O.A.

"We are not like you," Rose said. "We are not helpless until we are eighteen. At age six we are helping take care of our younger siblings and our grandparents."

"It's not like he'd starve to death," John said, reaching up to pluck a banana from a low hanging bunch just above his head. "There's food everywhere around here. Hell, he wouldn't freeze to death in the winter either. There *is* no winter."

"How have you avoided all the beasts?" I asked, looking for some sort of fallacy in his tale.

"I open bar. Sell them tuba. It keeps them drunk and happy."

"That was your bar?" John asked. June nodded confirmation.

"Who comes to your bar?" Rose asked.

"Mostly duwende. Sometimes sigbin. I get manananggal during the day. Before they change."

"Mana nang , wha… what?" John said, struggling with the names of the local beasts as much as Rose had with "Sasquatch" earlier.

"Manananggal," Rose said, rubbing June's hair one last time in affection- or for effect, I still wasn't sure- then pulling away. "Witch! They are shape shifters. They appear human by day, but at night turn into animals, mostly cats and dogs. They go around looking for pregnant women. When they find them, they turn back to woman and separate at the waist. Their top half grows wings and they take to flight. They go into house through roof to attack."

"And why do they want to attack pregnant women?" I asked, still critical.

"To kill them and eat the fetus." Rose said.

"I can't believe this crap," I said. "John, tomorrow morning, you and I are hiking out of here and getting the hell off this island."

"But my sister!" Rose said, pleading.

"Tell me about your sister," John said, resting his hand on her thigh, looking her straight in the eyes. If I had to compete against her beauty and sex appeal, I was done. John, or any red blooded male would take anything she said as gospel. Well, except for baklahs, but the baklah in residence was already on her side.

"Oh my God," I moaned, rolling my eyes in the dark.

"She was taken by Kapre. She is here on island with him. I cannot leave her."

"Do you give us your word?" John asked.

"Yes. I promise," she said, crossing her throat with her finger. In America, people 'crossed their hearts and hoped to die,' when promising not to tell a lie. Here in the Philippines, they cross their throats.

"You can't believe anything she says, John." I said. "She's a Filipina! Have you learned nothing since you've been here?"

"Excuse me?" John said. "Since when did you become a racist, Pete?"

"It's not a stereo-type if it's true!" I said. "Of course not all of them, man! Just the ones who want something! Shit man! You believe all this bullshit!?"

"I have no reason not to."

"So you believe in all this monster crap?"

"What were those… those…things back there?" John said, pointing back toward the trail.

"Inbreeds!" I said.

"What?" John said, incredulous. "Those were not inbreeds. You *saw* them!"

"That is his excuse for everything," Rose said. "He call the duwende king who bite him earlier inbreed because he is only two feet tall."

"Duwende?" John said. "The Philippine dwarves?"

"My best customers," said June, nodding his head up and down. "They just can't hold their liquor. But it is because they are so small."

"This is unbelievable," John said, shaking his head and rubbing his calves.

"John," I pleaded one last time. "Use your powers. That asshole projectile or whatever it is you call it. You'll see that this is all bullshit."

"It's called astral projection. You're the asshole projectile," he said. "And it only works in the spiritual and alternative universe realm. I'm afraid, Pete, that these things they speak of- things we've seen- are here in this world with us."

"So you're buying it all?"

"I trust the spirits in the other world," he said. "In this one, I've learned to trust my eyes and my gut. My gut is telling me to believe what my eyes have already seen."

"Please," Rose said, grabbing John with both hands. "You help find my sister. I pay you!"

"We'll help," he said.

"What?" I said, incredulous.

"That's an order, soldier!"

"I thought those days were in the past?"

"Not now," John said. "It's our mission to help those who cannot help themselves. That will *never* change."

"Whatever," I said. "Whatever happens from here, it's *your* fault!"

"Thank you," Rose said, squeezing John's hands.

"I'll help too," June said, jumping to his feet, excited.

"You're just a kid," John said.

"Could a kid do this?" June said, hunkering down low to the ground. Then he jumped, did a backflip, and grabbed a limb hanging above his head. He dropped to the ground, landing in a full split, hands karate chopping the air.

"I guess you're right," John said, amazed. "You can come."

"Ugh," I moaned, just before rolling over and going to sleep. I'd had enough bullshit and adrenaline rushes for three days.

I was out like a light.

20

I guess I'd better speed this up a bit. It's gettin' late and this place is gonna fill up fast. They'll start screeching with the videoke machine and you won't be able to hear me talk.

Where you stayin' anyway?

Oh, that's just right up the street. I'll get ya a cab when we leave, and he'll take ya on your way. Now remember, you gotta always ask if they have a meter and if it's workin'. They'll tell ya they got a meter, but you have to ask if it's workin' too. If you don't, they'll screw ya.

What? No, of course they're not all like that. The ones that you ask if they have a meter and if it's working aren't like that. The one's you don't ask... well.

So back to the story...

***

There's something John had forgotten about me from our time together in Iraq. I snore like a freight train. You've probably figured that out already, due to the whole duwende incident.

Well, John was tossin' back and forth. He couldn't sleep because of me. Rose and June had no problem. Rose'd no doubt grown up in a little ten feet by ten feet bamboo shack with a dozen other people, and sleeping with lots of noise was something she'd known her whole life. And June? Well, he was just June.

I'm glad I'd kept John awake with my snorin', or he'd never've seen the manananggal. He said at first he thought it was Rose checkin' on me. But when he'd squinted, he'd seen it for what it was. And then he heard it speak.

"Ah yucks!" it'd said, it's voice a hiss, like a snake. "Sigbin!" It was smelling the fresh bite on my calf. It switched to the other leg. "Ah, goods," the beast said. "I smell the kiss on the lips of the duwende. This kiss is from the lips of one who is with child!"

June and Rose woke up to catch the tail end of this. But they didn't dare wake me. Makes sense. Guess they thought I'd jump or something, and the thing would attack me.

"We feast!" the beast hissed, flying straight up, it's large, bat like wings attached at the waist. John described it to me later. He said from the waist up it was a woman with beautifully formed breasts. But its head was as nasty as that of medusa, minus the snakes. He said it had long, tangled, dirty hair. He said that from the waist down there was nothing, save for some bloody guts danglin' down.

She rose above the upper limbs of the tree above me, where five others like her followed in pursuit, hissing just as horribly as her.

"They go to the king!" Rose said. "His wife! The queen! She is pregnant!"

"I go there to warn them," June said. "You know what you must do here!"

"You'll never get there in time!" Rose said.

"I know short cut!" June said. He rose to his feet and kicked me. "Stop snorking and get up!" Yeah, they call snoring snorking here.

"What the…" I said. "What now?"

June was already gone. He was running through the jungle as fast as he could, on the way to the village of the duwende.

"Quick!" Rose said. "We must find the lower halves of the manananggal. Destroy them!"

"Is that what that thing was?" John said, rubbing his head. The buzz from the tuba had worn off, and let me tell ya, when that happens, it ain't good.

"Manananggal," she said. "Yes. I tell you of it before. That was it!"

"Not again," I said, rubbing my head, too. Damn that tuba!

"Pete," John said. "I saw it. It's real."

John was a weirdo. But he wasn't a liar. I know that I'd been seeing strange things this whole time, but my mistrust toward Rose, especially since I'd figured out the whole fake Muslim thing, kept me from wanting to believe what my eyes had seen. But now that John was wholeheartedly convinced, I finally allowed myself to become so, too.

"Let's do it!" I said.

"You make fire, Pete," Rose said. "We need ash!"

"Where'd the kid go?" I asked, rising to my feet. I gathered a few nearby twigs and dried leaves to make a fire.

"He goes to warn the king!" Rose said. "Come with me, John. We find lower halves of beasts."

"Not a big one," she said of the fire, looking back over her shoulder as she and John started to move out into the darkness. "We only need two handfuls of ash each. Just make it fast!"

"Roger that, Sergeant Rose," I said, and bent over to light the fuel I'd gathered with the lighter I'd had in my pocket.

***

"So what exactly are we looking for?" John asked, trailing Rose through the jungle. They were heading in the direction of what the moon revealed to be a large row of rocks, or cliffs.

"The bottom halves of six bodies. They will look like women's bodies."

"Are you serious?" John said, limping as quickly as he could. The malunggay had worked well, but it had not yet had enough time to work to its full effect.

"Yes," she said, slowing for him to catch up as she neared the rocks. "You will see. They separate at night and seek pregnant women to eat baby."

She stopped suddenly, and John nearly knocked her over when he ran into her.

"Sorry," he said, grabbing her, keeping her from falling forward. John was not a big man, he was about my size, but she was a Filipina; maybe five feet tall and ninety five pounds. It wouldn't *take* a large man to knock her over.

"They are here," she said, staring straight ahead.

John followed her gaze, and sure enough, standing like statues, there were the bottom halves of six women's bodies.

"Oh my God," he said, unaware he was speaking.

"You wait here," she said. "I go get Pete!"

***

June quickly passed the hut that served as his bar. Instead of going *around* the large gully that lay before him on the trail that would have gone the distance of three quarters of a mile, he leaped into the air, *into* the gully, like a man with the confidence of a parachute on his back. But he had no parachute.

As he began to fall, he reached out and grabbed a vine that he kept anchored on the limb of a durian tree. One swoop and he'd crossed the gorge in five seconds, saving him eight minutes.

He continued running, knowing the jungle so well he could traverse it at night as if it were day. He ran up a knoll, which was the remnants of an angry volcano a million years old, then down the other side, sliding on a large banana leaf six feet long like a sled to make good time. At last, he reached the home of the duwende.

"King!" he shouted. "King!" As he shouted, he looked to the skies, fearing what was to come.

"What do you want? Baklah!" the king said, exiting his chamber beneath the coconut tree, rubbing tired eyes.

"Manananggal! They come for your wife!" He was bent over, catching his breath as he spoke.

"Manananggal? She comes here?"

"Many of them, your majesty!"

"To arms!" the king shouted. "To arms!"

As he ran back into the coconut stump to tell his wife to hide in the cellar- the second cellar I guess you could say- his men came flooding out of the many unseen holes in the ground, brandishing spears and bows and slings.

"They are here!" One of them shouted, launching a stone from a sling into the night sky. It was a direct hit, and it sent the manananggal flying back and into a tree. It slid down the trunk, rubbing its forehead, but was quickly back up, and now it was pissed off.

Spears were flung this way and that, as were arrows and more stones as the great battle ensued.

***

I'd been on my way out into the darkness when I almost ran into Rose. I'd been carrying the ashes, still hot, wrapped several times over in a big banana leaf. It was like playin' that old grade school game 'hot potato.' I'd kept bouncing the pack back and forth between my hands.

"We found them," she said, steadying herself by use of my forearm. "Follow me!"

I did as she said, and soon enough we got to John and the six body halves. I stood in awe, just staring at first. Then I walked right up to 'em. I bent down and looked into one and almost gagged at what I saw. It was pure guts, and they were throbbing, like the beat of a heart.

"Don't just stand there," Rose said. She came over and took the banana leaf out of my hands and unrolled it. She took a handful of ashes and sprinkled them on top of one of the lower halves. "Like this!" she said.

***

Fight as the duwende did, they were no match for the manananggal. The witch-like beasts were clawing them out of their way, and they'd managed to get to the king's house. One of the evil winches stuck a long arm into the hole, and her arm morphed, like Stretch, the old comic book superhero, and it made its way through the house and found the queen. It pulled her out and threw her to the ground.

The duwende had been badly beaten, and they watched in terror as the witches surrounded their queen.

"No!" the king screamed, running toward his wife. One of the manananggal grabbed him and held him back.

"We feast," the leader of the horrible manananggal pack hissed.

Just then, when it appeared all hope was gone, the lead manananggal began to lean in toward the queen, but she kept going, wrenching over in pain. She let out a terrifying scream and began to melt like the wicked witch of the east on The Wizard of Oz. Her comrades did the same. The effects of the ashes we'd sprinkled on their lower halves a couple kilometers away had taken effect. They melted into steaming, oozing gobs of putrid evil muck.

"They made it," June said, and then nearly collapsed from exhaustion. He'd been doing his part, to little avail, in the fight as well.

John and Rose and I made it back to our campsite. We didn't sleep though. We were too anxious for the report from June. To see if we'd been in time.

He showed up about half an hour later and gave us the rundown. He said that the king passed his thanks on to us, and let us know that he would always be grateful, and that he and his court would forever be at our service, whenever we needed them.

"The sun comes up soon," Rose said. "We sleep. We reach the mountain tomorrow."

I wasn't focused on the mountain as much as I was the concept of sleep. It didn't take any of us long before we were out. And I'm happy to report that we slept through the rest of the night, what little was left of it, with no further incidents.

21

"You could bring her back with you, ya know," John said the next morning after we'd started our trek toward the mountain. We'd reach it by nightfall. We were close enough now to where we could hear the occasional cracks of thunder that followed the lightning. Looked like some pretty bad storms ahead, but where we were, there still wasn't a cloud in the sky.

And boy, were our heads hurtin'! Mine and John's. I'm happy to tell ya, that's the last time I've drank tuba!

"Who?" I asked. "Rose?"

"Who else?"

"Dude. There's nothin' goin' on between us. This is a job. She's payin' me a million pesos."

"I see the way she looks at you. And the way you look at her. And she's pretty damn hot."

"Aren't all of 'em, though?" I said, trying not to let John convince me, though I was afraid that I was already convinced.

"I'll admit," John said. "I've been to a few different countries, and per capita, the Philippines have the most beautiful women under the age of twenty five or so that I've ever seen."

"They just don't seem to age well though, huh?" I said.

"It's the lifestyle," he said. "You know that. Poverty is an ass kicker. But look at *her*. She's, what, about twenty five?"

"Almost."

"And single?"

"Says she is. Be she also expects me to believe she's a virgin. Holdin' out for Mr. Right. Sounds a little too much like a fairy tale to me."

"Hasn't this whole trip been like a fairy tale?" he said, and he was right. "I mean, we've had magical dwarves, evil witches, and now we're off to rescue Beauty from The Beast?"

"Isn't this the strangest damn mess you've ever been in?" I asked.

"Almost as strange as the night we got lit up in Iraq and the bullets went straight down to the ground, huh?" He looked at me and smiled. When my eyes met his, he winked.

"What the hell was that all about?" I asked. "You never did explain that."

"A little help from friends in strange places," he said, and he left it at that.

"We rest," Rose said, pulling a halt. John and I were happy to hear that. Our legs were starting to throb. June saw us wincing as we sat down, and he pulled fresh leaves off of a malunggay tree that was close by. The things are everywhere down here.

"What you do when we are finished," Rose asked John.

"I got back to The States," he said. "I'm tryin' to take Pete here with me. But he seems to want to stay."

Rose only looked down, saying nothing.

"I saw fresh hoof prints," June said, coming back with the magic tree leaves.

"Hoof prints?" I asked.

"From the tikbalang," Rose said. "Half man, half horse. He guards Kapre's palace."

"Palace?" John said. "Bigfoot lives in the woods. Sleeps under rocks and fallen trees. You're telling me the one over here lives in a palace?"

"Yeah," I said. "In an alternate dimension."

"It is true," June said. "My father cannot get into the palace, because we cannot see the portal. Only Kapre can see."

"Well, I guess with these centaurs runnin' around the place, we'd better start keepin' our eyes open and keep the noise down," I said. "I don't have any fresh legs for anything else to bite."

"What is centaur?" Rose asked. She and June looked at each other in confusion.

"I guess you could say it's the West's version of what your tik tok trot is."

"Tikbalan!" Rose said.

"There is an amazing similarity between our different folktales," John observed, thinking aloud more than anything.

We rested for about half an hour. We ate more dried fish and bananas, and June climbed a coconut tree- shimmied up it just like a monkey- and we had coconut juice. There was a papaya tree close by with some fruit on it so ripe it was about five minutes away from rotting. Just the way I like it, remember. We ate that too, and man, was it good!

"We follow the hoof prints," Rose said when we took back to the trail. "They lead us to Kapre tree."

We walked in silence for more than an hour. Then June almost gave me a heart attack when he screamed "Pesti!" in frustration. That's the F-bomb in Visayan.

"What?" I asked.

"The Tikbalang! They play tricks!" he said.

"What do you mean?" I asked

"Look!" he said, pointing to the ground about ten yards away. I looked over, and there were fruit flies flying and about a thousand red ants crawling all over our banana and papaya peals from earlier. There were so many ants, I was sure they'd be able to carry away the empty coconut shell.

"What the..." John said.

"Tikbalang. He is joker," Rose said.

In the distance, we could hear an eerie cackle. Then another.

"They lead us in circles," she said.

"Come on," I said, limping forward and toward the mountain. "I don't know why we didn't just follow our instincts before. They've gotten us this far."

"Yeah," John said, limping up behind me. "And *look* at us. A couple'a gimps."

***

We reached the base of the mountain just before dark, and we decided we'd keep moving while there was still light enough to see. It wasn't hard to figure out where we needed to go. The trail, well-worn with tikbalang hoof prints and the strangest tracks I'd ever seen, left by creatures I'd never even begin to imagine, pointed the direction for us. There was one set of tracks in particular that got our attention. I bet you can guess what they were. Here's a hint: Bigfoot.

We made good time, in spite of John and me limping. The path was almost like a road. And the hill wasn't too steep. Not until we got almost to the top. Then it really inclined, but we kept goin' anyway.

The mood of the forest was eerie. I mean, the whole island had an odd feeling about it. But this part was even more odd. The only way I can describe it, is that it was like walking through a graveyard, just before dark, and a week after Halloween.

Why a week after Halloween? Because you know the place is supposed to be creepy, but the excitement for the paranormal is probably at its *lowest* after its main holiday has just passed- adrenaline rush hangover if you will- but it still feels creepy anyway. Like it really is haunted, and we'd had every sign needed that this place was.

We'd hear the tikbalang laughing, off in the distance at times. And they'd move around a lot. Sometimes we could hear 'em, moving around in the underbrush, but most times we couldn't. And that was creepy, because we'd hear them cackling, say, a hundred meters straight ahead of us and then five minutes later we'd hear 'em cacklin' fifty meters behind us. It was terrifying knowing that they could maneuver around us so easily without us even knowing it. And I think that was their intent

Once, I swear to God, I felt somethin' breathing down my neck. It could have been my imagination. It could have been sleep deprivation. It could have been lingering remnants from the tuba from the night before. But I dared not turn around.

And then there were the cries. They sounded like lost babies, hungry and scared, out in the forest.

"Don't go to it!" Rose admonished me the first time we heard them. Every instinct within me told me it was an infant in dire need of help. But Rose said it was a monster called a tiyanak. And you pronounce that chaw- nock. And technically, she said, it *was* a baby. But one that had been aborted and the fetus had come back as a demon seeking revenge.

The tiyanak lure you into the woods with their cries for help, and then they kill you. I asked Rose if anyone ever tried to explain to them that they'd not actually been murdered, rather, their mothers had simply decided to terminate their pregnancies. She didn't understand what I was talking about, and I wasn't gonna risk bein' the messenger. I had reason to believe the tiyanak wouldn't exactly see things this way.

"We are here," June said, pulling up to a halt. We all stopped and looked straight ahead. It was too dark to see now, but with the intermittent lightning strikes, we knew we'd only have to wait a moment and we'd be able to see just where *here* was.

Sure enough, only after a few seconds, the skies lit up. About fifty meters before us stood what had to be the tallest tree in Southeast Asia. Rose would later tell us it was called a Bitaog tree. She said they lived for up to five hundred years, but I'll bet this one was twice that age. And being that it was down here, where there were no people to hack it down for firewood that was possible.

The tree looked as much like a palace itself, as any palace that may have existed on the other side of some inter-dimensional portal would, I'd imagine. It was draped in thick, glorious vines, and it just went up, up, and up. Into the clouds. I realized this tree is what I'd thought looked like a cell tower from so far away. I've never seen any tree like it.

We'd found the tree; great. The problem now was that there were two of those horsemen standing guard at the bottom of the tree. They had long spears and they weren't laughing. They looked on guard, and no doubt they were. For us.

"Now what?" I said.

"We must get my sister," Rose said.

"But how?" I asked. "Who the hell is gonna climb up that tree? And how are they gonna get into the other dimension? And before all that, how the hell are they gonna get past those guards?"

"All that might not be necessary," John said. The next lightning strike revealed his face plain as day, and it was a gruesome sight to see. He didn't look happy, but he didn't look sad either. He looked resigned. He wore the face of a man burdened with a job to do that he didn't want to do, but that he knew had to be done. I knew immediately what he was going to do.

"John," I said. "Is that safe? I mean, I don't know exactly what it all entails, but I remember every time you did it before, you came back... well... like you'd aged ten years in ten minutes. Are you sure it's safe?"

Rose and June had no idea what I was talking about, but they were looking at John like he held the key to all the magic of the Universe. There was hope in their eyes.

"It's the only way," he said. He took his backpack off and leaned it against a tree and sat down. It wasn't all out raining, but there was a light drizzle.

We sat down with him, and we were all quiet. I saw his eyes glaze over like I'd seen too many times before when he'd opposummed out on us in Iraq. His body was still there with us, but I knew that his spirit was gone.

22

What happened?

Well I'm gonna tell ya what happened. Then we gotta get outta here. Man, there're some weirdos that come in this place at night, I'll tell ya. Not the kind like we ran into out on that island. The kind with rat heads tucked between their legs. But weird enough.

Okay, but since we're nearin' the end here, we gotta get one more beer.

Guapa! (Beautiful!)

Damn! Look at that. We've been here so long they've done changed shifts!

That's the same girl?

Damn! This is why I go for half a year at a time without drinkin'. I can't handle this stuff.

Salamat, guapa. Yellow paki? (Thanks, beautiful. More ice?)

Okay. I'll go ahead and start while she's bringin' the ice.

Now this next part, I didn't know about until the next day. John told all of us what he'd seen, and what was goin' on in the palace as he saw it through astral projection. I guess we gotta just take his word for it. We did at the time, and it seemed to hold water, 'cause everything worked out in line with his story.

Why didn't he tell us 'til the next day?

'Cause when he came to, out of his trance, we weren't thinkin' about askin' 'im. Only thing we had on our mind was run!

***

Soon as his eyes finished glazin' over, I swear to God I saw a mist come out of his mouth as he let out a long breath. Like the breath of a dying man. June and Rose both looked at me with a look on their faces that asked me if he was dead, but I gave 'em a nod to let 'em know he was okay.

And they saw it too- the mist- and we all followed it with our eyes. It went to the base of the tree, between the two sentries who didn't even notice it. But lookin' back on it now, I swear I'd seen 'em take a chill as it passed. Then it started its way up the tree.

Now what John says the next day was amazing. He first described the portal. Said it looked like a crystal orb floatin' in the main forks halfway up the tree. He said you'd never see it with the naked eye. Humans wouldn't at least. He said animals had no problem seeing these things, and he attributes a lot of the difference between them and us to civilization and rational thinking. We've been taught to rationally convince ourselves that such things don't exist. I kinda understood what he was getting' at. Remember that whole 'seeing the world around me as it truly exists' stuff I was tellin' ya about? Yeah, but I'm still workin' on this dimension. Haven't even begun to make my way into any others yet.

So he says that passing through one of these things is kinda like the tube slides at the game parks, like Busch Gardens or Water World. Not that it's wet. It's not. He says it is actually hot in there because of all the electricity associated with the energy required to break on through to the other side, as 'ol Jim might'a said about it. But you go in lots of different directions like those rides and you're not really sure which way is next 'til ya get there. Just when you think you're going left, you turn right.

Anyway, when he-or his spirit, or however you'd say it came out on the other side, he was in a great hall. Just like a castle. He said it was long, like forty meters. The ceiling, the floor and the walls were ivory white. There were doors every ten meters apart going down both sides of the hall, and there were half a dozen candle chandeliers hangin' from the ceiling.

He drifted down the hall, and as he did, he glanced into each of the rooms he passed. He said half of 'em looked like bed chambers, or efficiency apartments. Only classy. Like a Crystal City high rise. And there were the most beautiful women inside each room that you could imagine. About half a dozen in each one.

The last two rooms at the end of the hall, just before gettin' to the main room at the end, which he said was a dining hall, were filled with gold and jewels and riches of every sort. He said there were lamps and chalices and even chairs that were made out of pure gold.

He said as he drew closer to the dining hall, he heard voices. Arguing. And they were both men. They weren't speaking English, or even any type of human language, but rather, some sort of guttural tongue. He said that had he overheard the conversation while he'd been in flesh form, he'da never understood a thing. But since he was in spirit form he could understand everything bein' said. Well, he didn't understand the subject of the conversation, but he could understand the language being used.

He drew to the door, and he said that he made himself spread out as thin as he could, to where he was basically a layer of fog covering the ceiling. It was a cathedral ceiling, twenty feet high.

He said he'd been prepared to see the mighty Kapre. And he did. And he confirmed everything the legends state. On this side of reality, or in this dimension, whatever you want to call it, it wasn't a big hairy man at all. Rather, it was like I said I imagined it was. A very attractive, olive skinned man with a long, western nose, jet black hair, and hypnotic eyes.

I asked John at some point while he was telling us this tale if he looked anything like a young Pierce Bronson, and he told me my aura was completely fucked up. But later that day, out of the blue, I think we were eating lunch or something, he looks over and he says, "You know, Richards? He did bear a remarkable resemblance to Pierce Bronson. But not the Pierce Brosnan from James Bond. The one before that, from that pussy television show Remington Steele."

So I was close.

Anyway, he wasn't ready to see the other creature. That one had really thrown him for a loop.

It's not that he was so much surprised to see it, as much as we've already seen, but he would have never imagined he'd see it here. Somewhere in the Cascade Mountains just outside of Seattle? Maybe. The Philippines? Never.

But he did.

John said that just below him, was Bigfoot. That's right. You heard me.

Sasquatch.

Bigfoot Sasquatch!

And John was scared for a minute, because as he was hoverin' there above 'em, the Sasquatch started sniffin' the air and lookin' around. John was afraid he'd smelled him, but he didn't know if that was possible. He said for a minute, the thing even looked right up at 'im, but then the Kapre said something and got his attention back and that was the end of it.

What were they arguing about?

Well, John was able to pass on some of what was said, but again, none of it made any sense to him, and it makes no sense to me either. But they seemed to be arguing about some sort of council. And it sounded to John like the Kapre had at some point been one of the key figures in this council, but he'd been asked to resign because he couldn't keep from meddling in the affairs of mankind.

The Sasquatch was saying something about the council had been in session and that they wanted him back. The Kapre was acting really cocky, John said. Goin' on and on about how now that they needed him for his ability to morph into a man, they'd finally realized his worth. And he was demanding apologies from the Sasquatch and everyone else. John swears he even heard him say something about that asshole Yeti and his bad attitude.

The Kapre kept wanting to know why if he'd been kicked off of this council they were talking about for always interfering in the affairs of man- and I'm assuming by that he meant going around kidnapping all these beautiful young women- but why, all of a sudden, the Sasquatch and the others had decided to interfere in the affairs of man.

The Sasquatch turned to pleading. He said his two granddaughters had been captured and were being held, and that their kind had sat by idly since they'd made their agreement with the great fathers of mankind for too long. And that they could no longer sit by and watch, as man did to each other things that no animal ever would. John said the Kapre became adamant over this, saying that man was the lowest form of animal ever to exist.

Long story short, these two beasts- creatures that until all of this happened I would have sworn on my own life only existed in fairy tales and urban legends- came to some sort of an understanding. The Kapre told Grace, that's Rose's sister, that he'd return shortly, and that when he did, she'd be of age, and for her to go ahead and plan the wedding in his absence. John said the girl broke down into tears, and the Kapre and the Sasquatch took off running at an all-out sprint toward the portal, and once they reached it, they dove into it, head first, and there was a loud, booming explosion, and then they were gone.

Now the explosion part, I can verify. Because it shook the damn ground. I'd been keepin' an eye on John's body this whole time. I guess I thought I should watch his vital signs or something. Like it would help. When the boom came, and it felt like one of those ten thousand pound dump trucks bombs that used to go off all the time in Iraq, I looked over to the base of the tree and the human headed horsemen acted like it was no big deal. Like they were used to it.

I looked back at John, and it seemed like he was startin' to come to. His lips were moving. Like he was trying to speak. One syllable.

I've never learned to read lips, but if I had to put money on tryin' that time, I'da bet on 'run.'

"Grace!" I heard Rose say. She didn't yell it. No. She said it as if she were in awe. As if she'd seen the dead comin' back to life.

I followed her eyes and saw that it looked somethin' a whole lot like that. Comin' down out of the tree, like a banshee onto the moonlit moors, was the most beautiful young lady I'd ever seen. She was wearing a long white gown, and her hair was as long as Rose's. Down to her ass. And she was floating on a white mist. Even the human headed horsemen were amazed. They never tried to go at her or come at us. They just watched as she descended. She bumped Rose into the number two spot for most beautiful woman I've ever seen.

Grace made her way to us in the mist, and I was so caught up in her beauty that it took me a minute to realize that John was now making noise. It was low and faint at first, but getting louder. I finally followed everyone's gaze down to him, and I saw that he was moving around now, and he was indeed saying "run."

We helped him up, and he was slow gettin' to his feet, but the whole time he just kept saying run, run, run, and he kept saying it a little louder each time. We got the point, and we looked back and where there had before been only two sentries, there were now about twenty, and they were coming right for us.

We took off haulin' ass. John kept coming to more and more as we went, and thankfully it was a downhill trek, but we were still only about fifty percent. Remember, we'd had hunks taken out of our legs by God only knows what.

We slid most of the way down the trail on our asses. The rain had come on full bore by now and the trail was more like a muddy stream than a trail. But for us, it was an advantage. The tikbalang were gaining on us, but they were having a hard go of it, because of the mud. But they *were* gaining.

Just as we got to the bottom of the hill, where the ground leveled off, things took a turn for the worse.

John collapsed.

I bent over to lift him up, and he told me to leave him. He said he'd had enough. Let him be the bait and get the others to safety. I looked at him, and it was the first time I really looked at him since he'd come to, and he looked every bit of eighty years old. Like I've told you, he's about my age, maybe a year older, but I can tell you, I've never looked that bad even after goin' on a three day bender of booze and whores and whatever else I could get my hands on. As bad as it sounds, I *wanted* to leave him. And not to save my own ass. But because I felt like it would be the more humane thing to do. Let him be put out of his misery by the tikbalang.

But thank God I didn't have to make that decision. Just as the tikbalang got up on us, arrows and stones came flyin' through the forest and hit every damn one of 'em square in the forehead. I looked up, and running out of the tree line were the king and his men.

"Run!" the king was screaming. Four of his men came over and helped me with John, and the king didn't have to tell any of us twice. We took off the way we'd been goin' and his men kept a constant rear guard. The tikbalang never caught back up to us. I didn't think they were tryin'. We got away. And that's all that matters.

If you were hopin' for a better ending, sorry to disappoint ya. But ya know, part of tellin' a story is tellin' it the way it happened. And makin' up the end to be more sensational ain't part of tellin' it that way.

What's that?

Well, I guess it's not the end, end.

John ended up stayin' here for a couple more weeks before goin' home. We were both nursin' bad legs, what with all the critters that'd attacked us. But we made the most of it. Mostly by goin' to high end girly bars and havin' the hottest damn women in the Philippines wait on us hand and foot in the V.I.P. rooms. Served us our food and drinks, and sang videoke for us. I'll tell ya, the people in the Philippines are the most musically gifted people on earth, as far as I'm concerned. All that private entertainment cost us, but hey, I had money again.

John and I keep in touch. When I do get online once a quarter or so, I get a message from him that says, "Yes. Are you?"

What's that mean?

Well, he'd sent me a message as soon as he'd gotten back to The States, askin' me if I was still alive, and I'd replied, "Yes. Are you?" So he replied, "Yes. Are you?" Anyway. That's the gist of it. Every quarter or so we let each other know we're still alive and kickin' with a "Yes. Are you?"

There've been times though, when I've felt like he's been sittin' here beside me. Like you are right now. Once I got online and messaged him and asked him if he was doin' that asshole projectile thing and coming over here and spyin' on me. Bet you can guess what he replied.

"Have I ever told you your aura is completely fucked up?"

I take that to mean that he's been here.

Rose?

Well, that's another story.

Remember earlier when I'd told you about that first girl I was involved with when I got here? About how she and her family took me for so much in just a couple weeks? Had me takin' the whole damn squatter's barangay to the Chocolate Hills and all that?

Well, ya remember me tellin' ya that unfortunately I'd been taken once since that time for way more?

That was Rose.

No, I'm not just talkin' about my heart. Of course she took that. I ended up fallin' in love with her, but the truth be known, and you've probably already figured it out, I'd fallen in love with her on the island. Hell, the truth of the truth is that the night I'd seen her bathin' in the river by the moonlight, I was a done man. She coulda stuck a fork in me then.

So, after John left, I started spending a lot of time with Rose. I never accepted payment, ya know. She'd pawned the family land for a million pesos to get the money to hire me. That was true. So I told her to take the money and get her land back. Besides, I had a couple million pesos in the bank and the card to access it now thanks to John. And I have some monthly cash flow now, so no more odd jobs for Morales or anyone else.

Well, June ended up shackin' up with Rose and Grace. Kinda like another little sister I guess, and they'd concocted this idea. I use my money to build a big house on their land, with a pool and everything. And you can do that here with a million and a half pesos, which again, is only about thirty five grand, U.S.

Well, I'm assumin' this means that Rose has fallen in love with me, too. So I'm like, sure, why not. Let's do it. Time to leave the girly bars and the booze behind, right? So we spent it all. The whole two million. I mean we made a nice place!

Wrong.

First thing ya gotta understand is that here in the Philippines, foreigners are not allowed to own land or businesses.

Oh yes. I'm serious.

What's that?

We put it all in Rose's name. Had to.

Well, you can own one small, primary residence, but the house we built was bigger than the parameters in that law anyway. So we had to put it in her name.

Only problem?

The family.

Listen. The family structure here works like the rank structure in the military. The oldest has seniority, and the males outrank the females.

Well, Rose and Grace's dad is a worthless drunk. I'd only met him a couple of times, and even then, it was upon my persistent requests. Rose was embarrassed to introduce me to him. See, she and Grace lived in their own little hut on one part of the family land, and the parents and their eight other kids lived on another part, about two hundred meters away. But the jungle was dense there, so it was really like they were in another village. Never saw 'em if ya didn't want to.

Anyway, I pay to have this house built. It took about four months, and the stories about that story I could tell you. Damn. Definitely for another time.

But after the house was finally built, Rose would hardly talk to me. I hadn't moved in yet. I was still living in my apartment in the city, but I felt really good about everything that was goin' on. Rose and I'd never made love. We'd kissed and made out, but never any touching below the belt. She really was different. And I have no doubt that she was a virgin.

Well, I was convinced that once the house was built, we'd actually get married and move in together and we'd all live happily ever after. Hell, the rest of this story seems like a haunted fairy tale, so that's how it should've ended, right? Fairy tale ending?

Wrong.

Haunted ending.

Rose's father really liked the house. Matter-a-fact, he liked it so much that he decided that he and his wife and their eight other kids that were still underage- the eight that never seemed to have rice unless Rose gave it to 'em, even though her father always had his damn tuba- were gonna move in. And they did.

Rose wouldn't stand up to him. The house was in her name, even though it was my money, but again, R.H.I.P. as we'd said in the Army. Rank Has Its Privileges. And her father outranked her. And even though the drunken bastard had never worked a day in his life, she gave him the respect you or I would give someone where we're from who's actually worked hard to accomplish something. Here? All you gotta do is be born first.

Anyway. I couldn't take it. The old man stayed drunk. He'd get in my face all the time and call me Joe and ask me how it felt to know that I'd gone to college in America, fought in a war, yet everything I had went to him. He'd brag about having not finished grade school nor worked a day in his life, and that he now lived like a millionaire. Kept callin' himself so wise. So wise. And remember, I told you how they misuse that word to make it mean quite the opposite of what it really does. This story's the best example of that.

Rose would never take up for me, or speak up for *us*. I tried to talk sense into her. I mean, here was a young woman that was smart! She'd proven her intelligence on the island. She'd known exactly what to do and when to do it, and she stood up to every type of beast that could be imagined.

But because of an ass backward cultural belief system, she couldn't stand up to a worthless drunk.

What'd I do?

Obvious, isn't it?

I left.

I loved her. I did. And yeah, she'd lied to me at first, but I could see her reasoning behind it. If she'da told me that her kid sister'd been kidnapped by some big hairy man who lived in the top of a big tree, and that we'd have to fight midgets and flying witches and human headed horsemen to cross a haunted island to rescue her, I would've laughed her outta the city.

I understand that I'm in the Philippines. But if a relationship is going to work between anyone, no matter where you are, and no matter what the cultural differences, there has to be give and take. Changing my location does not change who I am. I could tolerate the differences in diet. I've learned the language. I respect their way of life and I no longer judge them based upon how their way of life compares to mine. It's their country.

But when they impose on me, it's not an issue of respecting a culture, or where I'm located. It's about respecting each other as human beings. To tell me that I should just give everything I have to others because I have so much and they have so little is a no go. That's not culture. That's abuse.

But you know what? I'd learned a lot from Rose. She pointed out to me the faults in myself that I didn't want to see. She made me stop and realize how dangerously close to becoming a racist I'd become, because of the treatment I'd received here. And she made me see some things from perspectives I'd never considered. I'd been viewing everything through my eyes, never considering things through the eyes of others. Rose changed that.

Anyway, everything works out for a reason. And I'm more than satisfied with the woman I've got now. You've seen her. She's beautiful. And she's stood up for me. I went through the same thing with her that every foreigner goes through when they get involved with a beautiful Filipina.

The family.

But this one really is different in every way. She kept me away from her family for the longest time. Her province is quite a ways from here. Five hours on a bus, and to a poor Filipino, that's like traveling to a different country. Just the bus fare alone, small as it is, is more than a week's wages for 'em. That's if they even work.

Anyway, they'd known about me for almost a year. They were upset that we'd never come to visit, so they finally came to *us*. And they had a shopping list with 'em. Seriously. They'd taken the time to write out on a piece of paper- a big one- everything they expected their daughter's foreigner to buy 'em; appliances, furniture, tons of food, and they'd even demanded a monthly pension, as they called it. Ten thousand pesos a month. About two hundred and fifty U.S. dollars, and more than they'd ever made in one month in their lives.

What happened?

She kicked 'em the hell out of the house. She told 'em she loved me, that she was a grown woman, and she'd seen too many of her friends who'd been fortunate enough to get out of poverty, by their own means or through means of meeting and falling in love with a foreigner, only to be dragged back down into poverty by their greedy families, and that she wasn't gonna let it happen to her.

I was impressed. And no, she's not adopted. It's really her mother and father. And they'd brought six kids with 'em that she says are her siblings.

She's just different. She's unique. She really loves me and looks out for me. She looks out for us.

And I love her!

***

What's that?

Will I ever go back?

To the island? Hell no!

Oh, you mean the U.S.

Well, remember I told ya about that Michael Crichton novel, "Rising Sun?" There was a character in the book that'd lived in Japan for five years. He ended up goin' back to The States and being a liaison for Japanese businessmen residing in the U.S., and he'd become a detective, helping out in matters that involved Japanese visitors.

All throughout the book, his sidekick kept pointing out how much the Japanese seemed to love him. And he kept saying, "Yeah, here." And the sidekick would ask him why he'd left Japan, and he'd just blow him off and not answer.

Well, at the end of the book, you get his answer. And these are the character's words, not mine. But he said the reason he finally left Japan was because he got tired of bein' a nigger.

Yeah, it was shocking, because Michael Crichton wasn't a racist, nor was this character in the book. But he said it like that to bring the point home. Basically, he got the same treatment there, as I get here.

Now, if I ever get tired of it, will I go home?

No.

I'm a big boy. I can take it. It's only names, and I understand that they really have no clue how insulting they are being. To them, it's fun. I know the lives they live, and that for many, harassing a white foreigner on his way down the street, honest to God, is the highlight of their day.

However, if my heart continues to harden because of it, and I can feel *myself* turning into a racist? You'd better believe I'll be on the next plane out.

I've been to war. I've gone home from war to get rejected by the people who I'd gone to war to defend. I've seen third world poverty. Hell, you've seen it here yourself. And then of course there's all that I saw on the island.

I will attest that of all the things my eyes have seen, there is nothing I've seen uglier than racism. It's a poisonous concept that embodies hatred and ignorance and intolerance, all wrapped up in one package. If the heckling and the harassing and the skin tax and all ever gets to the point to where I start hating an entire race of people because of it?

I'm outta here.

Come on now. We've gotta get outta here. You've gotta cab to catch and I've got a long walk home.

No thanks. I'll walk. I might stop by and see if the princess is home.

Look. Here's a cab now. Let me talk to him.

Meron ekow meter? (Do you have a meter?)

O' O' (yes yes)

Trabaho ni? (Does it work?)

O' O' (yes yes)

Here. Take this cab. And remember, you always have to ask.

You take care too. You're good people. I've had a great day. Come back by before you fly out.

Hey! Look there.

Yeah, back there in the distance.

Get up on your tippy toes.

You see it?

There it went again.

Lightning.

The End